Neil Ferguson lives in North ~~~~~~~~~~~~ ~~~~~~~~~~
the Inner London Education Authority as a teacher of
migrants and refugees. He has written a sequence of
stories, *Bars of America* and one previous novel *Putting
Out*. He has also contributed to magazines and collections,
including *Interzone*.

i

DOUBLE HELIX FALL

Neil Ferguson

AN ABACUS BOOK

First published in Great Britain in Abacus
by Sphere Books Ltd 1990

Reproduced, printed and bound in Great Britain by The Guernsey Press

Typeset by 𝕬 Tek Art Ltd. Croydon, Surrey

ISBN 0349 1 0111 6

Sphere Books Ltd
A Division of
Macdonald & Co (Publishers) Ltd
Orbit House, 1 New Fetter Lane, London EC4A 1AR

A member of Maxwell Macmillan Pergamon Publishing Corporation

In Memoriam
The Inner London Education Authority
Abolished 1990

1

Eight hours after setting out for work, Vergil Wyman arrived home in a sweat, just in time to make the elevator gates before they closed in his face. Collecting his breath in the airless cabin he waited, inert, while it transported him towards the corner of the block in which his own condominium was situated. Time passed – or did it? – until the gates slid open. Vergil paused, momentarily balked. Why didn't he proceed? He couldn't think of any reason. Frankly, there wasn't one. If he declined to take the next step he might never reach his destination. Anything might happen. He could lose his footing, become a prey to chance. He might slide off the map altogether. Recoiling reflexively from such a prospect, he entered his apartment.

'Hi there Vergil!' the familiar voice greeted him.

Vergil peeled off his uniform jacket and threw it over the nearest chair.

'Did you have a nice day?'

The sweat rivuletting under his arms began to chill in the abrupt low temperature, giving him the unpleasant sensation that it was not his own sweat but some other person's. The AC of the condo was thermostated to the consensus of all the other condos in the block so it was not something he could do much about. His block was attuned to all the other VW residences in the city, as, for all he knew, Sanfran was plugged into the rest of the

Western Pacific States. In Vergil Wyman's opinion it was taking democracy a bit too far.

'No different than any other day,' he said, careful to leave out of his voice any hint of hysteria.

It was the truth. His day had contained no ups or downs, no contours to make it any better or worse than any other day.

'That's swell,' the TV said. 'So now you're ready. . .'

'That's to say,' Vergil continued. 'It was damned dull! I'm wasting my fucking time!'

He refused to pretend to himself that the duties he carried out as a Grade 4 security guard for the Protocol Organization could, in any honesty, be called work. Not if work meant making or doing something. There were elaborate differentials and a promotion-structure which gave his position the shape and form of a job, but when he considered the tasks which executives and technicians carried out he wasn't fooled. The substance of his duties amounted to very little. His current detail – to maintain surveillance over the security apparatus of yet another high-status guest-block – was no exception. He polished the glass on the observation panels and logged the readings for his boss whom so far he had not even met. That was it. It wasn't something you needed to be Einstein to crack.

'Try not to let it get to you,' the TV commiserated sympathetically, coaxing him back from the brink.

Vergil – aware that the TV's language production was programmed to respond to the modulations of his own utterances – said nothing. He didn't need sympathy. He needed to take his shoes off.

'So tonight's the night, Vergil,' the oral output signal effused. 'With your boy due to die any time, this is an important moment for you and Val!'

Vergil took off his shoes.

'I know you'll be wanting to get to the Clinic and be with him . . .'

Without responding, Vergil padded in his socks toward

2

the little kitchen where he poured himself a couple of fingers of whiskey and only then, after the hooch had hit the spot, did he confront the reason why he was alone in the apartment. His son, would be ending his life tonight and except for holding Val's hand there wasn't a damn thing he could do about it. If he was edgy, that was only natural. The TV was right. He should start thinking about getting over to the Clinic.

Nursing his drink, he sank down in front of the screen and lowered his eyelids. At this very moment Val was lying in the New Bethlehem Clinic on Potrero Hill while the technicians fussed over her, as they had been doing for six months now. Hardly a day passed without some new test had to be carried out on her. Vergil understood that this was unavoidable – since it was a legal requirement – but he was glad for Val's sake that it would soon be over. Soon Theo, as they had decided to call their son, would be dead.

He knew how it would end. He would proceed to the Clinic. He would support his wife while their baby's life terminated at precisely the moment the technicians predicted. The likelihood of an accidental series interfacing at this stage with their prediction was pretty remote. Luck, good and bad, had virtually been eliminated – although no one actually said it did not exist. Any false move on Vergil's part would reflect on his status. The Protocol Organization would be watching how he handled his child's death. They would not respect behaviour that did not conform to the matrices of his destiny. And right now he was destined to take himself over to the Clinic, like the TV said.

'We have the evening's episode of the Show on line, Vergil,' the TV said, adding: 'Soon as you get back from . . .'

'Quit harassing me!' Vergil snapped. 'Just get on with the Show!'

'Take it easy now!' the TV admonished.

Vergil felt uneasy about bickering with the TV. Like

3

most people he relied on it a great deal. Without the TV – in particular, the serialized drama of the Bernier family – he would never have the opportunity of seeing how other people fulfilled their destinies. TV made sense of the Protocol and the status-system and gave it continuity. Outside his own status-group Vergil hardly met anyone, and other VW's were not much different than Val and himself. Whereas everyone in the White House Show appeared to do what the fuck they liked and get away with it. Like most people he was fascinated by the goings-on in the high-status homestead: the President's family, the well-placed Gov-set and, above all, the manner in which the Protocol arrived at its decisions. And the Protocol, however low down in the Organization he came, was the business Vergil was in. Aside from everything else, the developments in the affairs of the Bernier family formed the main topic of people's conversation, so it never paid to miss too many episodes.

'We join the Show,' the TV said by way of introduction. 'With Archer and Ammarie continuing their discussion on the subject of Annie's future. Ammarie, you will recollect, is toying with the idea that their daughter marry the promising young MNEMOREX executive, Adrian Buckingham, with whom Annie has been playing a lot of tennis recently. Annie seems to like the idea too . . .

'MNEMOREX, of course, is the new relaxant from Farben-Bayer that's proving very popular. A single cap contains the effects of approximately one hour's meditation. No side effects. No addiction risk. Tested on the Government. So at the first sign that your afterlife is not progressing like you planned and little things start to screw up, consider MNEMOREX . . .'

Vergil must have dozed off during the sponsor's plug because when he opened his eyes the latest episode of the Show was already on screen.

*   *   *

'NOW DARLING, you know perfectly well . . .'

It was Ammarie Bernier speaking, the soft-spoken ash-blonde wife of Archer Bernier. They were both drinking green cocktails out of slender glasses on the recently-rolled lawn of some perfectly-maintained garden. Was it their château on the Loire, or one of their other residences? Fluffy white clouds billowed across the sky like racing yachts far out to sea. The sun winked through green leaves, pleasantly variegating the shade. Birds sang.

'. . . that MNEMOREX is an excellent product – everyone says it is – and Adrian has a fine future in front of him.'

'Sure, Honey, and they play tennis together,' Archer said. 'That don't mean they're *compatible*. I play tennis with her myself. I take MNEMOREX too. So do a billion other people.' He gestured vaguely with his cocktail toward the billion other people. 'Anyway, it was me told Adrian to take Annie to the Tennis Club in the first place. I figured it would take her mind off . . . What was that young man's name . . .?'

Ammarie was the President but everyone knew that she left the day-to-day running of the Protocol to her husband. Archer Bernier – elegant, affable, handsome – was a man you could trust. She nearly always went along with his suggestions. Anyone could see how much in love they were with each other.

'Why . . .' Ammarie giggled. '. . . That's funny, Darling! I told *her* to take *him* to the Club!'

'Then relax! Let them sort themselves out in their own time. Don't forget, Marie, the status of our friends is determined but not our preferences. Annie will marry someone like Adrian, sure, but it won't necessarily be him. So long as she's happy.'

Ammarie took hold of Archer's hand.

'You're right, dear,' she said, giving him that little girl smile which was her trademark.

'That's settled then?'

Ammarie nodded. Archer placed his unfinished drink on the marble table. He stood up.

'That case, let's us go up and say hello to Adrian.'

The President and her husband rose and crossed the lawn arm-in-arm. Birds sang.

Cut to an interior of the White House. Archer Bernier stood next to a large white marble fireplace that came as high as his shoulder. He was speaking into a vid-compact which he was holding in his hand.

'Did Adrian arrive yet, Jenny?'

The pretty face which Bernier was seeing in the tiny VDU filled the screen. Jenny Karbowska, Bernier's secretary, said: 'He just did. Do you want me to send him up?'

Bernier nodded.

'Yeah. Thanks, Jenny.'

He turned.

His daughter was watching him from behind plastic sunshades, her back flat against the lilac door, one white-shoed foot holding it shut. Naked sunburnt legs disappeared into a short broderie anglaise tennis outfit that was tailored around her slender teenage figure. A tennis racket in its press was crooked under one arm. Her sunbleached hair was tied back in a tail. The girl did not move nor say a word and in her shades it was hard to guess what she was thinking. Then, with a lazy swipe, Annie Bernier removed her glasses.

'Hi folks!'

VERGIL WYMAN turned guiltily away from the TV. He pulled himself to his feet. He sure liked to look at Annie Bernier — the way she smiled made his bones ache — but, fuck, his wife was in hospital, his son on the point of death!

Did people still play lawn tennis? he mused as he plodded in his socks toward the shower. He peeled off his uniform and stood under the warm water. He closed his eyes. The image of the Bernier girl, however, refused to go away. She was playing tennis, her body arching and stretching. What he'd do to know a girl who dressed in a tennis outfit that didn't hardly cover anything. Just the two of them – alone! His body tightened as the image in his mind's eye climaxed in response to the imaginary experience. He groaned. The warm shower relaxed his brief excitement, then washed away any evidence that it had ever taken place.

It depressed Vergil to realize that nobody he knew played tennis. None of his friends or work-colleagues did. Like himself they just worked, came home, bickered with the TV, screwed their wives – their own wives, mostly.

He stepped from the shower.

No one had to point out to him the absurdity of his infatuation with Annie Bernier. As well as being rich and pretty, Annie was an AB, daughter of the President. And what was Vergil? A VW – on the bum end of the status system – who lived in Arguello, not one of Sanfran's most fashionable areas. He was thirty-three and not losing any weight, with a dummy job and a wife who conversed with the TV almost as much as she did with him.

Vergil didn't mind that Annie Bernier was unaware of his existence and never would be. What hurt was the certainty that there was several million other VWs in the world no different than himself who felt exactly the same way about her as he did.

With a towel over his head Vergil groped for a fresh pair of underpants from the tear-off dispenser. His hand tore off nothing. The dispenser was empty, which meant the supply-roll was exhausted. Startled by this small acausal threat, Vergil was on the point of shouting his wife's name to have her fetch a fresh set when he remembered that she was away in the Bethlehem Clinic. Since he had no idea where she stashed the supply-rolls, he would have to put on the pair he had just discarded. Resigned, he stepped

7

into the already soiled undergarment.

FURIOUS AND frustrated Annie looked away. They had her cornered. For maybe the first time in her afterlife she didn't know what she was going to do next. But, being cornered, it didn't make any difference, so:

'Fuck you!' she said.

It felt good saying this to her mother and father and the concealed TV cameras which – how could she ever forget? – were monitoring every move she made. Omnidirectional mikes were picking up every word she said.

She turned her back on the two we-only-want-to-help-you people who were in the process of discussing her tennis engagement with Adrian Buckingham.

'C'mon, Marie! If she don't want to go . . .'

Archer, as usual, was trying to rescue the take. He didn't stand a chance. Ammarie was going at her for real. It was the old story, her father playing the soft-hearted cop while her mother took the role of the thug. The treatment was calculated to make Annie see that only one course of action was open to her.

Turning, she saw her exit blocked. She was facing the empty eyes, the in-love-with-itself mouth, of Adrian Buckingham. As, of course, she had known she would. It was in the script. On cue, his two hundred pounds were looming through the door like an obvious idea into a dull mind. He was standing over her, a large playful idiot dressed in tennis gear. They had her cornered all right. Nausea swept through her body.

Reflexively she scanned his mind, probing his intentions toward her. It was easy enough. She had done it often before. She knew Adrian Buckingham inside out.

'Hiya, Babe!' the young MNEMOREX executive said while his eyes leered over her body. 'You, uh, ready?'

Adrian Buckingham, like most high-status kids, had

8

attended psyschool but this did not prevent Annie from inspecting his inner attitude, most of which, she could see, consisted of uncomplicated lust. The carnality of his feelings came as no surprise. She expected it. What shocked her was, behind the poor mutt's primitive blocks, the presence of another mind, one much stronger than his own, fighting her on his behalf. It was a voice she had heard since she was in the cradle. Annie said nothing. She drew back her fist like a bolt and slammed it into the relaxed area of Adrian's abdomen. The shock might jolt the hold Ammarie had on him.

Adrian gasped, startled.

'Fuck you too,' she said.

She pushed him aside with one hand as though he were a large not-very-heavy bug which she was reluctant to touch.

'So you think you can do what you want?' her mother snarled behind her. 'You'll do like we say! And we say you cut along and play tennis with Adrian.'

Annie, to please her parents, had been in front of cameras since she was a baby. While she was a child this had been easy. She had never needed to act. It had been sufficient simply to be herself. Now being herself meant coming up against their idea of who she should be. As far as Ammarie and Archer were concerned, her affairs and behaviour were social duties, scripted, taped, packaged for the whole world to know about. Whom she married was an aspect of Government policy.

Well, not any more!

'Better do like your mother says, Annie . . .' her father whined. She pitied him, the way he jumped whenever Ammarie whistled.

Tossing a see-you-in-hell-first smile over her shoulder for the benefit of the TV cameras, she walked off the set. She ran the length of the corridor toward the elevator which, except for some ferns in pots, was deserted. Out of a side door a young man hurried, collided into her, his face aghast.

'Annie! You all gone crazy?' the ABC employee exclaimed. She had fouled up another rehearsal.

'We'll have to shoot that over . . .' he said.

She disengaged herself from his grasp.

'You won't, Charlie. Don't worry.'

'Look, you can't just . . .'

'I can! I'm through! You'll have to run the Show without me!'

'But it's . . . We're weeks behind schedule already.'

'I hate to say this Charlie, but will you just get the fuck outta my way!'

The elevator gates closed after her.

The Show would go out tonight the same as it did every night. And tomorrow night. Charlie could fix that. The TV company had enough pictures of her to keep it going for months. They didn't need her.

Alone on the tarmac she hesitated, dazed by the quietness of the kiteport, the clear sky, the absence of human beings. She inhaled the air. Below her lay the sky-reflecting Potomac. There were trees. There were fluffy white clouds. There was, stepping from behind a vent stack, the single most dangerous man in the world. Ben Cznetsov was rolling toward her on the balls of his feet, already smiling his never-taken-by-surprise smile. He waved to her.

'Hi there, sweetheart!' he called. Then, nearer: 'What's wrong? You upset? Is it Ammarie?'

Csnetsov – 'Uncle Benny' – had been around Annie longer than she could remember. He had a lot of affection for her and he had often interposed on her behalf with Ammarie. He was about the only person who could.

'Do me a favour,' she said without returning his smile. 'Take this . . .' She pushed into his open palm the butt end of the tennis racket. 'And shove it someplace, will you?'

Leaving the CIA Chief holding the racket, Annie Bernier ran across the apron of the kiteport to where her own kite was parked. Breathing fast, she ripped the velcro of the broderie anglaise tennis dress she was wearing and stepped out of the garment. She let it fall to the ground and leapt, naked, into the cabin of the kite and ignited the power halo. Fine dust petticoated from under the vehicle. Without waiting to obtain official clearance-permission from the port authority, or even to ask for it, she lifted the kite off the roof of the building, gained height and pointed it into the bluest part of the sky.

WHEN THE vid-console chimed Vergil was back in the kitchen fighting the ice-maker with a knife and fork in order to free sufficient ice for his third glass of fake hooch. Holding the drink, he returned unsteadily to the TV room, cracking his shin on the low glass-type table that stood between him and the TV. In place of the evening's episode of the Show the concerned features of a uniformed young woman watched him from the screen. He recognized Galina Hope, Staff Nurse at the Bethlehem Clinic.

'Mr Wyman,' she said. She smiled. 'You're in bad shape! What are you doing? There's nothing to worry about!'

'I'm sorry. I know nothing can go wrong. It's stupid of me but I feel, I dunno, kinda nervous.'

'Val's going to be fine! Don't get yourself in a state!'

'That's what everyone tells me. I can't help it . . .'

'Val's in good hands! . . .'

She held them up for him to see.

'. . . She has everything she needs. Except *Mister* Wyman! I wanted you to know that Theo is going to die *very* soon. I hope . . .'

'I was just leaving when you called,' Vergil lied. 'I'm on my way.'

'That's excellent. Don't let me keep you. And go easy on that stuff! She needs you in one piece!'

The attractive features of the mid-status professional faded from the screen. Vergil – he took a farewell slug of

11

the drink in his hand – tried to focus his thoughts on Val but it was the image of Annie Bernier in skimpy tennis clothes that reappeared on the screen. That was all he needed! He found his shoes and stumbled out of the apartment without relaying his intentions to the TV and had the elevator transport him to the kiteport where he called for a cab. While he waited he dropped a couple of MNEMOREX in the hope that they would counteract the effect of the alcohol.

The kite which turned up was a beat-up old Cessna but, given the status of the neighbourhood Vergil lived in, he could probably count himself lucky. He climbed in and posted his Protocol key, directing it to take him to the Bethlehem Clinic, real quick. The senile vehicle took its time verifying the necessity – and therefore the legality – of the request but when it had gotten the green light it had, grinding gears, taken to the air. Vergil sat back in the faded upholstery and closed his eyes.

He had often wondered what kind of afterlife was in store for Theo but there was a sense in which he already knew because he had seen it for himself on his copy of the child's SollyChart. And the Sollyheim Uteroscope predicted that his son was due to lead a normal healthy a-life. Theo would be a TU and that was an improvement on themselves. Vergil had been relieved to find this out. At least his son wasn't going to be a Zapper. At the same time, he had been disappointed. Theo would rise moderately in status so he must have put up a better show in his previous life than either Val or himself. TUs cut a lot of ice in the community, whereas VWs were just very hard workers. But they didn't cut *that* much ice.

They said he had nothing to worry about. They said the boy would be fine. Kids today learnt quick because they didn't harbour doubts about the future as people of Val and Vergil's generation did, just as Val and Vergil, in turn, had not been as edgy as their own parents during the era of 'Phrenia Plague'. Young people take for granted what the previous generation has to learn the hard way. The children dying today would grasp the importance of the uteroscope before they knew how to talk. They would grow up with an understanding of the principles of Death, the a-life and being Returned. It would never cross their minds that they were, as people had once said, alive.

The taxi crossed the Panhandle on its way toward Potrero. The functional outline of the service-worker condo-blocks, built on what had been the fashionable neighbourhood of Richmond in the prequake city, gave way to the elegant pyramids of Mission and Bay View. Vergil tried to recall the circumstances which had led to Gottlieb Sollyheim's ideas taking root. It wasn't easy. Imagining the world as it had been before Sollyheim was like imagining it before electricity or the compass. Like everyone else who watched TV, Vergil knew about the work of the great genetic physicist whose experiments into perinatal experiences had clarified the nature of the afterlife. But it was Sollyheim's remarkable interpretation of his findings as much as the experiments themselves which had caught the public's imagination. According to Sollyheim, what took place during *life*, that is, *in utero* – created the preconditions for what happened after death. It was his revolutionary redefinition of death which had, literally, changed people's lives. Before Sollyheim's flamboyant TV appearances – only the first decade of the century, incredible as it seemed now – everyone had held to the superstition that their day-to-day experiences constituted *life* and when they were Returned they *died*, as they had used the term.

Sollyheim's ideas had taken hold of people's imaginations during a period in history when a lot of folk had begun to forget who they were. There had been inexplicable mass outbreaks of doubt in the validity of perception. The prevailing world view had begun to collapse long before Sollyheim came along. Vergil could not recall the innocence that had prevailed before a scientific advance of

13

such magnitude. Once you know the world is round, it's hard to see it any other way.

By the time Vergil was old enough to understand, Gottlieb Sollyheim had been approaching the end of his own afterlife, his mind beginning to go. He began to make a fool of himself, speaking out against the Compulsory Sollyheim Readings Ticket on which the Dover Administration had been elected. The silent old doctor in the films of that period did not resemble the fellow he had been in his prime. But when he finally went and his body was placed in the mausoleum on Capitol Hill everyone was genuinely sorry. Crazy or not, people had loved him.

The taxi was approaching Potrero. Already below loomed the exclusive ABBACCA ROOM on Harrison and 16th, conspicuous by the huge holographically modulated palm-trees with which it syringed the sky. 'MNEMOREX PICKS YOUR BRAIN . . .' the 3-dim advert on top of the building reminded the world '. . . CLEAN.'

Almost immediately the bright lights of the Clinic complex, massive and self-contained like a small town, soared out of the darkness. Vergil was able to see through the huge transparent walls to the lighted interior where white-coated personnel went about their business like minute organels in the cytoplasm of a cell under magnification. It made his head spin. A lethal cocktail of epinephrine and booze was rollercoasting through his veins. His wife was somewhere inside the Clinic, his son inside his wife. He was outside the both of them. Separate. A speck of dust. One out of a billion spermatazoa jostling toward the egg.

Vergil, to his own surprise, threw up.

The taxi politely requested a clarification of the instruction.

'Juss land this fucking flying saucer, why dontcha?' he rasped through his vomit, impatient to be with Val. Every second was crucial.

The aged machine, hopelessly outmanoeuvred by the

newer faster models, slowly located a vacant parking slot. After Vergil had retrieved his ID – the enormous cost of the short journey already deducted from his next pay-cheque – the hatch swung half-way open. Vergil had to kick it the rest of the way. He chose to do this at the very moment the hatch opened fully of its own accord. His feet, kicking air, dove toward the tarmac and by the time the rest of his body had caught up with them they were already tucked up in bed and fast asleep. The bright lights of the Reception Foyer faded. A gentle oceanbreaker of sadness pushed through Vergil's veins into every capillary in his body until, snug, he let go his hold on consciousness. MNEMOREX . . . he recalled . . . PICKS YOUR BRAIN CLEAN.

2

Joe King – he could hardly hear himself think – had no idea what time it was. He was not even sure what, precisely, Time consisted of – if he had ever known. The drug he had taken was having the effect of amplifying the discrete functions of the organs inside his body into a soaring pibroch. He tried to recall what it was he was trying to recall. It was hopeless. A gale howled down his throat every time he opened his mouth. His lungs boomed as the muscles connected to his heart contracted and relaxed in concert with the wooshing ebb and flow of his blood. Juices oozed. His alimentary parts hissed and squooshed like a Chinese laundry. The drug had evidently hooked up his conscious mind to his parasympathetic nervous system. Consequently he was experiencing himself as a machine, an artificial intelligence. The experience was not unpleasant but it was distracting him from the immediate problem facing him.

The blood vessels surrounding his eye-balls glowed and dimmed with each beat of his heart as he studied the beautiful face of. . . what the *fuck* was it?

'19.10,' Joe said, startled by the sound of his own voice.

The time his old chronometer kept, like the moving parts inside it, was circular. On the occasion he had disassembled the intricate mechanical device – as Joe King did most machines sooner or later – he had discovered the principle driving it: centrifugal force! He had found a

16

minute self-contained universe driven by an accurately weighted fly-wheel unwinding a coiled spring at the exact rate at which time flowed in the outside world, the inertial drive mechanism ratcheting not only at a speed relative to the rotation of the earth around the sun but in response to the same forces! Beautiful!

But if it were 19.10 — a fact corroborated by the luminous digits set into the eyes of the little wooden dog on Val Wyman's chiffonnier — then he was on duty and it was a while before he came off shift. He was at his place of work. He was assisting his colleague, Jerry Kittow, to disengage the Sollyheim apparatus that was hitched up to the body of Valerie Wyman. Val was nearing the end of her term — as Theo Umman neared the end of his — but it did not look as if it was an occasion she was especially happy about.

'Where *is* Vergil?' she pleaded to no one in particular.

A wave of pity for the unhappy woman flooded Joe's own drug-induced sensations. Val was an ordinary sweet-natured low-status woman who had never hurt anyone.

'Don't worry, Val,' Jerry said from the other side of the room. 'He most likely got caught up some place.'

Jerry took hold of Val Wyman's hand.

'Sure,' Joe said. 'He'll be here soon as he can.'

Joe could understand why Val was getting worked up. Her husband was behind schedule. If he didn't arrive soon he might miss his son's death altogether. Only a chance-series could interfere with the causality behind Vergil Wyman's behaviour. Complications of such a nature during the child's incarnation could — technically — result in a down-grading in the kid's status-rating. It wasn't unheard of. The Protocol did not approve of accidents.

Having mapped the matrices of the boy's *in utero* experiences himself, Joe knew all about Theo already: his tastes, disposition, mannerisms. He was already an old friend. From their readings of his mental activity they knew he had been having a good life, demonstrating a normal interaction with the activity of his uterine contemporaries in his intelligence-band. Theo would forget most of this after he died but his performance within the hierarchy would be preserved in the computer and on the basis of that the course of his afterlife could be accurately projected. Joe and Jerry had traced his participation in the life urges shaping the destiny of the world. For Val's amusement they had separated and amped up Theo's own unique bath-tub song-of-life. It had amused her but in the end it would be this data relating to his previous life which determined the framework of Theo's personal SollyChart.

'Joe. . . ?'

Joe started.

'. . . You okay?' Jerry's voice spoke quietly into his ear.

'What?'

'What the fuck did you take this time?'

'I think,' Joe told him, 'it began with M.'

'Mellodrin?'

'Could be. Why? What does it do?'

'It's a thalamus repressant,' Jerry said as a matter of fact. He turned back to the uteroscope. 'You'll probably go insane.'

Joe felt pretty sure the drug had not been Mellodrin. Jerry was trying to scare him. Jerry was a good friend but he made no secret of the fact he disapproved of the way Joe took drugs randomly, sampling them on the basis of their colour and shape in preference to a more informed system. Like most people, Jerry Kittow considered it irresponsible to mess with chance.

Val Wyman groaned. Joe and Jerry glanced at each other in silence. They could see she was frightened but what could they do? Jerry spoke into his lapel pager.

Bizarre scifi noises continued to woosh and buzz inside Joe's body but that was nothing compared to what must be going on inside Val Wyman's. The four feet separating him from her might have been a million miles. She was upset and probably in pain while he was marooned inside a drug the name of which he thought began with the letter M. He could have cried himself. The drug was making him experience himself as a machine. He could do nothing for the human being suffering a few feet from where he was standing.

'SWEET VERGIL! Help me!' she murmured.

The pressures of another contraction were building up inside her. The upper part of her uterus began to lean down on the baby like a piston, forcing her lungs to make rapid inhalations until she heard the voice of Galina Hope inside her head, calm and clear, say: 'Breathe in slowly, Val.'

The contraction gathered momentum. It had nothing to do with her. She was alone in a crowd that was turning ugly.

'Now breathe out – slowly.'

She lifted the entonox mask to her mouth and inhaled according to the remote instructions her brain was issuing, which had the effect of relaxing her whole body except the arm holding the mask. The constricting muscles of her uterus clung to the skull of the little person inside her, refusing to let go. She grew detached from her body, a peaceful country invaded by a power that was forcing from it everything it had existed for, her crop. Aloof – she could hear the clicking whirr of the valve on the entonox cylinder – she surrendered to the necessity of the contraction.

'Breathe in!'

She breathed in but she was no longer in control. The voice of the Staff Nurse was piloting the floating vessel of her body and its precious cargo.

'Now breathe out.'

The contraction peaked. Oh boy! The mask dropped from her hand onto the bed. The whirring of the valve ceased. She could breathe easy again. With each contraction she had to accept that Theo, from having being been part of her for so long, was saying goodbye. He was pushing away from her, becoming separate. Dying, in fact. She knew that this was something that had to happen but could she hold on until Vergil arrived?

'What time is it?' she said.

Worse than the contractions was the prospect that Vergil would not show up at all. How could the moment they had worked so hard for pass without him being present to participate? It was too fearful to contemplate and yet in the lulls between the contractions she didn't have anything else to do except contemplate it, think the unthinkable. An unpermuted occurrence – happenstance – had interfered with the most important moment in her son's life, his death.

'19.10,' one of the technicians said.

'Where is Vergil?'

'Don't worry, Val . . .'

Someone took hold of her hand.

'. . . He most likely got caught up some place.'

What did he mean 'caught up'? That sounded terrible. Accidents happened, sure, but it had never occurred to her until this moment that one could happen to Vergil. It would be a real setback. People who trusted in luck never got anywhere.

'Sure, Verge'll be here soon as he can,' the technician said.

Joe King and Jerry Kittow were nice boys. They were only doing their best, she knew. They had been real nice to her since the day she attended for her first routine Sollycheck. But couldn't they see that right now she just wanted to be left alone? Already another slow-motion whiplash of pain had begun to uncoil from the centre of her being, an incubus exorcizing itself. The present contraction was identical to the contraction preceding it – and to the one preceding that. Their unchanging nature wrung her like a rag that was already well enough wrung. One part of her was tense like just before an orgasm while the rest of her was limp, like just after one. She didn't have the energy even to cry. Her son was leaving her for ever. Her husband was never going to arrive. She was all alone.

'Val . . .'

She turned her head on the pillow.

'I just called your husband again,' Galina Hope approached the bed and laid a cool hand on Val's hot forehead. 'He's on his way over!'

'He is?'

'According to the TV he already left for the Clinic. He'll be here presently.' The Staff Nurse smiled. 'You just try and relax!'

The two technicians left the chamber along with the Sister, the door closing silently after them. She breathed in. She breathed out. The pressure on the tip of her tailbone – the head of her baby – welled like a sea wave. She was bobbing on the ocean, far from land. Her eyes watched the wooden clock carved in the shape of a dog – Vergil had given it to her during the period in which they had first tested their compatibility with each other – until its green eyes blinked: 19.17.

3

As evening descended the lights of Oakland and Alemeda winked across the Bay. Quick irregular shadows altered the surface of the Bay itself whenever a fragment of cloud passed in front of the face of the moon. A breeze was blowing off the ocean. On the edge of a roof garden high up on the Bayside of the city open azalea flowers, their purples and vermilions made unearthly by the moonlight, trembled in the gentle turbulence. The white-haired octogenarian leaning against the safety rail of the same roof-garden, drawing on his cigar, welcomed the cool current, enjoying the small discomfort it caused him after the servile warmth of his apartment. At least it possessed a will of its own. He smoked his cigar here at this time almost every evening but he had never noticed until now how much the rapid play of light and dark on the silver water resembled the passage of memories over the surface of his own mind. Urgent, beautiful, illusory, pointless. The fragrance of jasmine pervaded the air on the hem of the breeze like the presence of a woman.

Through open french windows a lighthearted piece of chamber music serenaded, unaware that it was serenading a deserted chamber. This grieved the old-timer because it was a piece which had always been dear to him. It had been a number of years, however, since even Mozart had lightened his heart. Lately he preferred to watch the sea-

22

encircled city as night closed upon it, active with human beings whose destinies were colliding by chance and appointment. It wasn't the same city he had known as a young man, of course. The earthquake had almost completely erased that lovely old town. All the same, he had taken a liking to the new metroplex which had risen out of the ashes of the devastation. He had witnessed for himself the extent of the destruction immediately after the disaster – 8.5 on the Richter – and what the quake had left standing the government bulldozers had finished off. Inevitably his own schemes had become tied up in the reconstruction programme and, just as inevitably, he had fallen in love with the city all over again – the delicately gimballed incarnation of the old phoenix.

'*Seid umschlungen Millionen. . !*'

He muttered the words of the Schiller poem to the city to which he had given so much of his life but which had eventually rejected him.

'*Diesen Kuss der ganzen Welt!*
Brüder! Überm Sternenzelt
Muss ein lieber Vater vohnen.
Ihr stürzt nieder, Millionen?'

He sighed. What was the point? Poetry, music. Cigar smoke carried off into a beautiful evening.

From his aerie high up on the promontory of Hunter's Point he was in a position to take in the whole of Sanfran at a glance, which he liked to do at this hour when the taxis were plying the Bay. He liked to imagine the ordinary human desires and fears paying for them. He knew that the vehicles would, for the most part, be ferrying AB customers to the AB pleasure zones, returning mid-status executives to their single storey houses in Redwood and Freemont. It still moved him to see the species carrying out its business the way it always had, seeking out the comfort of bright lights and hearth in the face of night's uncertainty. Downtown, above the massive Protocol Centre on Union Street, a pair of pale blue SkyPol kites hovered.

Everything – and nothing – had changed. He stood on the same terms with the city as he had stood with his fellow creatures throughout his career. As a spectator. He was surveying a world – vast and beautiful and ignorant – from the vantage point of a knowledge which he had tried and failed to impart. He had done his best to put across his ideas but without any luck, and now luck was not just against him, it was against the law. The huge illuminated complex soaring almost to the height of the roof-garden, not a mile away on the neighbouring hill, was a poignant reminder of his irrelevance. The variously sized carriers trafficking around the building, arousing the tender emotion that ambulances always do, took no account of his existence. He observed the activity around the Bethlehem Clinic with a mixture of affection and resentment. The place compounded the mixed feelings aroused in him by humankind itself – love, irritation, despair, anger, pity, forgiveness, you name it. This was not surprising. He had been betrayed by both. He knew the Clinic better than anyone. Had he not worked inside it for seventeen years? Had it not been constructed according to his own detailed specifications? As a government consultant had he not overseen its planning and development? As its first Director he had steered through its original charter which had become a blueprint for hundreds of similar institutions all over the world. The hospital on Potrero Hill was his baby. His fame was founded on its success. And the eighty-six-year-old Doctor of Medicine smoking his cigar on the moonlit roof-garden was just about the most famous person in recent history.

But what he had created, the achievement for which he was famous, had destroyed him. He had spent a lot of his time – the third quarter of his life – setting up the Sanfran Clinic programme. Too much time, perhaps, because it had been during that period that his theories had taken root and in the most unexpected imaginations. By the time he had come to see what was happening it was too late.

The perversion of everything he had stood for was complete. He had been a foolish old man who had allowed himself to be used. Now, if no less foolish, he was an even older man, passing his last days in a paradise customized for his comfort. He had everything he could ask for. He smoked the rare *Romeo y Giulietta* coronas on the roof of the Schryer Building, one of the tallest and most prestigious residences in Sanfran. He dwelt in the city of his choice and his simple Old World tastes were satisfied. A fresh doughnut and coffee for breakfast – real coffee. He had his cat Mitzou. He had Mozart. He had an intelligent and gentle 'personal requirement supervisor', as they termed the young person who brought him his tea in the morning and mixed his milk and cognac before he retired. He had his favourite books – Tolstoy, Dickens, Goethe. He had his own garden to cultivate, a miniature Eden of common and exotic shrubs and trees. He had peace, fresh air and a Sterling Smith and Corona typewriter. What more could an old man ask for?

One thing this one would have asked for was a vidphone – or even an old telephone. A door he could walk in or out of as he chose. An elevator that would take him down the ninety storeys to streetlevel. Neighbours who would greet him by name when he stepped out to fetch his doughnut from Righi's for himself. He would have liked to take a cab to Mission Rock for fried fish and spicy vodka, to pass a sunny afternoon playing chess on the benches along with the other old-timers, to start conversations with people whom he did not know and who did not know him. King's pawn to King Four. Knight to Bishop Three.

But he would never do any of these things. For reasons of State Security his freedom of movement had been taken from him. Knight takes Bishop. The Administration had nothing against him personally. It was what was inside his head that they had been keeping out of circulation – for the last fourteen years. The Truth. He had it and they knew he did. They wanted to make sure that he could no more tell the world what it was than he could run for President. Rook takes King's pawn. He possessed no ID, without which no door or elevator would open for him and, even if he had, the elevator doors would have opened onto an apartment occupied by the resident SkyPol crew. Check. It was an arrangement he had accepted without complaint, while the Administration, for its part, made sure that his confinement was comfortable and lacked nothing. He could, within reason, have anything he wanted. All he wanted was to stop being dead.

Mate. *Shāh Māt*. The King is dead.

'Honey . . .'

A slim arm encircled his waist.

'. . . You're brooding. I can tell!'

At the other end of the arm the warm body of a young woman came into contact with his own and conducted to earth the electricity inside his brain. He knew she was thinking he was going to catch a chill if he stayed much longer out in that sea breeze. But if she was, she wasn't going to say. She understood that old men can't be shielded from all the dangers all the time. Such small risks were all they had left.

'Clinic's busy tonight,' she murmured.

'Babies come in phases,' he said. 'Like coincidences.'

She was silent. His gentle taunt lay between them. However close she got to him – which could be pretty close – he never let her pretend to herself that he accepted any of the Chance and Necessity crap that characterized the New Orthodoxy. '*Eppure si muove* . . .' as the old Italian astronomer had muttered under rogation. The world was round and it rotated on its own axis around the sun. Always had, always would.

'I wish I could . . . *do* something,' she said eventually. 'That could help you!'

Turning his gaze from the city lights to his young companion, he pushed her short black cat's hair against

26

the growth the way men of the world do to their kid brothers. Cheryl Duvall, of course, was no kid. An attractive twenty-eight-year-old woman, she had probably learnt a good deal more about the world than he had himself and in a quarter of the time. For this reason he felt sorry for her. The kind of world she had learnt about was heartless and mechanistic. Free will, including her own, had been eliminated from it. Having agreed to ride herd on a potentially embarrassing public figure, she had surrendered herself to a will stronger than her own.

'You do help me, Cherry!' he told her. He batted her an eyelid. 'You fix my nightcap like no one else could!'

'Oh, I forgot! Here! Drink it before it gets cold!'

Lunar shadows masked the more obviously female contours of her body. She might indeed have been some man-of-the-world's kid brother. He smiled at the thought. Cheryl Duvall's delicate features belied the trained reactions of a crack CIA agent, one of Cznetsov's people, licenced to carry a gun.

He took the milk and cognac from her, aware that on occasion she added something to it besides Courvoisier, something that made him sleepy and took away his dreams. If the opportunity presented itself he would slop the confection into one of the flowerbeds, preferring a wide-awake night to the amnesia which the drug induced. Perhaps tonight there would be nothing in it. If there was, it probably meant she had a date. She had some place to go, someone to meet out there in the big bad city. If she did, he didn't want to stand in her way.

Tilting back the glass – wisps of cigar smoke were still troubling the face of the moon – he finished the drink. Behind them, on the other side of the open glass doors, the painfully cheerful *divertimento* arrived at its conclusion – no less painfully than its cheerful composer had arrived at his.

* * *

NOTHING COULD be any different from how it was. The apparently random cross-town traffic was running according to an everchanging unchangeable schedule. The numerous transit vehicles streaming back and forth between Market and Mission, North Beach and Pacific Heights, Bayview and Oceanview, were all headed for the same place: a destination logged in the memory of the central communication computer which recorded and processed every travel request, regulated every flight course and thereby eliminated the opportunity for human error – collision. The world moved purposefully on sonar rails. Streetlevel, in contrast, was growing quieter and more sombre by the minute as the interstices between the banking and commercial institutions were surrendered to the night. Soon they would be inaccessible altogether, sinister no-go areas inhabited by vermin and vagrants.

Rock bottom among the daytime jetsam, a figure – shabby and shadowy – took shape among the piles of uncollected garbage bags, a species emerging from the habitat to which it had become adapted. A cold wind buffeted shadows and scraps of light like litter. The moon was in and out.

'Sure's a beautiful night.'

The collar of Spight's Navy greatcoat was turned up over the flaps of his wool cap. Both his hands were in the pockets. One of them clasped the warm silver of his old Hoffner B flat, the other a comforting half pint of brown rum. His situation was not so bad. He had been worse.

'Time to get off the streets,' he told himself.

Although he did not officially exist – Spight's name was on no Protocol computer file – he could nevertheless get himself spotted and picked up by a passing curfew evasion scanner. What he needed right now was to find a place where he could curl up and decant the rest of the rum from the bottle to his belly. In order to make room for it, should that happy opportunity arise, he released the contents of his bladder against the steel bars of a locked access-gate while he considered his position. It was already too late to break into the warm vent of a service garbulator shaft. Streetlevel access, even as he stood there, was closing down around him.

It'll just have to be one of the public buildings,' he concluded aloud, shaking his penis before re-introducing it to his pants. 'Them places is always open.'

Spight, though capable of recognizing the factors contributing to his immediate situation, never consciously *did* anything. Unable to differentiate himself from his environment, he participated mystically with it, relying on instinct and intuition. Consequently things happened to him without his being aware that he had played any part in their coming about. Suffering as he did from the variety of left-hemisphere cerebral dysfunction known as Korsocoff's syndrome, he had no recollection of the passage of time. He inhabited a continual present, a series of *nows* which never added up to a *then*. When he found himself in the vicinity of a towering public access building, this was a fortuitous event rather than the consequence of a causal chain he might have contributed to.

The nearest public building rose up, bright against the night, on the crest of the nearest hill. Spight made his way towards it. Crouching among the shadows before they disappeared completely, he waited while white ambulances and other self-regulating carriers rose and descended over the open tarmac around him. He couldn't take it seriously. In whichever direction he turned he was faced with the same meshing of purpose and result – a world running on circuits. Doors opened – people passed through them, doors closed. The functions of the humans and the artificial intelligences were so nicely attuned that – so far as he could see – there wasn't much to choose between them, no margin for error.

The activity on the landing apron continued for some minutes, or hours – for Spight the clock had stopped long ago – until an old Cessna cab taxied unsteadily onto a vacant space near to where he was crouched in ambush

29

for just such an occurrence. A single passenger – a young man in a big hurry – leapt out of the vehicle and immediately collapsed onto the tarmac, a casualty depositing itself on the Emergency Bay of the City Hospital. The man, either too drunk or concussed, did not move. But Spight wasn't interested in the passenger. Already white-uniformed AIs were hurrying out of the foyer. In no time at all they had the unconscious arrival scooped up and wheeled through the sliding doors.

The rat in Spight's heart leapt – this, after all, was the moment it had been waiting for – while the cat in his brain did not move a muscle. At the mercy of his instinctual fears, he stole up on the stationary kite – a warrior stalking prey, made invisible by his magic. He ducked under the gate in the sonar-field of the vehicle's security system, diddled open the rear hatch and rolled into the trunk. He lowered the hatch lid after him.

He lay still, soaking up the human warmth which the interior of the cab retained. Already the steps he had taken to pass from the dangers of streetlevel to the relative security of his present situation were beginning to fade from his memory. He had made it, that was all that mattered. He had not done anything. It had just happened to him. Grinning at his good fortune, he pulled himself comfortable – head propped, knees bent – in the narrow but adequate luggage compartment and brought out the two things that were stashed in the pockets of his Navy greatcoat. He unscrewed the cap from his short dog and sipped the scalding nectar. While the anticipated happy feeling spread through his body, he gave the old B flat an affectionate smack with his palm. He put it to his lips and blew into it.

'*Excuse me . . .*'

Spight – the cat leapt and the rat froze – stopped playing in the middle of the bar. He looked up. He was alone.

'You have entered this public transit vehicle in violation of the Protocol regulations . . .'

30

The communications facility of the cab's computer was addressing him.

'Please state your intentions and dime your ID.'

Spight giggled.

He had no ID. The very idea! Oh boy! How could he? Since he had gone AWOL from the Marines – quite why he had not been able to recall for some years – nobody had been able to put a line on him. He had no legal status. So far as the Protocol was concerned he was dead. He had slipped through the net. He lived among rats and cats in old sewers and abandoned heating and ventilation conduits, the labyrinths of streetlevel. He had got by without the aid of ID, thank you. He wasn't dead yet.

He returned the harmonica to his mouth and punched out a few chords:

F – G – C – C7 – F – A♭7 – G . . .

Then he sang some:

'I'm a zig-zag wanderer . . .'

'You are . . .'

'I'm a zig-zag wanderer . . .'

'You are . . .'

'I'm a zig-zag wanderer outta zig-zag time . . .'

'You are a. . . ?'

'Zig-zag traveller through zig-zag miles . . .'

'You are a musician, sir?' the kite's communications facility persisted.

'You got me!' Spight laughed almost silently. 'Fast and bulbous!'

'Fast and . . . Is that F?'

'Flat!'

'A. . . ?'

'Seventh.'

'Fast and bulbous!'

Spight licked out the rhythm on his mouth harp while the old cab, keeping correct time, enunciated the words with precision.

'Fast and bulbous!'

Spight paused to take a pull from his bottle. He hadn't felt this good in a long while. The rhythm of his songs — the *now* and *now* and *now* — was the only kind of time he felt easy with. He let his head fall back onto the upholstery in order to finish off the last of the rum. As he did he caught sight through the cab's observation panel, of the moon reeling — fast and bulbous — through brilliant clouds.

'Sure's a beautiful night!' he murmured, lowering his eyelids. Warm and happy.

'Fast and bulbous!'

'You got me!'

4

'. . .He picked his way among the disembodied limbs that were entangled in the wreckage. Heads and torsos of varying hair and skin colour lay in contorted attitudes of pain and ecstasy. Exotic fragments of lawn and faille and crêpe de chine snared the eye and provided camouflage for the butterflies. . .'

Joe King, sitting out the remaining minutes of his shift in the technicians' quarters, re-read a favourite page of the old pulp fiction classic. It gathered his mind into one place while the effects of the drug he had taken – which, he was now satisfied, had not been Mellodrin – wore off. He found, on re-entry that the unfulfilled prophecies and future visions in the reading matter of a previous genera- tion counteracted the chemistry of hallucinogens. Brave, moving, silly, they broke his fall and, in addition, took his mind off his own unfulfilled dreams of being a writer of such books.

'. . . Billowing overhead, a canopy of tall evergreen leaves, palm fronds and tree-ferns reticulated the light onto his face and hands. Rivulets of clear water trickled out of a carpet of mossy liverworts and clumps of horsehairs and fern thalluses. . .'

He could have written this stuff. He knew it in his bones. If he had not written this, it was not his fault. It was his misfortune that he had been born in the wrong period of history, one which did not possess sufficient naivety to let itself enter and partake of an alternative world. It wasn't his fault that the convention of buying and reading books of fiction had broken down. In a society without readers, what role was there for a writer?

'I guess I'll take off.'

His colleague, Jerry Kittow, across the room from where Joe sat, was in the process of exchanging his white uniform trousers for his blue jeans.

'You coming?'

'Uh-uh . . .' Joe murmured without looking up from his book. 'I want to finish this chapter. I'm still a bit wired.'

There followed an awkward silence. Joe pretended to read, hoping that it would go away.

'Are you still planning to meet that girl – the one you told me about?' Jerry said.

Joe looked up. He knew what Jerry was getting at.

'You bet!'

Jerry stood velchroing himself into his old air-jacket. 'One these days,' he said. 'One these days they gonna catch your ass inside a high-status environ! They'll kick the shit out of it when they do.'

'Why should they catch me? I can go anywhere my Protocol ID key permits me to!'

'The fuck you talking about? It's not *your* key! You stole it from the store and you tampered with it! The Protocol, they ever find out, will cut your brain out!'

Jerry didn't understand. It wasn't people who gave their identity to machines, it was machines gave their identity to people. Dismantling the ID key hadn't been difficult. The hard part had been retriggering the device with a new set of information, repersonalizing it with the aid of the restricted data and specialized tools which his position as a Sollyheim Technician gave him access to. With details of his own physiology encoded into the modified status-rating, the key – whatever Jerry said – was his. Doors, kites, elevators, AIs and other restricted utility mechanisms accepted and processed his requests.

'Whyn't you come along?' he taunted. 'Some of those AB night spots are hot!'

'Too hot for me,' Jerry said. He moved towards the door. 'And you're forgetting something. *I* don't have a key! Here . . .' He tossed his lapel pager to Joe. 'Sign this out for me, will you? Later!'

Alone, Joe glanced down at his watch. 20.47. In just a few hours he would be with the woman whom Jerry considered it his duty to warn him against. He was looking forward to seeing her, of course, for the very reason that disturbed Jerry. It was a dangerous liaison. He knew little about her and she even less about him. Nevertheless, in a short time the barman of some ritzy lounge would be bringing a pair of cocktails to the booth where a girl wearing an expensive silk gown would be seated opposite him.

'*. . .An electric cobalt butterfly approached the gaping labia of a splendid creamy-purple lily-orchid, circling it several times. Dithering fetchingly, the butterfly eventually settled onto the fleshy blue calyx of the flower and, putting out its proboscis, began to imbibe the nectar. He watched, horrified, as the beautiful petals closed very slowly over the intoxicated insect which realized too late the peril of its situation and beat its wings pathetically against the closing walls. . .*'

A high continuous bleep interrupted his reading. His hand pushed the contact switch on his lapel pager into the on position. The bleep, however, did not go away. Joe leaned across and picked up Jerry Kittow's pager, which lay on the chair beside him.

'Technicians' Room,' he said into it.

'Hi! It's me, Galina . . . I'm in the ante-theatre.'

'Hi, Lina. Can I do for you?'

'I need your help. Are you busy?'

'As a matter of fact I was just about to come off shift.'

'Oh . . . I'm sorry . . .'

'I mean, I'm free. I don't have anything on.'

35

'It's Val Wyman's husband, Jerry. He still didn't show up yet and frankly I'm getting worried. I checked he already left his apartment. As you know, it's kinda critical Theo Umman doesn't trauma . . .'

Galina Hope, Joe realized, was mistaking him for his colleague, Jerry Kittow.

'What do you want me to do?' he said, wondering how to disabuse her.

'The baby's due to die inside the next hour, right? That's if Val can relax. We have to induce Theo, he'd be sure to lose status. You and Val got pretty close while you were working on Theo's chart. She told me. . . If you wouldn't mind . . .' The Staff Nurse faltered. 'She wants you to be along for the incarnation. You know, to hold her hand. She asked for you, Jerry.'

It was already too late. How could he tell her now that he was not, in fact, Jerry Kittow but Joe King? She would think the misunderstanding had gotten this far because he had deliberately prolonged it. One of his jokes.

'What do you think?' he said.

'In the circumstances, Jerry, I think it might be a good idea. If you don't mind. I could arrange for you to be her DJ.'

How could he begin to explain? Val really hit it off with Jerry but Jerry just went home. How could Joe inform her that Jerry, like Vergil Wyman, would be unable to attend?

'I'll be there in two,' he said. There was nothing for it. He would go up and explain in person.

Galina Hope thanked him and blew him a kiss over the airwaves.

Jerry let the switch of Jerry Kittow's pager return to the off-position. Rising, he closed the old paperbook, placing it under the cushion of the chair he had vacated, and made his way up to the ante-theatre of the Music Chamber where Wyman's son's afterlife was scheduled to start.

The ante-theatre was empty. Staff Nurse Hope was already in the chamber. Joe – he was not going to be able

36

to explain anything – undressed and took an antiviral ray douche and climbed into the folded green autoclaved theatre smock which had been laid out for him. He hooked the disposable face-mask over his ears and stepped into a brand new pair of disposable clogs. The opening doors announced his arrival.

The air was virtually ozone, clean but without the chilly dryness of standard sterilization. Joe blinked at the illusion of daylight, a soft crepuscular desert light, clear and blue. Val Wyman floated on her arms in a pool of water and a young attendant in a black crossover bikini swimsuit floated alongside her. Galina Hope was standing over by a mobile incubator on the other side of the pool in conversation with a pair of assistants who, in their identical theatre gowns, could have been anyone.

Joe hesitated, momentarily intimidated by the fresh air, the artificial daylight, the atmosphere of professional calm and, more than anything, by the situation. In his theatre autoclaving he was being mistaken for someone he wasn't. It was becoming ridiculous. He headed towards the incubator. He would have to tell Galina Hope straight.

'Hello, Jerry . . .'

From the bathing pool came the remote voice of Val Wyman.

'I'm sorry . . .'

Joe paused.

'Do you think I'm being silly?'

He glanced towards Galina Hope who was still talking with her students.

'You just relax now,' he said behind his sterilized mask. He took her hand and squeezed it the way he guessed Jerry Kittow would have done. I'll be here, you want me. Tell you what . . .' He released her hand. 'Whyn't I go sort out some sounds? Young Theo has a taste for early Italian music. Right?'

He headed for the JVC, sweat breaking out on his forehead. What a mess! He shouldn't be there! He wasn't

Jerry Kittow, nor was he Vergil Wyman. It wasn't *his* hand she wanted to hold! But how, now, could he explain that to her?

He ran his eye down the music index file. The mobile high-toned quality of the Baroque repertoire was what Theo had, *in utero*, responded to best. He located a Pergolesi concerto for flute and strings. The delicate tracery of the *ritornello* would encourage Theo during his last minutes, possibly even persuade him that life after the womb was not so bad after all.

Val Wyman, wrapped in white towelling, lay on the couch panting and weeping alternately. Joe did what he could to encourage her as her contractions – Theo's death throes – increased in intensity. He let her hand grip his as hard as she wanted, which was pretty hard. What else could he do? It was becoming clear to him why Vergil Wyman was in some bar instead of doing his duty at his wife's side.

Shit!

Joe suddenly recalled his own date. He had forgotten all about it. If he didn't start moving soon he was going to miss it.

SQUATTING ON the floor with her back against the hard couch, Val Wyman was barely conscious of the masked figures peering down at her as if she were something on a plate they were about to eat. One of them had given her his hand to hold. You'd think *he* was the one having a baby! Another was the Staff Nurse, talking her through her contractions which were steadily accelerating. In many ways the experience was like the stages of erotic arousal – without the erotic part.

It wasn't Vergil's fault, she knew that. He had penetrated her often enough for her satisfaction. She had no complaints in that department. It wasn't his fault which egg his sperm had fertilized, nor when it had been re-introduced into her uterus by the Protocol clinicians. It hadn't been Vergil who had determined which genetic information it should carry. All he had done had been to screw her. It had been the Protocol Organization that had gotten her pregnant.

'I can see him, Val . . . He's coming!'

The pressure increased. She wanted to push.

'This time,' Galina Hope urged. 'I want you to take one big deep breath and hold it.'

Val, wondering how she was supposed to take any kind of breath with the stubborn weight heaving down inside her like a lump in her bowels, grabbed as much air as she could and held onto it until the pressure it created began to weigh upon the counter force of her baby, hanging in there for dear life.

'Stop pushing!'

She stopped pushing.

'And pant!'

Val – she didn't wait to be told – lapped the air like a dog in the shade of a hot day. She wanted to push but, instead, her diaphragm relaxed. Her lungs contracted. Suddenly, without encouragement from herself, her vagina opened. It possessed a will of its own. Panting involuntarily, she surrendered to the extraordinary metamorphosis her body was undergoing until the contraction, in its own sweet time, began to ease off and when the baby's head slipped out she was surprised. She wanted to laugh. She wanted to cry.

'Good, Val! Now breathe easy!'

It was all over. The corpse of her son – viscid, vocal, taking sly little looks at her between each noisy exhalation – was placed onto her breast. She was so happy, having finally decanted her reason for being into the world. She was so sad. Her baby's departure left a hole inside her, an emptiness which only he – who would never return – could ever fill.

VAL WYMAN'S baby died at 22.23. Joe King reluctantly witnessed the awesome event. On time Theo left the womb and, after his first huge breath, released a howl which almost drowned out the adagio section of the Albinoni concerto which the JVC was reproducing. The moment the placenta had broken, Theo had lost consciousness and all memory of his perinatal experiences. If he was like anyone else the trauma would influence his behaviour for the rest of his time on earth. It was the Clinic's job to make sure that the rupture between an individual and his psychogenesis was not so painful that it would scar his ability to fulfil his life's promise, the topography of which had been recorded so that the direction it was disposed to take, its distinctive homeorhesis, would not be forgotten. Theo's afterlife would unfold according to its own morphogenic destiny. As well as trivia such as his preferences in music, his Sollychart contained the matrix of his personality and from that could be predicted fairly accurately the kind of career he was cut out for, his disposition to succumb to any of the major diseases, the nature of his sexual partner, in short the kind of person he was going to be.

Val, radiant, the dead child on her breast, wept happily with the release of emotion. It no longer seemed that Vergil's absence was important.

At 22.27 a Doctor from the Protocol Section arrived. It was his task to supervise the Staff Nurse while she affixed the plastic Protocol coding to the tiny ankle of Theo – no longer Wyman, now: Umman. This, Joe was interested to learn, was the Doctor's only duty and aside from checking his watch, it was all he did. It obviously wearied him to have to change into theatre autoclaving for the routine inspection but he had no choice. It was the Law. At 22.38 – Joe checked the time on his own watch – the Doctor left. The ordeal, for Joe King, if not for Val and Theo, was

40

over. The professional calm among the staff relaxed as soon as the Protocol physician departed. Masks came down and faces were smiling. Lina Hope approached Joe who, alone, had not removed his mask.

'Thanks, Jerry, you make a great DJ, you know that?'

Joe shrugged. What could he say?

'Yes, Jerry . . .' Val beamed through her tears. 'Thank you. You were a terrific help!'

Everybody loved him – or, rather, Jerry.

A look of bewilderment crossed the face of Staff Nurse Hope. Her eyes were scanning the ID tag on the front of his gown. Her lips mouthed the name printed under the photograph, '*Joe*?'

He shrugged. What could he say?

He said goodbye. Abandoning his uniform in the ante-theatre, he hurried to the Technicians' Room for his own clothes. The effects of the drug he had taken earlier in the afternoon had worn off completely.

BEYOND THE light, the darkness.

One ear of the cat which was reclining in the sphinx position along the arm of the chair, feigning sleep, twitched. Sollyheim glanced up from his book. He raked a finger through the soft hollow nape of the cat's neck while he contemplated his cigar. Either Mitzou had seen or heard something on the other side of the luminous halo thrown out by the floor lamp, or the nape of her neck suddenly itched. And the former was impossible. There was nothing out there. They were alone in the apartment. The shadows on the far side of the lit perimeter were made even shadowier through the smoke-filled beam of the lamp, as if to demonstrate the truism that the Unknown appears even more farouche when viewed from within the safe bright prism of consciousness.

Or prison.

41

To dwell within the circle of what was known, the comfortable and the intelligible πr^2 of human achievement, was his fate – as it always had been, only now more poignantly than ever. In his escape-proof apartment Gottlieb Sollyheim was free – freer, anyway, than most – to consider the cosmos as constructed by Artists and Philosophers throughout history. The greatest poetry, the major works in physics, biology, medicine, music, were all within reach, in his library or on his computer. Euclid and Paracelsus were inside his head. Civilization was on disk. Mozart's little *Rondo in A Minor* for pianoforte – a facsimile of the original manuscript of which lay open on his lap – was a perfect example. But, no matter how perfect, the bounded is always loathed by its possessor. The most elegantly constructed statements about the universe, if unleavened by reality, become anathema – especially to the artist and to the philosopher. To one immured inside the Truth, Mozart's dots and squiggles on the manuscript might just as well have been Einstein's shopping list, for all the difference they made.

The apartment had been rendered escape-proof to the satisfaction of Sollyheim's captors. Amusingly, while a number of wealthy citizens ached from having been denied the privilege of getting inside the Schryer Building, the small penthouse surrounded by its wide and beautiful garden had been re-engineered to keep one particular citizen from getting out. Even if Sollyheim had discovered by chance the combination to the exit – which, of course, was impossible since chance had been illegalized – he would not have gotten any further than the quarters of the Skypol crew who spelled each other in the apartment below. The Administration, convinced that this embarrassing old man had been isolated from the rest of the world, was prepared to be generous in the luxuries they allowed him. Within reason he could have anything he wanted. Archer Bernier and Ben Cznetsov weren't gorillas. In fact, they were almost human.

During his long incarceration Sollyheim had seen Cznetsov maybe six times – and none of the interviews had been pleasant. The reason for this was that he had once liked Cznetsov who, along with Archer Bernier, had been his friend. At one time Sollyheim had been both Ammarie's and Cznetsov's personal physician. He knew things about them which they probably did not know about each other – for example, the small melanoma so perilously near Ammarie's appendectomy scar. But there were a great many pieces of information which the Administration did not suspect Sollyheim of being in possession of. One of these was the fact that the penthouse was not as escape-proof as they liked to think.

And the beauty of it was that it had not been by chance he had discovered the camouflaged hatch of the neglected maintenance-shaft to the service-systems grid – it had been inevitable. Completely overgrown by evergreen creeper, the hatch must have been deliberately screened before his own occupancy of the premises, perhaps because it was not particularly attractive.

Inevitably Sollyheim, being blessed with a green thumb, as doctors often are, had come across the hatch while he had been working on the garden, and he wasn't surprised when he did. He had been incarcerated for being the person he was. It was because he was that person he had discovered a means of escape.

The hatch had been overlooked, he deduced, because no one had thought of ascending as far as the roof-garden. Outside the design plan in the computer in the engineer's consultancy that had conceived of the Schryer, Sollyheim was probably the only person who was aware of the existence of the roof-exit. The computer had never been programmed for the contingency of the penthouse apartment being transformed into a high-security jail.

In the nine months since he had known of the shaft's existence the opportunity it gave him to escape made his enforced residence ridiculous. All the money being spent

43

on his confinement was being wasted. The fact that he could escape any time he chose to meant that all the time he did not choose to he was staying there of his own free will. This knowledge, however, did not console him on those occasions he wished he was in Golden Gate Park playing chess with one of the other old-timers. Ninety storeys were a long way down.

The impulse to lift the hatch and attempt the descent by the metal rungs all the way down to streetlevel had been slow arriving. The hatch was heavy but not as heavy as the collective weight of what he would be leaving. His garden. Mitzou. His books and his music. His typewriter. Climbing rung by rung down the steel ladder in the dark with only a cable-harness clipped to him every storey was not something he was looking forward to. Saying goodbye to Cherry Duvall was not going to be easy either.

And he knew what to expect down there. Out there. Beyond the light, the darkness. The world he would be escaping into, by its own admission, was dead. People led their lives on predetermined courses which they were forbidden to depart from, like prison inmates. The machinery of the State had constructed a nightmare for the citizens to inhabit − and not by force. It was an arrangement everyone was prepared to collude with. Having been sold an idea which justified this state of affairs, they were content. Sollyheim regretted, with all his heart, that the idea had been one of his own.

It had taken some months for Sollyheim to adjust to his discovery and summon the will to leave the comfortable environment to which he had become accustomed. His resolution to do so had gestated inside him, an egg hatching in its own sweet time. It had been a process he had been unable either to accelerate or retard. Now − he got to his feet and, as he did, the pages of pianoforte notation slipped from his knees and fell open onto the carpet − the moment had arrived. He left the pages where they lay. They would be of little use to him where he was going. He stepped out of the lamp's brightness and headed into the shadows. Having prepared himself for this moment, he did not need to consider his actions, now that it had arrived. He went straight to Cheryl Duvall's private room and dug out the white Dacron shoulder bag which he had already decided would serve his purpose. The room smelt pleasantly of her.

Into the shoulder bag he packed a change of clothes, his razor, an unbroken box of his coronas. He typed a short note to Cherry and left it on the typewriter where he knew she would find it. Then he dimmed the lights, stepped through the french windows and left the apartment which had been his home for more than a decade. Overhead ribbons of cirrostratus cloud were streaking nervously past a brilliant moon. Sollyheim understood that this was the moment he had been waiting for. The clouds' restless formations were like his own instinct to be gone, the solid mass of the moon his own steady purpose.

He had to lift the heavy maintenance hatch manually. There was no other way. With Cheryl Duvall's bag slung across his back he fastened the first harness around his body and lowered himself into the narrow vertical tunnel. As his face drew level with the hatchway it was nuzzled by a black shadow.

'So long, Mitzou,' Sollyheim murmured. He ruffled the cat's fur. 'You take good care of Cherry, now.'

He pulled the hatch cover shut over his head, sealing himself inside the unlighted liftshaft. It would probably be too heavy to lift if he should happen to change his mind. He began his descent.

'One . . . two . . . three . . . four . . . five . . . six. . .'

On the platform level with the storey below he unclasped the harness, hauled up the next one, fitted it and continued down. His mind became empty of everything except the position of his hands and his count of each of the sixty rungs between storeys.

'Seven . . . eight . . . nine . . . ten . . .'

After twenty minutes he had completed five storeys. In other words he was parallel with the eighty-fifth floor. Eighty-five was his present age. He became a machine for forgetting why and remembering how. Gravity leaned down on him. His fingers wanted to curl up and go to sleep. At each platform the length of time he paused for breath grew longer and he let the harness take his weight.

'Eleven . . . twelve . . . thirteen . . . fourteen . . .'

The storeys felt like years – the years of his life. Nearly ninety of them, assuming he lived that long. *Sixty*. A good year. When he was sixty he had first gone on TV to discuss the differentiation principle involved in the morphogenesis of the developing embryo. Boy, the dust that raised!

Fifty-nine: 1997. The year of the San Francisco earthquake. Flying in soon after the disaster in the Army Lockheed jet, seeing through the window the city gutted, fires raging. The most beautiful bridge in the world collapsed into the straits, its back broken. The TransAmerican Pyramid alone standing its ground. Along with everyone in the aircraft, he had wept.

Automatically now, as he counted each rung and each story, incidents from his life entered his mind – memories, some of which he had long forgotten, belonging to the year which coincided with the level of his descent. He was going back, as he went down, through the most important stages of his life.

Fifty-four. He had been fifty-four in the year of the Colorado Nuclear melt-down. In fact, he had been flown into Boulder to take charge of the genetic reparation programme. He had fought to save the lives of the unborn. During that period, after analysing so many malformed and impaired embryonic structures, he had – literally – stumbled across the simple principle by which the complex polar co-ordinates of a cell function determined the position of cells during gastrulation. The principle was simple in the sense that the simple folds in a piece of paper produce the complex 3D origami structure – as long as you knew what they were. The determining factors in embryonic growth – seen in the light of so many dysfunctioning structures – had provided him with the clue to how the coordinates aligned themselves. The tragedy had given Sollyheim's team the opportunity to study in mass the misdevelopment in the human foetus which, otherwise, only a Nazi hospital would have allowed him access to. He had never forgotten the part played by coincidence – so called – in determining his discoveries. He felt certain that his method of discovering the laws of cell-instruction followed closely the method of the laws themselves.

He had been walking back to his quarters after twelve hours in the theatre. It was dark and he was weary. His team had failed and failed to reverse any of the dysfunctioning embryonic structures. Babies were being born dead. Exhausted, numbed by failure, he had stumbled and fallen and, in the moment between stumbling and hitting the ground, a memory from early childhood had flashed into his mind, unlocking the problem. By the time he had picked himself up and dusted himself off he held the solution to the conundrum.

Forty-three . . .

Leila, his second wife, as he found her, lying dead in their apartment. Her blood on her favorite blue dress and on the telephone . . .

Thirty-eight . . .

A hot August. Rome, via Gioachino Belli, 67. Stepping out of her new blue dress to reveal her beautiful naked body, Leila, smiling for him, on the day they were married.

Thirty-six . . .

The years passed. Fragments of conversation and experiences came back to him. Sollyheim ceased to be aware of the difficulty of lifting hands and lowering feet and placing them on the rungs one after the other, or of his fatigue or the effort of inhaling the fetid air.

Twenty-five . . .

Marching all day in the rain, as a student in England, along with many thousands of other people, young and old, singing folk songs, defiant against world paranoia. It was the first occasion he had really appreciated the light in that country, unlike the light in any other, changing from one moment to the next.

Twenty . . .

Sollyheim had been climbing for four hours. The darkness inside the shaft was total and the air was growing thick and sticky. It was no longer important to him whether he was climbing to his death or to a new life.

Ten . . .

He looked out, aged ten, at the round portal of the falling sky as the rust-red Dutch grain ship *Prins Hendrijk*, dipping like a camel in soft sand, hove out of the unhappy port of Gdansk, where the sky was always falling.

Eight . . .

Seven . . .

Six . . . May 1944.

Inside each of the locked cattle cars ninety people were jammed. The stench of the urinal buckets, which were so full they overflowed, made the air unbearable. The train of deportees, forty identical cars, had been rolling endlessly for a week, first across Slovakia, then across the territory of the Central Government, bearing occupants to their unknown destination. Peering through a gap in the side of the car in which he and his mother were compressed, six-year-old Gottlieb read the names of the stations they passed through. TATRA . . . LUBLIN . . . KRAKAU . . . Scarcely an hour outside Krakau the train ground to a halt and he was able to read the gothic script of the name of the station they had arrived at which, like all the others, meant nothing to him. AUSCHWITZ-BIRKENAU.

The line of cars began to move again and some twenty minutes later stopped with a prolonged strident whistle of the locomotive. For the first time in a week the seals were broken. The doors of the cars opened. The deportees – Sollyheim and his mother among them – slowly oozed out with their accumulated stench. Further along the platform black uniformed SS officers were standing around, relaxed, smiling, tapping their leather batons against the heels of their boots.

The deportees huddled together with the people they understood. Townies in their ridiculous dishevelled once-smart city suits and dresses. Country people in their rough woven cloth clothes. Each person clutched the dearest thing left to them. A suitcase. A manuscript. A child's hand. A violin case. A wool doll.

Gottlieb – pressed in the throng towards the light and air – was jostled away from the hand of his mother. The spill of people instantly filled the distance between them. Her face – the last memory of her he possessed – cried out silently to him. Gottlieb stumbled backwards toward the track. He fell. As he fell – he watched it happen very slowly – the black arms of the uniformed officer leaned towards him and plucked him from probable death.

Gottlieb – he never saw his mother after that moment – had a vision in the moment of his falling, which, later, he often tried to recall in words.

We dwell on earth in different flesh to do different things, that we may do one thing, be one body.

Labouring between the fifth and fourth storey of the Schryer Building, Sollyheim did not remember the exact form the words had taken. He experienced, seventy-nine years later, the same vision. His fight to escape prison was the struggle of all humankind. If he failed, humankind would fail.

Three . . .

Two . . .

One. His foot touched *terra firma.* His hands, groping, found the exit-hatch. He breathed with difficulty but the air was on the other side of the hatch. He pushed and pushed. The steel mechanism would not budge. He beat it with his last strength. Nothing gave. This, he knew, had always been a possibility. It was a gamble he had taken. Limp, he slumped against the metal rungs of the stairway. His heart was pumping slow clumps of blood into his lungs where there was no oxygen. He got ready to die. It wouldn't take long.

Then, laughing at his own stupidity, he remembered that he was on the inside of the screw mechanism and that therefore the direction of the thread was reversed. He threw his weight clockwise against the hatch which slowly swung open. Air imploded into the shaft and into his lungs. He had made it! Head-first he tumbled through the narrow opening and lay half in, half out, panting, laughing, weeping. He turned his eyes up to the brilliant white face of the moon looking down on him like a midwife.

5

In the subsurface section of the ABBACCA Room comprising the cocktail lounge affectionately known to its customers as the Fish Tank, Joe King sat alone at the bar staring down at the glass precariously balanced in front of him on top of an identical glass upside down beneath it. Below the two glasses a fashionably unshaven high-status young executive was returning his stare with a fixed expression. The young executive's face gave the impression of being even more washed-out than Joe King was feeling himself even though, of course, this was impossible.

An aqueous pallor originating from within the glass walls was diffused equally over Joe and the other night owls present. Behind the walls real sea-fish were swimming peaceably about in real sea water, establishing the calming illusion among the customers present that they were not inside a chic night-spot in the vaults of the metropolis but some grotto on the floor of a tropical ocean. While wealthy citizens drank cocktails and discussed real estate prices, groups of parrot-fish, blennies, demoiselles, guppies, electric eels, patrolled the coral and marine flora. It was an hermetic environment as balanced ecologically between prey and predator as the bar itself, although none of the customers was paying much attention to the fish and not many of the fish were paying attention to the customers.

Joe drank without getting drunk. The stools on either side of him were empty. His date was not in the bar, which meant he had missed her. By how much he didn't know. She had either left thinking he had stood her up or she had not shown up at all. Which of the two he would never know. Consequently tonight he was the person in the bar everyone else kept away from, the one who wasn't there. The dangerous loner who drinks by himself without getting drunk. There's usually one in every bar in the world.

He didn't particularly notice the two brown skinned teenaged mermaids entwined on the dance-floor like a pair of elvers, sliding in and out of each other to the rhythm of the music being amped out through the surrounding holomorphic vegetation. He wasn't struck by the diffractive glint their short chain skirts and vanadium jewellery made off the polished zinc and mirror-glass bar fittings. His thoughts were preoccupied with the hypothesis that he was in this situation — waiting for a date to arrive long after it was too late — because he had been infected by his proximity to Val Wyman and Val Wyman's bad luck. Had his situation, as Adrian Buckingham would have said, become transmuted into hers? Was he . . .?

'Hello, Charlie . . .'

A tiny shiny fish swam leisurely into the shell of his outer ear and then into the semicircular canals of his middle ear, from where it headed — just as leisurely — towards his brain.

Her voice.

'. . . Penny for them?'

Joe — looking up from the puzzlement on the washed-out face looking up at him — was momentarily puzzled to be addressed by a name that was not his own. This was obviously the night for it. Straight ahead, reflected in the mirrors behind the bar, was the woman of his dreams. His date. Smiling. Oh Boy! She was standing behind his stool inside an antique oyster and air-force blue silk chevron-patterned dress, open at the neck. It might have been water falling over the surface of a rock, the way it looked on her. She was wearing red lip-gloss and a white wet-leather purse over her shoulder.

'Oh, hello . . .' he said as coolly as he was able.

He turned to face her, wishing he had known her name so that he might call her by it.

'You made it!'

FOR THE second time that night she entered the aquarium bar and stood at the door and surveyed the assembled company for the man who called himself Charlie Dickinson. The place was still quarter-full with the same couples and posses and for the second time that night it didn't look as if he was present among them, which came as no big surprise. On the earlier occasion that she had looked in it had not been with much conviction that she would find him. It had been one of those take-it-or-leave-it assignations, the kind any attractive woman receives from men all the time. It hadn't been anything definite

Which was why she had come, the reason she wanted to see him again. It hadn't just been a pass. He had meant it. He was real. He had leaned across – in the elevator – and spoken to her in a tone that suggested he already knew her. What he had said had been – in socio-linguistic terms – completely inappropriate. Taboo. He had broken all the rules. She was intrigued to meet him again if only to find out if it was his looks and personality she was interested in as a woman or, as a law enforcement officer, his irregular behaviour.

It was – she didn't need to come to find out – both.

The good-looking young status-evader was sitting up at the bar with his back to the door, lost in his own reflection. Out of his depth. None of the other customers sat anywhere near him. They could tell there was something

53

funny about him, the way all mammals can tell about one of their own. The same way she had been able to tell herself.

Skirting the dance-floor, she snuck up on the suspect real slow and engaged with him inside the terms of reference he himself had already established, just as she learnt to do in Police School. As an object of desire.

'Hello, Charlie . . .'

She had only ever seen a vamp on TV movies but it was unlikely he had ever seen one anywhere else either.

'. . . Penny for them?'

He raised his eyes from the bar to the mirror facing both of them. He looked at her for a while. The way he looked, his expression, made the parts of her body that were located inside her stretch silk undergarments go all mushy. The muscles in her diaphragm contracted. Her pulse rate accelerated.

'Hello,' he said. 'You made it!'

It was the *way* he looked at her, she could tell both as a woman and as a law enforcement officer, that affected her. He didn't care what happened to him. He was reckless – and he didn't even know he was. She felt suddenly very vulnerable in her high-heeled fuck-me shoes because here he was, in the flesh, the man she had been waiting all her life to meet, just when she was about to give up hope. A man who wasn't afraid.

He turned to face her.

'I was just trying to imagine what it would be like if I didn't ever see you again.'

She took his hand.

'Well I'm here now. So you won't have to worry about that.'

She climbed onto the next stool to his and caught the barman's eye.

'Are you drunk?' she said.

'Not especially.'

The carp-faced barman took her order and left.

'Don't you think I should know your name?' he said. 'I mean, assuming you don't mind telling me.'

'I don't mind. I'm Cheryl. Cheryl Duvall. My friends call me Cherry.'

'Cheryl. Sounds like some kind of rare fruit.'

'What about you?'

He looked from her face to the reflection of both their faces in the mirror.

'My name . . .' He exhaled air slowly '. . . isn't Charlie Dickinson.'

'I know.'

'Oh, you know.'

'Sure.'

'OK I ask how you do?'

Cherry had decided to tell him the truth concerning her feelings about him – she was attracted to him and would probably agree to sleep with him if the occasion presented itself – but she had no intention of breaking her professional code. She was not about to tell some guy who had cruised her in a public elevator that she was a CIA Lieutenant.

She shrugged and he gallantly let it go.

'Well my name . . .' he started to say.

Before he could finish, the black-coated carp paddled into their conversation with two identical glasses and a bottle on a silver salver. The barman transferred the glasses from the salver onto the two coasters on the counter in front of them and poured freely from the bottle.

'. . . is Joe King.'

'You're joking?'

'No. That's my name.'

'You're *not* joking?'

'I *am*!'

'What?'

'My name is Joseph L. King. My friends call me Joe. You don't believe me?'

Cheryl Duvall didn't know what to believe. She had

easily found out on the restricted access Protocol Tracer that no person in the city currently existed under the name he had given her but, on the other hand, it was difficult to believe that a low-status evader could pierce the security-web of the ABBACCA room and get away with it. At least, she had never heard of such a thing happening before.

If he really was a mid-status evader like he claimed, he ought to have been jumpy as hell. She didn't understand how he had penetrated the security organization but right now that was not her concern. She wanted to know why he had trusted her with the information, someone he had only met once. In an elevator. He didn't know who — not to mention what — she was. She wouldn't have to work for the Government to have him hauled out of the place. Anyone could have it done.

'I believe you,' she said. 'But if I do that means you got in illegally — right?'

Joe King nodded.

'Aren't you going to tell me how?'

He said nothing.

'You're going to have to sooner or later. You say you're a JK. Fine. Your secret's safe with me. But an up-status club like this, how did you crack it? We both know they cross-check ID with the medical records of everyone who crosses the threshold. Just anyone can't walk in.'

She took hold of his hand and held it in her own, unsure herself whether she made this gesture as an off-duty Protocol Officer or simply because she liked him. She said, as convincingly as she was able: 'I want to know all about you.'

'People have known all there was to know about me since before I knew anything about myself,' Joe King said.

'You're supposed to be . . .'

'Sure I'm supposed to be home watching TV. I know. I'm a JK. I work for JK pay in a JK job. I eat JK food. I live in a JK part of the city. But I can get into any CD environment, see, because I work in the Bethlehem Clinic on Potrero Hill as a Sollyheim Technician. It isn't bad, the work – fairly routine stuff – but it gives me access to ways to fuck the Protocol.'

She wanted to smile, fairly confident that he would not fail in his ambition.

'You're telling me you forged your identity?' she said.

She took for granted he had not forged his medical records.

'Well, in at least one sense of the word, I guess I did. Yes.'

He was fearless and vulnerable and they would get him sooner or later. She knew they would because she knew who they were, being one of them herself.

'I constructed the matrix of an identity for myself,' Joe King confessed. 'On the Bethlehem Computer. With a new SollyChart I can get by anywhere in the world. But that's about it. I could never date one of the doctors or move into a more fashionable part of the city. Not unless I could invent a CD history for myself as well. But at least I have a legitimate Protocol key. I can penetrate most local access controlled facilities.'

He disengaged his hand from hers and reached for his drink.

'Like elevators?'

He met her gaze – his glass midway between the bar counter and his lips. She raised her glass to touch his and into her mind's eye appeared the unwelcome image of Gottlieb Sollyheim, alone in his empty apartment. Perhaps she should have put something into his nightcap after all.

'Especially elevators!'

They both drank. She felt pretty good, buoyed on a sudden wave of panic, the exhilaration that came from not being completely in control of the situation. If Joe King was out of his depths she was out there with him. There were plenty of contradictions between them. He was a status evader, she was a Protocol cop with a firearm in her purse. Nevertheless she felt, somewhat to her surprise, pretty good. She wanted him to kiss her.

Leaning across, she grabbed the furthest lapel of his black jacket – just as she might have done if she had been making an arrest – and slowly rotated him on his stool. She pulled him towards her and forced his mouth gently against her own until neither of them could bear it any longer. Then she spun his stool so that he was facing the dance floor and the exit. She had to get him out of there.

On the floor the two young ectomorphs of mixed race were orbiting each other in opposite directions, both attired in slinky mail shifts which drew their inspiration from the jet-and-chrome look of Zapper girls, a Canal Street couturier's quotation from streetlevel style. The girls were executing a well-rehearsed erotic mimicry of the infamous Double Helix Fall, the mere illegality of which was almost as titillating as the motion of their limbs. At ritual points in the dance their fingertips, noses, breasts and shoulder blades almost touched, but not quite, deliberately hinting at the danger such proximity to Chance would engender. The two daughters of high-status executives must have witnessed the manoeuvre on TV because it was unlikely they had ever encountered a Zapper girl – not to mention a Zapper – for real. They would have fainted from fright if they had.

'I better get you out of here, Joe King,' Cheryl Duvall said. 'How did you come here?'

'We're back there again?'

'Silly! I mean, what kind of transport do you have?'

'Taxi. I came straight here from the Clinic. I paid it a retainer so it must still be lurking around some place!'

'Fine. Let's find your cab and go home.'

'Whose home do you have in mind, Cherry,' he said with hardly any intonation, 'yours – or mine?'

She just looked at him. There could be only one answer to that question.

Joe stepped off his stool. He took her hand.

'Did you ever visit the JK dwellings over on the Western

Addition?'

Cheryl collected her purse from the bar, relieved that he accepted her without attempting to understand the things she did not wish to explain.

Joe King forged the cheque with his forged Protocol key. They left the Fish Tank with the two toy Zapper girls swaying to the invisible music and, behind the walls of the aquaria, luminous teams of angelfish snaking and diving with a mastery they had learnt in the freedom of the ocean they had forgotten.

6

The Emergency Wing of the Bethlehem Clinic was open throughout the night. It was not the only public service building to which citizens could gain access after curfew but it was probably the only one from which they would not be turned away. Some nights the foyer might be empty, other nights you could hardly move for bodies. Empty or full, it made no difference who you were to the Artificial Intelligences conducting the injured and sick from the landing bay into the emergency theatres. It made no difference to the AIs who they were themselves, of course. Wasn't that the great thing about them?

Momentarily the Wing was quiet. This evening's squall of activity – the consequence of a skirmish between the SkyPol and some Zapper kiters – had been and gone. In the lull the night clerk had one eye on an old movie on her monitor screen, the sound turned down low. Around the brightly-lit foyer exhausted and bewildered friends and next-of-kin tried to stay awake on the hard plastic furniture that had been specifically engineered to make sure they were successful in their endeavour. Some gazed vacantly with half-finished pieces of conversation on their lips. Others dozed, woke, stood up, sat down, unconscious that they were wearing combinations of clothing appropriate for discordant social situations. Bedroom shoes and a works uniform. A swimsuit. Odd socks. A girl in a Zapper's black leather jerkin drew on a cigarette, unaware that the cigarette was no longer alight or that the jerkin hung half-open, half-revealing her chest. The girl didn't care. She was wrapped inside her own private nightmare, like everyone else. An ancient street person with uncombed white hair was trying to talk some sense into the coffee dispensing machine. When the machine finally released a cup the old man, still trying to figure out what had happened, ferried it to the bench opposite the bench occupied by the young Zapper girl. Neither the girl nor the old man made any sign of acknowledgement of the other's existence. Here no one acknowledged anyone. This was limbo, the ante-chamber to Hell.

'Rosie . . .?'

A grey-haired Duty Sister emerged from one of the side cubicles. Padding down the corridor, she approached the Arrivals Desk.

'Rosie . . .?'

The Arrivals Clerk looked up from the VDU in front of her.

'. . . The patient who collapsed out on the kitebay . . . Vergil Wymann. We can't elicit his purpose in coming here. He'd been drinking pretty heavy, apparently, so we gave him a pump and a sed.' The Duty Sister handed Vergil Wymann's Protocol ID to Rosie. 'Check out records, will you. See what we have on him.'

Rosie punched out the situation onto the keyboard — thereby erasing the old movie from the screen.

'We don't have a pathology reference to any Vergil Wymann, Sister . . .' Rosie looked up. 'But we appear to have a Valerie Wymann here in the Clinic already. His wife. She's in one of the Music Rooms right this moment.'

The Arrivals Clerk and the Duty Sister looked at each other in silence for a moment.

'You mean, *she has a child dying*!' the Sister said, deliberately keeping her voice low.

Rosie nodded.

The Duty Sister turned and hurried back down the

61

corridor. Rosie returned to her movie. The young woman in the Zapper jerkin set fire to her cigarette with her lighter, tears running down her face. The wild-haired old street person rummaged inside a grubby woman's shoulder-bag, eventually drawing from it a soft wood container. He ran a thumbnail through the paper seal of the box. He prized open the hinged lid and lifted out a silver tube. After carefully returning the wooden box to the shoulder bag, he proceeded to unscrew one end of the tube and allowed the contents to slide into his hand. Nobody noticed when he bit the rounded tip of the incongruously fine-looking cigar, remove the piece of leaf from his tongue with his finger and then, leaning forward, address the young Zapper girl facing him.

'My dear child,' he said. 'May I trouble you for a light?'

I killed him!
I killed him!
I killed him!

The silent words repeated themselves endlessly inside her brain like images reflected from one mirror into another. Her brain was a chamber of mirrors inside which the same thought ricocheted into infinity. No corner or shadow existed for doubt to lurk within. It wasn't even a thought, it was a fact. She *had* killed him. She was the answer to an easy sum. No matter how many times over she made the calculation the conclusion, with mathematical certitude, remained the same. Mute with fury she wanted to smash the flat mirror-walls of her brain with her small clenched fist of a hope:

I didn't kill him!
I didn't kill him!
I didn't kill him!

Fuck it, the bastard was going to kill himself anyway!

62

The two contrary truths raced in opposite directions to and from her brain like alternating current. She was a naked high voltage cable, unearthed.

She was a Zapper's girl. Consequently she knew even before he had gotten into his Black Shadow that sooner or later Zeb was going to push his luck a little too far. She had already pictured the scene: Zeb stepping into his kite, kissing her goodbye as he always did. When the moment *had* come and he *had* kissed her goodbye she had been forced to watch it again as if it had already happened, knowing that it had not, his kite spinning out of control, ploughing into the side of the mountain after failing to pull out of a Double Helix Fall. She had tried to warn Zeb. Zeb had laughed in her face and kissed her on the mouth – as she knew he would. She had watched Zeb's kite catapault him earthwards, leaving him no opportunity to eject. And if the opportunity had existed Zeb would have missed it because, like all Zapper kites, his illegalized Black Shadow had not been fitted with the heavy government-standard ejector. She had watched him crash twice, first in the blind spot in her mind's eye where her fears and intuitions were focused into images of the future, and then again in the clear moonlit skies of this very evening. The final enactment had corresponded almost exactly with her premonition, from his last casual kiss to the arrival of the SkyPol and the ambulances to carry off his body like Valkyries in a climax of sirens and flashing lights.

How could she have warned him? He would never have listened. He was a wild mean stubborn bastard. He enjoyed doing things which people said were dangerous. He was a Zapper, which was the reason she had loved him. Everything about Zeb was dangerous. She had known this the first time they had met in Sam's bar, just as she had known how it would start and how it would end. She had tried to put this knowledge out of her mind because she had wanted to be wild and illegal too, a Zapper's girl whom Zeb wanted. Paradoxically, she could only be his girl by not telling him what she knew was going to happen to him, by acting dumb and as if she didn't give a damn. It wouldn't have changed anything if she had told him. He hated – more than anything – people telling him how things were going to work out, which was why he was a Zapper who lived outside the Protocol. He would have laughed and left her and gone ahead and driven his beautiful kite into the dirt of Stanislaus County just the same. Maybe sooner. She didn't have to have precognitive powers to see he wanted it that way. It was obvious to everyone. She hadn't killed him. He had killed himself.

Zelda relighted her cigarette with her Zippo.

It gave her a helpless feeling of isolation to reflect that she had not been able to influence Zeb's fate one way or the other. Now he was gone – *dead*, he would have said – and she was alone and had no place to go. Zeb may have been a crazy fucking Zapper but she had loved him and he had looked after her. She could never go back and live among the Zappers without him although, after having lived among them, she would not be able to live anywhere else. Zs were the end of the line. From there you only went where Zeb had gone.

It was not that no Zapper would take her. There were plenty of them who would give Zeb's girl a ride – but Zelda was not sure that any of them would be strong enough to keep her or hold off her enemies. On the other hand, after the Zappers there was nothing. Z for Zero. No one liked them and they liked no one. They refused to conform to the rest of society. They stuck to antiquated degenerate ways of behaving which got the Government mad. No one could tell Zappers anything, they were so dumb – and, of course, violent. They still believed that 'life' was something which took place while their fancy fast kites executed difficult ritual manoeuvres in the night sky, sometimes fatally, like Zeb, in the terrifying Double Helix Fall. To them only their nightly sky-duels with their chances of survival made any sense of their existence. It was, as the Protocol often said, childish regressive behaviour. And, inevitably, most Zappers finished up on a stretcher in the Bethlehem Clinic sooner or later, which only confirmed in the eyes of the world the reason why they were Zs. For their part, Zappers expected to *die* – as they persisted in saying – since it was the only way they could be sure that they were really living. This and other dumb attitudes gave them a style and a language which other status groups found hard to comprehend. They gave the finger to the Protocol and anyone else unfortunate enough to encounter them. As far as Zappers thought – in so far as they did think – members of all other status groups were wooden puppets who were, as they said themselves, *dead*.

Zelda had been flying with Zappers, drinking with them and making love with them long enough to know them pretty well. She had experienced her share of close shaves in dog-fights with the SkyPol. During that time she had never been afraid. Why should she have been? She knew she was never going to get hurt in the same way that she knew that Zeb was going to kiss the earth. If she could never change the things she knew were going to happen, at least she had no reason to fear them. Which was why Zeb had kept her around. Had she attempted to explain to him the reason why she was so fearless he would have shrugged and walked away. Looking into the future went against everything Zappers believed in – and Zelda knew a lot about the future. Hadn't it been to forget it that she had thrown in her lot with the zero-rated outlaw group in the first place?

Zeb, however mean he acted, had not been dumb. He had tried to give her clues about how to forget the things he guessed she was running away from. He seemed to know all about the useless fucked up kind of knowledge a well-heeled family puts into a daughter's head to make her like them. 'Babe, you know, the only way to handle the present is to live it,' he had told her one time, 'which you do by not treating the future like it's already happened.' At the time this had been about the most illegal thing she had ever heard.

She would have cried but for the fact that she had never cried. She did not know how to. Crying was something she had never gotten the hang of and her parents had had her seen by the best specialists. Instead, she did what she had learnt to do whenever an event she had tried to prevent finally came about. She *looked away*.

It was just a trick but sometimes, she *looked away* quickly and on impulse, sometimes random circumstances infected the sequence of events she saw stretching ahead of her like a road on a map. She had *looked away* from her mom and dad, from her childhood, from the habit of wearing real cotton undergarments. By turning her back on the pre-determined world she had been raised to understand, consistently doing the dumb thing, she had tricked everyone and, so far, gotten free. Her impulsive response to random factors had accelerated her retreat down the status-rating into obscurity. Making out she was dumber than she was smart had paid off.

She looked into the smiling face of a person already watching her, waiting for her to speak.

Taking her time, she perused the features of the person sitting opposite her. She took in his age, the cumulus of windswept white hair, the dust-streaked out-of-fashion clothes, the woman's shoulder bag. Everything about the old fella added up to street-person, which is to say didn't add up to anything. Except the eyes, grey like wet smoke, gentle, not hiding anything. They were not the hard bright predatory eyes of a high-status individual nor fear-filled like those of the lower social groups she had encountered – and by now she had encountered all of them. He was off the scale.

'My dear child,' he said. 'May I trouble you for a light?'

Zelda flipped the cap of her Zippo and held the flame towards the polite old-timer's fine-looking cigar.

She watched him puff the cigar alight as if he had all the time in the world.

He said. 'You are crying.'

'What . . .?'

She touched her cheek. It was true. Her fingers were wet.

'But . . . I . . .'

She could hardly believe it. Tears in her eyes!

'. . . I never cried in my life!'

The old man showed no surprise. He nodded.

'Indeed? . . . In that case something of singular import-ance must have happened to you.'

'My fella's . . .'

I'm crying.

'. . . kite exploded.'

Because Zeb is dead.

'I saw it happen . . .'

I should have stopped him.

'I killed him!'

The old stranger in out-of-fashion clothes moved across the aisle, seated himself beside her and put an arm around her. She let him. She let her head fall against his shoulder, tears falling onto her leather jacket.

'No, my dear,' he held her gently in his arm. 'You didn't kill him,' he said. As if he knew.

7

'We're ... I'm telling you we're ...'
        'Doing nothing!'
        '... We're doing all we can, Marie!'
'Yeah? Did you check every point an apprizer can trace her to? Taxis? Payphones? Entertainment zones?'
'Of course we did. But she obviously isn't using her own identity. If she was, we'd have her already. Officially she isn't ...'
'She has to be some place!'
'According to our computers she doesn't exist.'
'Christ, Bernier! I'm trying to get you to move your fucking pink ass and locate my daughter, all you can come up with is she doesn't exist!'
'She is *my* daughter too, don't forget! You don't seem to appreciate the problem. It isn't so easy to trace ...'
'Don't try and shuck me!'
Archer Bernier was forced to look away from the face sneering at him out of the screen. He was seated at the big desk in the important office at which, on the TV Show, he play-acted the calm executive. At the present moment he didn't feel either big or important but he did attempt to remain calm. The bitch was trying to make him lose his temper. She wasn't having him find Annie because she cared about her. Ammarie didn't even like her daughter! All she cared about was avenging herself on Annie for daring to break out. He ought to lose his temper and wring

68

Ammarie's neck.

'I know you'd like to kill me,' she said as if this was the thing she wanted herself more than anything in the world.

'Look, I'm not trying to shuck you, Ammarie.' Bernier said, his voice as taut and slow as a length of wire slowly tightening around her neck. 'I just want you to understand how it is.'

The Chief of Protocol and the President stared without any love at each other across the vidlink.

'Go 'head,' she said. 'Tell me how it is. I'm listening.'

'We've eliminated, like I said, the situations Annie could be traced to. That leaves us with the semi-legal places . . .'

'What semi-legal place you talking about?'

'C'mon, Marie! Don't *you* shuck me. You know every city has them! It must be with them that Annie is holed up. We know she was headed West before she went off the screen. We picked up her kite and interrogated her first associates, a screwy bunch, too dumb to know how dumb they are. We couldn't shake anything out of them. Annie was careful to leave no indication of her intentions. There is no pattern to her actions. All the same, one of our men – well, not one of *our* men, a West Coast private operative – claims he has picked up a rumour of a girl he thinks . . .'

'Bernier!' Ammarie interrupted. She spoke slowly as if addressing a child: 'You pay the wages of every peace officer on the Administration payroll. Why truck with a private cop? She can't be so hard to find as your lazy employees make out.'

'They ain't so lazy and I don't pay their wages. I run the Protocol – remember? I don't have authority over State or Fed law enforcers. You want I turn the country into a police state in order to find one young girl who has run away from home?'

'Yes, if that's what it takes.'

'Do I have to remind you that so far, outside our private staff, no one knows that Annie Bernier has gone? This is a very delicate operation. We're not in a position to mobilize all our resources. Even if we found her that way, the damage it could do would be unacceptable. As it is we can only keep putting the TV show out by clipping archive material together. We can't go on doing that for ever. Sooner or later people are going to pipe to what's happening. Annie is a determined eighteen-year-old . . .'

Bernier, experiencing a sudden heartbeat of compassion for his daughter, left the sentence unfinished. He didn't feel any anger towards her. His heart wasn't in this hunt for her. In fact, he didn't blame her at all. He wasn't having the State Security apparatus locate Annie because he wanted them to but because this woman he was married to wouldn't give him a moment's peace until he did.

At that moment the welcome features of Jenny Karbowska appeared on his second vidscreen.

'There's a call for you, Mr Bernier, from California. The one you said to give priority. Shall I put it through?'

Bernier told Jenny to stack the call. If Ammarie found out that it was the investigator on Annie's trail she would be sure to hook herself up and tear into him for a son-of-a-bitch and prise out of them whatever he had discovered.

'Who's that on the other line?' Ammarie said.

'A Protocol man doing some work for me,' Bernier lied.

'Must be the only one who is. What kinda work?'

How did she do it? Somehow, by following her intuitions, this stupid woman was able to get what she wanted out of people. Bernier had come to accept that she accomplished her ends *because* she was stupid. As far as the world was concerned Ammarie was the attractive easy-going wife which she portrayed on the White House Show. Millions adored her. Only Archer and a few other top-ranking members of the Administration knew that her power did not lie in her TV image or in her position of President but in her skill at manipulating people into situations which left them only one course of action, the one she had had in mind all along.

'He's working on status evaders?' Archer said, which

was, in a roundabout way, the truth.

'What's there to work on? It's against the law.'

'Yes. However, our checks and tracer-systems are processed to monitor on the assumption that citizens are only going to be motivated to falsify their status upwards. Which, so far, has been the case.'

Ammarie, unbelievably, said nothing.

'We're beginning to get reports of citizens of high-status – Es and Ds – who are working under false low-status aliases. Cznetsov's people are watching them . . .'

'Who the hell would want to falsify their status *downwards*? Less privilege. Scum jobs. Curfew. Nothing to do but watch TV?'

'To find the answer to that, sweetheart, I guess we better ask our daughter. If we ever find her.'

'Go fuck yourself,' the President rejoined.

The screen went blank.

Bernier could not understand how it had all gone so sour. His marriage. His optimism. Now even his own daughter rejected him and everything he stood for.

He had Jenny route the California call and the face of the investigator who claimed he had a lead on Annie appeared on the blank screen. Such as it was. Through the graphic scrambling device the man did not look like any ordinary citizen. Every indication of his status was blurred. All identifying characteristics had been modified into a uniform composite. This was a security convention which most private eyes took advantage of, their rights to anonymity having been upheld in the Supreme Court on the grounds that it guaranteed protection from their clients necessary for the free practice of their trade. When it came down to it, Archer Bernier knew as much about the identity of the man he was facing as he did the whereabouts of the girl the man had been hired to locate.

'Right, mister,' Bernier began, unsure how to address a private eye. 'Give me the plot!'

'The "plot", Mr Bernier,' the featureless face said, 'is

that your wayward daughter is running from home. She doesn't want me or anyone sleuthing after her.'

'Look, I got work to do. You were hired to give me information I don't already have. Fact, your contract . . .'

'Take it easy. Let's not invoke the laws of tort just yet.'

'Are you going to tell me what you've found out?'

'Sure. Before I do, I want you to understand that whatever I might have found out is not a commodity. Information — contrary to the popularly held opinion — rarely is. Your daughter will only feel safe from your computracers by burying herself inside illegal groups involved in illegal practices. Whoever goes looking for her — me for instance — is going to find himself a target for some of those practices.'

'If it's too much trouble . . .'

'Trouble . . .' the scrambled image of the mouth attached to the voice appeared to smile, 'is my business. Dressing up like a World War Two Nazi flyer and risking myself in some sky-crate that would never approach Federal minimum safety requirements, kissing ugly Zapper girls with no teeth, chewing their cheap meth cut maybe with strychnine, on the chance they have something to tell me about your daughter, is also my business. Before I tell you what they told me I want you to understand what finding her will mean. I need to know what you plan doing when you have found her. I'm sorry, Mr Bernier. These are questions I have to know the answer to in order to continue my investigation.'

'The President and I want our daughter back. Quick. Any price. Could it be more straightforward? If you require the assistance of the Protocol or the local Police, that can be arranged. As soon as you find Annie . . .'

'I have found her, Mr Bernier,' the voice said without intonation.

Archer Bernier stared at the display.

'You found her? Well, that's terrific! Where is she?'

'Not so quick. When I say I've found her I mean I've

72

located a girl who answers to your daughter's physical description. If it *is* her, she's way off the map.'

'Don't worry. I'll have the SkyPol go in and take her out . . .'

'Send your bulls in after her and it's an even chance she'll stop one herself. Her new friends won't be carrying walking-sticks. You best let me handle this.'

'Listen, you've found Annie, that's swell. Your job's done. You can haul yourself off the case. We'll take over from now.'

'Sorry, Mr Bernier. You haven't grasped my meaning. *I* may have found her. *You* haven't. Before you do anything you have to find me. I have to tell you.'

Bernier waited, wondering what form this cheap snooper's blackmail threat would take.

'Either you want me to frontpage how young Annie is giving head to a gang of Zappers,' the cheap snooper said, 'and have the SkyPol kites blunder in so one of their Glory Boys can maybe stop her running forever – or else you have her found quiet and in a shape that's worth finding. Like you hired me to. So far's I know only the President's staff knows that her little girl isn't in the Lilac Room embroidering linen handkerchiefs or playing tennis with that beef-barrel like how she is on the Show recently. And me, of course. *I* know.' Again a smile scrambled across the graphic distortion of the investigator's face. 'So far you've succeeded in keeping it in the family. I don't know how. Appearing on TV every night. But you play it wrong now, you're going to start a bigger scandal than your Admin can handle. It's not going to look good, the President's cute daughter molling out for a gang of Zappers – outlaws with bad chromosomes.'

'How much do you want?'

'Please. This isn't a shakedown. I don't want any more than is owed me. I'm sorry you think I do. You're my client. I'm half-way through my assignment and I'd like to finish it. I'm making my report. All I want is for you to

73

say you're happy with the progress we're making and you agree I continue. It's your choice.'

'She's my daughter. I don't have a choice.'

'Sure you do. I was just kidding when I said I would open the file on Annie to the world. If you want to find her your way, go ahead. I won't interfere. I'll collect my cheque and wish you luck. But you made a right decision the day you called in my agency. There's no way your surveillance agents would have gotten this far. They're big and mean but in a situation like this they have the finesse of the Seventh Cavalry – and you remember what happened to them.'

'You saying you can handle Annie's associates unaided?'

'I'll soon find out. If I can get close enough to Annie I'll try and speak to her, let her know she can communicate with you through me. But I'm sorry, I won't be bringing her in at pistol point like a cheap criminal. You wouldn't want that. She'll only come home and stay home under her own terms. I can negotiate on your behalf?'

'Anything.'

'She might, say, refuse to marry the beef-barrel.'

'Fine. I hope she does. How d'you plan persuading her?'

'By my personal charm.'

Bernier doubted that it would be sufficient but he kept his doubts to himself.

'What if I want to contact you?' he said.

'You won't be able to. When I'm on a case even my own agency aren't in a position to say where I am. So don't piss in my well. I'll talk with you just as soon as I have something to say.'

The screen blanked abruptly.

Bernier considered his options. He could have called the investigator off like the man suggested. Annie had put a lot of distance between her and her family. He only wanted her to be happy. On the other hand, the Protocol demanded that she get back to the White House. The TV Show couldn't continue much longer without her and without the Show where was the Protocol?

Unannounced, Jenny stepped into his office. She was carrying a small tray. Bernier watched the young woman as she moved unselfconsciously toward him. Her smile was genuine. It had nothing to do with the problems he had to deal with.

'I brought your coffee and doughnut, Mr Bernier,' she said. She placed the tray on his desktop, a nurse attending to a patient whom the doctors had given up on.

'Thanks, Jenny,' he said, unable to meet her eyes. 'Listen, get onto Ben Cznetsov, will you? Ask him what we have on that agency we're using for Annie, the one in . . .'

'Petaluma.'

'Right. Everything he has on them. Have him call me back when he can.'

He watched her leave the room. She moved with the grace of an animal unaware that it was being observed. As far as Jenny Karbowska was concerned he was Mr Big. She believed in him. It would never have occurred to her that he was drifting through this mess like a kid's balloon. Or that he would have thrown it all up for a quiet time with her. On a farm. Ten acres and a mule. Jenny, wearing a plaid shirt under denim coveralls, holding onto him, keeping him from drifting . . .

The face of his secretary appeared on one of the two screens.

'I have Mr Cznetsov on line.'

Bernier nodded and saw the familiar smile of his buddy, Benny Cznetsov, appear on the second screen. Like everyone else, he liked Cznetsov – they had been through a lot together – but that smile of his still worried him.

'Hi, Ben. What do you have for me?'

'Hello, Archer. Not too much, I'm afraid. I warned you about employing private agencies. I have a good team here on the CIA payroll if anyone can find her, we can. Trust me.'

'Benny, *you* don't trust anyone!'

Cznetsov grinned. A great compliment had been paid to him.

'Well, the California agency is working under an alias. They often do, of course. In this case the alias company does business in its own right. We'll have to take a closer look, you want us to uncover the investigator handling the case for you.'

'What line of business they in?'

Cznetsov glanced across to another screen. 'According to my information they're a West Coast firm calling themselves QUASAR ELECTRONICS. They're small time but have quite a reputation in their field. They specialize in high quality homeoactive devices, autopilots, home-helps, that sort of thing. I see here they just landed a State contract for a self-regulating fireservice. They're legit.'

'Nothing to do with security?'

'Not that I can see.'

'Then how'd they ever get a licence?'

Cznetsov winked at Bernier. He obviously had some-thing unpleasant to tell him. 'I hoped you would ask that. *They don't have a licence*!'

'Shit! You mean . . .'

''Fraid I do.'

'How did they land the California contract?'

Cznetsov shrugged. 'His agency answered the advert. Why? Did he come up with something?'

'Uh-uh,' Archer Bernier lied. 'I'm checking out all the agencies. For Ammarie. You know what she's like.'

'You want me to take a closer look?'

Bernier shook his head. 'I'll be in touch. Thanks, Benny.'

Bernier cut the link. He felt depressed. The only clue he possessed regarding his daughter's whereabouts was in the head of an unlicenced private investigator whose identity nobody knew. It was little better than no clue at all. And there was nothing he could do now except wait. Trying his best not to think about his daughter – or his secretary

– he dunked his doughnut into his cup of coffee and waited.

BEN CZNETSOV, reclined in the maximum reclining position of his omnidirectional swivel-chair, staring at the ceiling, shook his head and ran his palm against the day's stubble under his chin. By degrees the odd fragment of the ceiling he was looking at came into focus, ceased looking odd and started to look familiar again. During the taped recording of the conversation he had just watched he had experienced another attack of *déjà vu*. The second that day. The face of the West Coast private investigator whom Archer Bernier had been talking with – the investigator's scrambling device reversed by Cznetsov's own terminal – had triggered off another disconcerting chain of false memories. He had seen that face before. The attack had been painless and brief – as they always were – but the sensation that he knew intimately everything that was about to take place and about to be said disturbed Cznetsov. Because he knew that it was not true. It was an illusion. He had never seen that face before. It disturbed the CIA Chief to learn that he was vulnerable to any kind of illusion.

Putting the attack out of his mind – what else could he do with it? – Cznetsov overviewed the situation. Of all the agencies that Archer Bernier had brought in, only this one, the illegal and unlicenced Petaluma outfit, had come up with anything. Cznetzov had, of course, had every one of them wired and there was a file on QUASAR – he knew all there was to know about them – but only now did he have a picture of the operative on the case. Cznetsov liked the look of him. He seemed to know what he was doing, especially the way he had not let his client intimidate him. In fact, he had talked all over Bernier. The thing to do now, he decided, was to mail the tape to the Sanfran District Office. Who was in charge there? Captain

Dalgano, a good man. Then follow out himself and lean on QUASAR himself. They wouldn't know what hit them.

As for Archer Bernier, he had not looked so good. His face was tired like an old cop's face — which, in a way, was what it was. Archer was acting like a person who had lost everything and blamed himself for it, who thought there was nothing he could do that would get it back. It was not just that he was old or a cop. Archer was not so old, he just wasn't young any more, and he had never been much of a cop. He simply wasn't the idealist co-architect of the revolutionary social venture whom Cznetsov had known when he had been young himself.

Cznetsov lowered his eyelids. He had never been any kind of idealist himself, that went without saying. It was not truths which interested him but the layers of deception which concealed them. Bernier always tried his best to hide how much he loved his daughter in order that she didn't catch hell from her mother who used her as bait to manoeuvre him where she wanted. Cznetsov, in his old-friend-of-the-family role, had watched her bitch whenever Archer gave a piece of himself to the girl. There had been occasions when Cznetsov would have preferred not to have been party to their precarious marriage. On the other hand there were several reasons why he had no choice, chief among them his own personal interest in Annie. Everything personal to Cznetsov was secret but nothing more so than his feelings for this wilful eighteen-year-old with psychotic hallucinations of the future. She meant more to him than anything. He loved her.

Annie was fond of him too, or so he liked to imagine. She kissed him and hit him whenever she felt like it. She was the only person he had ever known who had absolutely no fear of him, certainly she was more fearless than a daughter could ever have been toward a father. He had waited a long time to find a person into whom he could not strike terror. Whether he liked it or not everyone he met was afraid of Benny Cznetsov. He could coerce them into fearing and feeling affection for him at the same time without even trying. He had waited a long time to find a person on whom his charm did not work. Annie Bernier had grown up into such a person and, quite incidentally, into a beautiful young woman. He wasn't going to let go of her without a fight.

Cznetsov recollected the first heady years during which the Administration had been jockeying to establish itself. Old man Dover had chaired the alliance of Western multinational companies and coordinated their piecemeal takeover of the remaining currencies. They had all been younger in those days, and keener, and none of them had held the positions of responsibility which they held today. He and Archer Bernier had been two among a cluster of rising stars and Ammarie an attractive young woman who had gotten Archer to fall in love with her enough to want to marry. If he could help it Cznetsov never thought about his own loveless affair with her. It had been brief, like all his affairs, and fun while it lasted, but neither of them ever spoke of it anymore. It might never have happened. He, Archer and Ammarie had been three junior members of the Dover apparatus, unwittingly forging the eternal triangle which would – much later – form the psychological basis of their present unassailable triumvirate.

And while they were busy screwing each other, higher up the organization those two old men, Dover and Sollyheim, had been circling each other like a pair of old buzzards. Along with a lot of government personnel at the time, Cznetsov had decided that only the formulations of scientific truths from the world of pure research could give back to people the sense that they were still all part of the same race – which some of them were beginning to forget – and at the same time give authority to the moral code which the Administration had sought to engineer. They wanted a dogma which would support a societal *gestalt* again and in Gottleib Sollyheim's popular discoveries they had found one. Sollyheim, later, had begun to see things differently and might have won over Dover himself if he, Cznetsov, had not suggested to him the obvious expedient solution. His present position as Chief of the Central Intelligence Agency owed itself to that well-kept secret.

Sollyheim might have won in the end. He was nothing if not persuasive. Dover had been cunning and powerful but lacked the necessary ruthless streak. He could only have beaten the Doctor by killing him and risking losing the credibility he hoped Sollyheim would provide. As for Sollyheim he may have been right but he had been right in the wrong way, at the wrong moment in history. He had discovered the preparation of gunpowder and refused to let the generals make use of it for their own ends. They had asked him nice but when he refused they had taken it anyway. As they always do.

This had been the world Annie had been conceived in – Cznetsov remembered the time and the event. Harder to recall were the intervening years during which old Dover had been Returned and the Protocol had grown into the powerful embodiment of people's unconscious yearning for a strong paternal authority against which it would not want to rebel. Ammarie had aged into a sharp-tongued harridan – President of the Union. His friend, Archer Bernier, had become the defeated idealist he had just watched being pissed on by a faceless nobody. As for Annie, she had retreated into the widespread AB neurosis that she was able to see the future.

Cznetsov was aware – having encouraged it himself – that Annie's delusion was necessary to members of high-status groups. They nearly all attended classes in some kind of psychic therapy. It allowed them to exercise their social privileges in the comforting knowledge that history – as well as their own destinies – was already determined. It couldn't be otherwise. The Protocol had come into being in order to put an end to the mass uncertainty about the future and by degrees it had begun to happen as the government wanted. A lot of citizens, under the impression they knew the direction history would take, helped determine the direction it did take. The delusion of possessing precognitive powers was necessary for any group wielding power over the rest of society. The rich, in one form or other, had always possessed it. Cznetsov, however, knew that he never had, which was the reason his current attacks of *déjà vu* were beginning to disturb him.

Annie, after having been given everything an AB kid could ask for, had turned her back on the safe fate awaiting her as if it were a movie she had already seen and didn't care to sit through again. She had sought out the company of losers who shifted for themselves on the edges of society, breaking every rule of the Protocol in order to do so. Cznetsov – because she was Annie – found it hard to blame her. His reasons for wanting Annie back home were the same as Bernier's: he couldn't bear not having her around. But he was not after bringing her in like a delinquent runaway child.

So it was a stroke of luck that this northern Californian private investigator had located her. Cznetsov would get hold of him somehow. He was confident some arrangement could be reached. Bernier would do nothing, that was certain. The not-very-veiled threat which the scratch investigator had made to him had been effective. Bernier would wait until the situation gave him more room to manoeuvre in, although there never would be more room. There rarely is. Archer Bernier was trapped. Part of him needed to find Annie in order to get Ammarie off his back but another part – the best part – did not want to find her at all. Leaving her alone was the only thing he could do now to protect her from the hiding she would catch from her mother if he ever did. However long Bernier could stall Ammarie was how much time Cznetsov had to get to Annie first.

It wouldn't be the first time he had gone behind the back of his boss. The CIA was the unconscious will of the government. At some level Bernier probably understood this. Whether he understood or not, this was not the time to back off from QUASAR. Cznetsov had too much shit on them, enough to persuade them it would be in their best interests to release themselves from their professional obligation to respect their agent's incognito. They had a greater obligation to stay in business.

Leaning forward in the multidirectional chair, he lowered his eyes from the ceiling and spoke into the communications screen.

'Captain Dalgano . . . of the Sanfran District.'

8

Investigator: Rick Stator
File Code: RS/7
Report: 12

When I got my first sight of the subject – RS/7 – I was sucking ice and watching lizards chase each other up and down the walls of an out-of-town bar in a desert corner of the State. You don't mind, I'll keep the name of the bar under my hat for the moment. I'll just say it was not the kind of establishment a nice girl would want to be seen drinking in. Drinking would probably not be the only thing she would be doing.

The particular lizard I had my eyes on was examining my face while it paused in its journey across the big mirror behind the bar. The dumb reptile didn't know this, of course. It had made a big mistake a long while back in the history of its species which it had been paying for ever since. It figured it was real smart, you could see that, the way it jerked its stiff little scaly neck around. Reminded me of a retired army colonel looking at a world it didn't understand anymore. It figured it was smart but history had passed it by just the same.

The bar in question was an original polished redwood and painted-mirror tavern with a long bartop which Sam – who runs the joint – keeps clean as a morgue-slab. Another thing he keeps is an antique iron repeating action

83

Navy Colt down his trouser leg, a trick almost as old as the Colt. It was a Zapper bar I had been hanging out in recently, getting my face familiar. I even bought some respect on account of the kite I fly is a zapped-up Silver Wing. I was on nodding terms with one or two of the Zappers but no more than that. Your average Zapper is as approachable as a conger eel. By the time you have approached him it's often too late. By then you are either a Zapper yourself or worse. And there is only one thing worse than being a Zapper.

Most of Sam's clientèle are oiled-up-to-the ears outlaws who don't put an especially strong emphasis on personal hygiene. That kind of attention they reserve for the pieces of rocketry parked in the dirt out front. Kite-flying is the only thing they think or talk about. It gives them a preoccupied expression you could mistake for an absence of feeling. They sit quiet and drink hard, play a bit of poker and watch you drink with the quiet hard eyes of poker players. The truth is that the scowling tattooed mug looking through you is probably worrying about a fault in the ignition-halo of his illegal machine. Or the fuel injector. Or the sonar-orientation system. With kites, if it's not one thing it's something else.

Zappers may be bad talkers but they are great mechanics. They need to be. They have to out-pace, out-manoeuvre and generally outfuck the assembly-line crates the SkyPol send up to keep them out of the air. They're at war with the police and the government every waking moment and their kites have to be better than just good to keep from getting in the way of one of the SkyPol's nasty new fission cannons. Hence the scowl. They know they are the asshole of the status system. You can't blame them for making a career out of paranoia.

Why Sam puts up with them I haven't figured yet. He's just the opposite, always in a fresh white shirt, black bow tie, pink face scrubbed clean as a widow's son. Stands out like a choirboy at a coven. I haven't figured why the

Zappers put up with him either.

So there I am, drinking beer in Sam's bar, watching the mirror, with no better reason for being there than I am beginning to run out of places I might encounter the subject. Outside, a hot desert wind is blowing up, the kind of wind that makes you reach for the bottle if you are the drinking type, and if you are not the drinking type makes you wish you were. Inside the bar you couldn't see it or hear it but you knew it was out there. I tried to sit still and drink slow. The lizard hadn't moved for ten minutes.

I had the description of a recent acolyte of this chapter of Zs which matched the picture of the girl whose trail I had lost down in Orange County last month. I didn't know if she was the subject or not and it didn't make any difference because I had no way of contacting her short of asking the Zappers outright – which, from an actuarial point of view, would have drawn short odds on my chances of benefitting from hindsight again. I had poked my nose about as far as it would go without working up her friends' suspicions. Meanwhile, I had learnt a lot about the merits of this kite over that one, how tight to adjust the throttle-sleeve to achieve extra loop in a spin. I'm becoming an expert in the art of illegal kite-flying.

I knew the subject had attached herself to a particularly mean Zapper and I had been throwing a line out on him whenever the opportunity arose. There is no hierarchy among Zappers but I had never heard this one's name mentioned without a certain respect. So although I had never seen him before I recognized him the moment he entered the bar. You can usually tell when someone entering a room has authority over the people already present. There are small signs by which people recognize it, a minute stirring of unconnected gestures which, taken together, add up to a tightening of an unspoken bond.

The big fellow they called Zeb approached the counter – I was watching in the mirror – with a girl alongside him who appeared so slight I almost didn't see her. When I got a good look at her I saw she had cut off most of her long blond hair, now dyed black. With the leather-and-chrome garb and the scowl she could have been just another young Zapper girl, enough to fool even her own mother. But I'm not her mother. I'm meant to be a detective.

She was sure pretty. There wasn't a man or woman in the place who didn't think so. Suddenly there wasn't enough air to go round. Or perhaps it was just we all wanted the same piece of it.

The two of them walked over to some people they knew. I heard his voice raised, laughing at some pleasantry. From where I was I couldn't see them anymore without moving my head and I was in no hurry to do that. I continued studying the lizard and waited. I had a feeling I wouldn't need to do anything. Events were going to take their own course. I was just one of a number of different ingredients that had been mixed together. All I could do was react the way I was going to have to react.

I didn't have to wait long. The big Zapper moved down the length of the mirror towards where I was sitting, his arm riding on the shoulder of the girl beside him as if the pair of them had business together. I kept my eyes on Sam who, behind the bar, watched them until he was looking straight through me and I felt like that damned dumb lizard.

'Excuse me,' the man growled into my ear. 'You mind I ask you a question?'

In the mirror he loomed over me like an avalanche about to happen. I only weigh a hundred and ninety-five stripped. He was smiling at me as if someone had just told him of some exploit of mine he liked the sound of. I know the trick. I refrained from smiling nervously along with him so that he would succeed in defining the mood.

'. . . My friends say you been putting a line out on me,' he said.

I held his gaze for a moment in the mirror, then turned – the lizard darted for cover and my heart went out to it.

I stood off the bar stool to face him. He stepped back to give me room. He was displaying a fine set of white teeth through a rough-trimmed black beard in which there were flecks of grey. He was big and strong and healthy-looking and happy to be that way.

I was guarded in my response.

'I don't know,' I said. The way he looked at me, his eyes laughing, made me want to quit acting tough and be friendly. 'Depends who you are.'

'I'm Zeb . . .'

He stuck out his hand for me to shake, the way Zappers still do. I took it. He didn't try to break my arm. He was a charmer. He had that smile, that rare quality of being able to make you feel special. Most people would do anything to put themselves in good with him, break the promises they had made to themselves rather than fail him. I was going to have to try to be an exception.

'. . . And this is who we call Zelda.'

Only then, on his invitation, did I look in the direction of the mean-faced runaway I had tracked across three counties. She didn't give me her hand. She didn't give me anything. Her violet pure-blooded Caucasian eyes were hooded with suspicion.

'Rick Stator. Pleasure to meet you.' I said. 'Sure I put a line on you, you're the dude with the Black Shadow. I been looking forward to meeting you. Some the boys were telling me it's an ace kite you have yourself.'

'You're interested in kites?'

'That's my Silver Wing out front.'

No conversation with a Zapper can get off the ground without this kite rap. The time I spent chewing the match with Zeb's aquaintances had not been wasted. I knew what direction the conversation was going to take. We were going to discuss the merits of different machines. It's commonly held among Zappers that the Silver Wing is a plodder. It has the torque but lacks the acceleration of lighter kites.

'Descended from the old longhorn hog,' he said. It was a polite way of saying my machine was a respected traditional vehicle. Reliable. A plodder. Out of date. 'You must like the pace.'

It's also a commonly held opinion among the Zapper fraternity that the Silver Wing has no pace to speak of.

'I like going in straight lines,' I said.

'Zappers usually go for more mobility than that.'

'That's OK,' I said. 'I'm not a Zapper.'

Now we were talking.

He shrugged. 'Who is? You think I am? Is Zelda here? A Zapper isn't a category of person, just the opposite. It's a non-category.'

'I guess I'm not there yet,' I said.

Sam poked three glasses of beer in front of us. He didn't say a word, although we each nodded to him and took a glass and drank.

'But . . .' Zeb continued, beer-foam on the whiskers of his top lip. 'You like flying a kite like a Zapper?'

'I love it.'

And this was no lie. Ever since I had started impersonating the style of the lowest status-rated social group I had learnt to appreciate the beauty of flying. I began to understand the kick they get from it, especially the dangerous Double Helix Fall which legally and symbolically defies everything the Protocol stands for.

'Love, huh?' Zeb said. 'That's a tender emotion for a lump of micro-circuits and tempered plastics. We keep love for people, surely? I mean for *living* things.'

He had deliberately stressed the outlaw semantic emphasis. It was a trap, of course.

'It's not the machine I love. It's being up there in control of something that can can *kill* me,' I said.

He nodded. 'That's a good definition.' He looked down at the girl while succeeding in giving the impression he was looking up to her. 'What d'you think, Sweetheart? Is it true? Do you have it in you to kill me?'

For the first time the subject spoke.

'Fuck off! I'm not a machine! You don't control me!' As if she was addressing a fly on her sleeve, she added: 'You're going to kill yourself anyway. You don't need any help from me!'

There followed an awkward pause. They looked at each other the way lovers do when one of them has spoken privately in public. For a moment I think they forgot that I was there. Finally Zeb said: 'Zelda would prefer I use an ejector . . .'

'I never said that!' she spat.

'You didn't have to say it.' He looked at me. 'What position do you take on the question, if I may ask?'

I repeated the credo: 'Ejectors can be safe but too much safety can be a dangerous thing. They slow you down.'

Zeb shook his head and sucked his teeth ironically. 'Anyone crazy enough not to use a government ejector, Rick Stator, *must* be a Zapper!'

He smiled at me. I smiled at him. But the girl, when I glanced at her, she wasn't smiling at anyone. She was watching me with cold hatred, almost as if she could read my mind and she knew I was a private dick her father had employed to find her and bring her home . . .

'QUASAR ELECTRONICS . . . Oh, good morning, Mrs Bloomingdale. You look worried. What can we do for you? . . . Your Homehelp is giving you trouble? What kind of trouble? . . . Oh, I'm real sorry to hear that . . . Again? Same as last time . . . I see. Okay, Mrs Bloomingdale. Leave it with me. I'll have a repairman drop by and take a look. I'll book you in for tomorrow. No. I'm sorry, that the earliest I can do . . . Don't mention it. Goodbye, Mrs Bloomingdale.'

In the repair lab contiguous to Larry McAlister's office Osip Pelig, QUASAR's Chief Repairman, overheard the booming voice of his partner without catching Mrs

Bloomingdale's half of the conversation. He heard McAlister get out of his chair, leave his office and approach the bench where Osip himself was tinkering with the intricate and, as far as he was concerned, mysterious magnetic rivers grid which he had removed from the dysfunctioning receptor of an artificial intelligence. He was progressing slowly – as far as he was able to tell. It was no secret that Osip Pelig's title of Chief Repairman was more honorary than a reflection of any skill he possessed at repairing homeoactive devices. It was a reflection of his position as third partner in the company.

McAlister was standing over him, he could tell. His wheelchair was very sensitive. Osip had not needed the chair since he had learnt to use the pair of prosthetic legs one of the QUASAR engineers had designed for him, but having sat in the chair for so many years he retained a strong emotional attachment to it.

'That was Mrs Bloomingdale again,' McAlister boomed. He was a big man who worked out in the health parlour every morning. His big voice expanded the importance of everything he said. 'You know, we want to have Szmidt take a look at her warranty certificate. That's the third time this year she's complained. Says her homehelp is refusing to obey her instructions. Shit, how can an automatic construct refuse to obey her? No one else complains!'

'They do, Larry. A lot of them. They expect things from Joesy that the J Model was never programmed to perform. They're only meant to clean the apartment, take out the garbage.' Osip spoke without looking up from the circuitry that was laid out on the bench in front of him. 'Hey, Larry. You're standing in my light!'

'What the fuck you talking about? What kinda things?'

'Oh . . . Interpersonal union.'

'What? You mean . . .?' Larry McAlister moved around the workbench to face the Chief Repairman. '. . . *Marital duties?*'

Osip knew that it troubled McAlister to acknowledge

90

the sexual practices which Joesy, the QUASAR Homehelp, was being subjected to. Ethical questions of any kind troubled him. They didn't – he liked to think – belong in the sphere of business. And the business McAlister was in was simple: the manufacture and marketing of useful and reliable domestic and public-service auto-appliances. Period.

Whereas Osip had given the question a lot of thought.

'That's right,' he said. 'I played over the memory of the last model Mrs Bloomingdale sent back. You should take a look yourself sometime. I fed it into one of the Joesys lying about the shop. The damn thing didn't stand a chance! You know it had to . . .'

'I don't want to hear about it!'

'Face facts, Larry! They nearly all do it. The trouble is we can't write it into the warranty certificate. I spoke to Szmidt. He told me that if we tried to we could be arraigned for failing to conform to the description of our trading licence.'

'So why don't we take them to court, using the memory tapes to show the kind of hammering our products are taking?' McAlister growled humourlessly at the thought. 'Mrs Bloomingdale would pay plenty for us to lay off!'

'Larry. Think of the publicity!'

'Yeah. We'd be finished.' Then: 'We could show Mrs Bloomingdale the tapes. Let her draw her own conclusions.'

'We could. They call that kind of thing blackmail.'

'Well, what *can* we do? Just sit by while these horny high-status matrons screw QUASAR to bankruptcy?'

Osip shrugged. 'Give her one that works. I mean, modify a model to provide the service our clients appear to require.' He looked up. He wanted to see McAlister's face when he heard this idea.

'Christ, Osip! They do most everything already! We can't afford to process for individual . . .' he groped for the word, '*appetites*! That kind of thing is unacceptable! We don't have it in the bank either. If it wasn't for the State Fire Department contract we'd be wiped out by now. Some of your ideas, Osip, are plain irresponsible! You know how much I value your work but, Christ! First it was this private investigator scheme, which isn't just irresponsible, it's illegal! Now you want we break into the male-whore racket . . .'

Osip smiled into the circuitry while his colleague got the bit between his teeth. McAlister saw everything as a two-dimensional construct like a sheet of paper, only one side of which had any writing on it. He had no depth of field. He lacked vision. Unconsciously he probably wanted every enterprise to go wrong.

'That reminds me,' Osip said. 'Szmidt wants to talk to you. Something to do with the Fire Department contract. He says he isn't convinced we should handle it. He was muttering something about we never took on anything this big before.'

In order to float his own projects, Osip had learnt it paid to keep his two partners at cross-purposes with each other.

'Szmidt's a shyster,' McAlister sneered. 'He doesn't understand our product. Never has. You know as well I do that it isn't quantity that counts when you're dealing with high-effect auto-systems, it's production quality. Once you've evolved your prototype you set the reproplant to turn out as many versions as you think you can sell. Szmidt's a company lawyer. What the fuck does he know about production assembly techniques?'

'Oh I think he'll go along with us. He knows we don't have a choice. He's just cautious, given our financial situation. You know what he's like. What's eating him is he can't trace how we came by the contract in the first place. We didn't tender for it. In the second place nobody else did. And in the third place why not? It's kind of coincidental we were offered the contract when we were on the point of having to call in the receiver general. What's more the State, according to Szmidt, was not budgeted for a refit in the auxiliary services.'

'What has this to do with QUASAR? We clinched the deal, didn't we? We're back in business! Your job's still here. So is Szmidt's. What's he beefing about? We're making money. Isn't that the general idea?'

McAlister was pacing the length of the lab, gesturing into the air, crossing in front of Osip's light every time he passed.

'He says it's lucky for us a major order appeared on the book just when we were on the point of insolvency. And uncanny. He told me it was the oldest double deal in company history, for large corporations to farm out – for them – small orders which make all the difference between business and no business to five-cent companies like ours. Then, after they – *we*, in this case – have sunk their assets into the design and production of the order, to threaten to withdraw the contract. The five-cent company finds itself geared to the requirements of an order from a single major client who says the deal's off. The five-cent company can't fight IBM or TI or whoever. What does it do with all the work it has already put in on the contract?'

Larry McAlister stopped pacing. He was standing in front of his Chief Repairman.

'What does it do?' he said.

'It has no choice,' Osip said flatly. 'It sells up lock-stock-and-barrel for nickels and dimes to the only people interested in the line of business they are now specializing in. Naturally this is the transState company, through one of its subsidiaries, which placed the order in the first place. That's how they got to be a big transState company. Market cannibalism, Szmidt calls it.'

'Szmidt said that?'

'He gave me a lecture on monopolistic practice and let me draw my own conclusions.'

'Osip, the State Fiscal Agency may be crooked but it isn't a private company. It's a public body!'

'It's a powerful client. The same reasoning should apply.'

'How can it? The State is not allowed to renege on its

contracts. Why should it? Did you ever see a State Agency that didn't have a hatful of reasons before it spent a penny of taxpayers' money?'

'I never did, Larry. And nor did Szmidt. That's why he can't figure out why they should want to rescue us from the bankruptcy court. What do they stand to gain?'

'An efficient labour-free auto-fire service is all!' McAlister barked over his shoulder. He headed for his office. 'And cheap!'

The door slammed behind him.

Alone, Osip continued his examination of the circuitry of the magnetic rivers which he had taken out of the receptor. He was not, as he had implied to McAlister, repairing it. Not exactly. There had been no dysfunction in the mechanism. It had been working fine before Osip had disassembled the thing. He was simply trying to figure out how it worked. There was a good deal to do with the engineering that went over his head, even though much of it had been manufactured to his own specifications. It was a frustrating paradox that the ideas had been his but the design engineers understood more about the principles they involved than he did himself. QUASAR Electronics prided itself on the calibre of its graduates – they were the best – but no one pretended that Osip Pelig was one of them. Whenever they sat around discussing the information theory behind the molecular structure of microcrystal cell technology, say, or comparing different sonar-orientation systems, Osip felt undereducated. He was not a real repairman. He was only an inventor.

It wasn't every day you found Osip Pelig leaning over one of the workbenches manipulating a tension-gauge. He could diagnose and correct a fault in a Homehelp as well as any of the repairmen, but he worked more slowly and he made elementary mistakes. Accidents, it had been claimed, had a tendency to happen around him. For these reasons Osip carried out most of his work at home. It was in his old stone cliffside villa while practising arpeggios on his cello that oddball variations on the theme of high-effect self-regulating systems proposed themselves to him. Or while he walked – since he had taken possession of his new QUASAR prosthetic legs – along the beach at low tide. Or, at high-tide, while he sat at the foot of the stairway cut into the side of the rock, watching the motion of the waves. He had come to the conclusion that it was probably because so much was still a mystery to him that he asked the obvious dumb questions which the graduates were too bright to ask but which, so far, had kept QUASAR in business.

The more Osip bowed his cello and watched the ocean's rise and fall, the more he became convinced that all the vibrations in the universe, including those inside human beings, wanted to obey the same simple law of octaves. In all wave-motion activity the difference between what we call the notes, the intervals in their varying pitch, are simply pauses, broken places, in the necessary direction of the octave. At these points of discontinuity the wave alters and eventually develops into its own opposite. This, he intuited, was why all movement in nature was cyclical. Any escape from the circle – when say, one species evolves into another – has to coincide with one of these intervals. It is the timely random mutant chromosone that rescued a species from extinction. Chance screwed by Necessity.

In the case of humans, whose complex moods and thoughts are fluctuating all the time, the lesion between the fixed laws of probability and aleatory occurrences are infinitely more frequent. What takes a species a million years to effect, a human being accomplishes every time he puts on his green pants instead of his blue ones.

Osip had worked hard to persuade the bright graduates to encode this simple principle – which he called The Aleatory Factor – into the decision-making cortex of the homeoactive constructs that QUASAR was turning out. It was not sufficient to manufacture a machine capable of responding to a programmed code. They needed one which could recognize and act on the interference of acausal phenomena. For a construct to be able to acknowledge the synapses in physical reality it had to be in a position to assess events at the moment at which they could be changed. An epistemology of its own mental process – consciousness – would enable the construct to develop and to take part in its own development.

But to find out what progress they had been making in this area depended on the success of their latest self-directing artificial intelligence: the one they had called the K model hominoid.

Osip was still diddling with the magnetic rivers of the K model's feedback terminal when, an hour later, Larry McAlister re-emerged from his office. He was waving a hard copy print-out in his hand.

'Osip . . . I been tidying up the file on the East Coast high-status kid the K Model is supposed to be finding.' McAlister made no attempt to hide his disapproval of the scheme. 'We don't seem to have very much. In fact, we don't have anything!'

Osip looked up from his work. McAlister was standing in his light again.

'That's true, I'm afraid, Larry,' he said. 'There isn't much. Most of what there is to know about the girl – like who she is, or even who the client is – only Rick Stator, I mean the K Model, is in a position to say. It was the K which made the connection in the first place. It has the client's confidence. So anything the K has found out – if it has found out anything – is still inside its memory.'

'You don't say?'

'The K – Rick Stator – would regard it as a breach of professional etiquette if he thought we knew. He couldn't function. Don't forget he possesses an above-average sense of ethics. He would – like Mrs Bloomingdale's homehelp – refuse to work.'

'So how do we get to find out? That's the idea, isn't it?'

Osip was aware that in this private investigator venture

he stood alone among his two partners. McAlister was still a long way from being sold on the idea and Szmidt could hardly bear to hear it mentioned. They had only agreed to go through with it because they had been forced to admit that it provided the best quick return on their one-off K Model prototype, the most sophisticated hominoid QUASAR had ever turned out. And, in terms of production costs, the most expensive. But it still existed in a market vacuum and the company, faced with the possibility of having to wind itself up, had taken the decision to lease out the K Model as a high paid private investigator. It had been a decision taken in desperation. With the Fire Department contract in the bag, the situation had changed. Osip had come under fresh pressure to call the K back in. Neither of his colleagues had been persuaded by his special pleading, in particular that the new hominoid was excellently placed as a private investigator, operating independently of QUASAR, to test a specifically ingrammed social-role matrix. McAlister and Szmidt professed they could not see the advantages of this and that, whatever they were, they didn't count for much against the fact that running an unlicenced investigation agency was not entirely ethical and almost certainly illegal. Osip was convinced that the K, left to itself, would reach the edge of its current skills programme sooner rather than later. QUASAR would be better placed to make the necessary modifications before launching it on the market.

Osip often found it hard to square the vertical thinking of his two partners with his own long-term plans. Szmidt thought only in dollars and McAlister morbidly identified with the success or failure of the company. Osip failed to see what McAlister was getting steamed up over. From a production point of view it didn't matter whether QUASAR knew the whereabouts of some runaway rich kid. That was Rick Stator's business to find out. The business of QUASAR was to work out how he did.

'One way we can find out,' Osip said, 'is by asking it.'

McAlister shot him a look.

'You mean,' he said, measuring his words hysterically, 'that we, the company which assembled the plastic fellow you call Rick Stator, we gotta ask its goddamn leave to be put in the picture?'

'That's no way to talk about one of our best products, Larry. No, we don't have to ask its leave. We can get a pretty good picture direct. We can see and hear everything Rick sees and hears the moment he does. Or we can,' Osip grinned at his partner, 'soon as I fix this terminal.'

Osip nodded towards the circuitry laid out on the workbench. The disassembled terminal was their sole means of finding out what the hominoid was doing or thinking at any particular time. Osip had deliberately put the terminal out of commission, however, in order to make this impossible. He was in no hurry for contact with Rick Stator to be established. Just the reverse.

'Is that what you're gumming up there?' McAlister sneered. 'You should give it to one of the boys. You'll as likely paralyse the thing in midsentence.'

'No chance of that happening. This thing is discon-nected.'

McAlister, turning to leave, froze.

'Wait a minute! You're telling me that one of our hominoids – the K model no less, our best! – is running around out there and *we have no way of receiving information from it*! Like whether it's taken off for Korea or Singapore or some other place they can replicate our work!'

'Larry, relax! It's not that bad. We still have our regular videolink security arrangements. As far as Rick is con-cerned we are his employers. He's phoning in his progress reports regularly like we fixed. We programmed him, don't forget!'

'Can't we suggest it drops by for a chat? Like next time it's in the neighbourhood?'

Osip grinned at his partner's heavy sarcasm.

'That might be tricky, Larry,' he said. 'Rick would want to know why. He's a cagey bird. Like a good private dick should be. It's how we made him!'

'*He*? Sure you don't mean *it*?'

Osip had noticed that there was one aspect of the experiment which deeply disturbed McAlister, that Rick Stator was working as a private eye without understanding that he was a prototype hominoid from the QUASAR workshop. It unnerved McAlister to know that the machine was ignorant of the extent to which it had been duped. On the occasions they had met together, McAlister had been extremely ill at ease, unable to conceal his anxiety. Rick had obviously picked up on this and wondered about it. He didn't trust McAlister – his boss. Osip had watched the autonomic detective succeed in making his big weight-lifting partner paranoid.

'When is it due to check in next?' 'McAlister asked.

'It already did this morning. You want to take a look? I'll run it through. I think he's making some progress.'

'We had the terminal you're fucking up, we wouldn't have to rely on what the thing chose to tell us.'

The Director pulled up a stool and the Chief Repairman wheeled his chair in front of the video monitor. Osip touched some keys and had the recorded message replay itself.

The pleasant clean-shaven face of Rick Stator filled the screen. His grey eyes – pigment G/37, which Osip had chosen himself – looked at them, clear and unworried.

Rick grinned briefly.

'*When I got my first sight of the subject – RS/7 – I was sucking ice and watching lizards chase each other up and down walls of an out-of-town bar in a desert corner of the State. You don't mind, I'll keep the name of the bar under my hat for the moment . . .*'

'Shit, we don't mind.' McAlister growled.

9

The Emergency Duty Sister flipped back the paper sheet covering the face of the body lying on the trolley. It was a Zapper's face, overrun by an unpleasant growth of black hair and it reinforced the opinion she already held about Zappers. They were an unpleasant growth on society. Who needed them? This specimen had been brought in after his kite had flipped out of control, failing to complete one of those senseless illegal manoeuvres which, so she understood, Zappers forced their machines to perform for their own incomprehensible reasons. In her time she had seen plenty of Zees – all of them, like this one, lying on trolleys with their eyes shut, very few of whom had ever opened them again. She despised the crass illegality of their behaviour though she knew from her social harmony course at school that the degenerate status group was necessary for an integrated societal equilibrium. She knew but she didn't comprehend. Even lying with his eyes shut on the trolley the big Zapper offended and threatened her. She hated him. He smelt.

She threw a glance towards the young girl who had entered the cubicle to view the body – obviously a member of the same status-rated group as the laid-out male in front of her, her black leather jacket barely concealing her breasts. It was disgusting! And, behind the girl, a really decrepit old wino. Urgh! What a great pair they made! At the sight of the ex-Zapper the girl grabbed hold of the old wino's hand. The gesture pleased the Duty Sister. It was in the natural order of things and it immediately removed the affront these people made to her authority. She was in control. It was only right that such a young, disturbingly pretty girl should be reminded of what all Zappers had coming to them sooner or later: grief.

'Not a nice way to end up . . .' she said.

ZELDA OBSERVED the scene unfold as slowly as she had foreseen it would. First the disaster, now the aftermath. Her foreknowledge did not hurry it up any, however. She watched the steel-jawed lady nurse draw back the sheet – again. Suddenly there he was, the beautiful face of her lover lying on an ambulance trolley, without her, as if all he needed was a good shake and a cup of strong coffee. The event was finally overtaking her forememory of it.

All the life in her wanted to flow out of her and into Zeb. But this was impossible. Her fingers felt for the hand of the old man who was standing behind her.

She knew it was not Zeb's death which was so disturbing. Hadn't she been teaching herself to accept it since she had first met him? It was her immediate feelings of separateness from him which made her heart beat, something her prescience had not prepared her for. He was dead, without her, and a bit of herself was still locked up within him and must, therefore, have died with him.

SOLLYHEIM ESCORTED the grown-up child – Zelda, she said he was to call her – into the cubicle which the Arrivals Clerk had indicated. He stood by as the Duty Sister, with barely concealed contempt, drew back the sheet. Cold fingers squeezed his hand and tugged at his heart.

The body was too big for the trolley. The sunburnt

bearded face was not the kind you were ever likely to see looking at you from behind a desk in the Protocol Building. It was a strong-boned old-fashioned human face that had laughed a lot, you could tell, and cried too maybe, although that was less easy to tell. The features, in their final repose, radiated the pure honesty that can only be practised outside the law.

But humans had always been outlaws. That was how they had got to be humans in the first place, by breaking the rules, leaving the trees and taking to the river, inventing new uses for the thumb. And there were still – as there had always been – plenty of monkeys around who didn't think it was such a good idea.

What a waste that this young man with so fine a face should be lying on a hospital trolley as if this were the best end he could have hoped for. If it was, humankind had surely cut itself off from the instinct for life and risk which had pulled it out of the forest.

'Not a nice way to end up . . .' the Duty Sister said, somewhat unnecessarily in Sollyheim's opinion.

'THE FUCK you know?'

Zelda put her hands on her hips, deliberately exposing her chest in order to provoke the nurse.

'Well, I . . .' The nurse faltered. 'I know that this man didn't have to be lying here with the smoke taken out of him!'

'Lady, that's where you're mistaken! He *did*.'

'You're saying he wanted it to be like this?'

'What he wanted? Shit, what's that got to do with anything? It's the way it happened! There was nothing he could do to stop it!'

'Then he was a fool – or a coward,' the nurse said. 'Or both.'

'Like fuck he was! You don't know . . .'

'Police say he wasn't taking legal precautions.'

'Police don't know shit too! You can't drop into a Double Helix with a half ton of ejector up your ass!'

The grey-faced nurse gave a sour triumphant smile.

'What's so necessary about flying a kite upside down?' Zelda held her ground.

'What's so necessary about anything, Lady, is it makes you feel your *life* is in your own hands! It's something good that belongs to you yourself and not to some fucking government department computer!'

'A person's afterlife is a co-ordination of all factors contained in that person's SollyChart. There is no . . .'

'Zees don't have SollyCharts. Why should they? They don't have no fucking future!'

'Because they are outlaws.'

'You bet they are! For us life is something that happens to us when we breathe and eat and fuck and fly fast kites, not when some fool quack said twenty years ago!'

The nurse, nettled, drew herself up inside her uniform. 'Please remember it was Doctor Sollyheim built this Clinic. It's only thanks to him that we . . .'

'. . . Are all *dead*!' Zelda jeered. 'Sollyheim . . .'

'. . . Was an old fool.'

It was the old man who had spoken and put an end to the unpleasant conversation. After a silence equally unpleasant the nurse replaced the paper sheet and handed Zelda a brown plastic package and left the cubicle.

The package contained Zeb's beautiful leather jacket, a leather belt and a pair of leather boots. It was all she had to show of her relationship with him. But she was a Zapper girl and she had to do what was expected of her. She took the belt and clinched it round her own waist. The two boots she replaced on the feet of their owner. The jacket she passed on to the next man in her life.

'Here, Old Man. Put yourself inside this.' She handed him the jacket. 'Go on, put it on. This was how it was meant to be!'

She helped the old man into the Zapper jacket.

'Now you're a Zapper!' she said. 'Let's go.'

Together they walked through the foyer towards the exit.

'Where to?' he said.

'Back to where I came from, I guess,' she told him. If they would have her. 'If they'll have me. Unless you have any ideas.'

'Ideas, Zelda, is *all* I have. Unfortunately you can't sleep inside ideas. I can't go back where I came from. I am – like your friend – a kind of outlaw.'

She slid her arm around the old guy's waist. He needed looking after.

'If you're like him, you're like me,' she said.

They stood in the quiet ambulance bay while the old man relit his cigar with Zeb's Zippo which he had found in the jacket pocket.

'Where does a Zapper go at this time of night where he can buy a drink and lay his head?'

'Only one place I know,' she said.

FORTY MINUTES later Zelda's kite, having picked its way through the desolate Diablo Range, settled onto the dirt in front of the bar where, only a few hours before, she had said goodbye to Zeb and then stood and watched him manoeuvre through the sky with that weird piece of bad luck, Rick Stator, the only person she had ever met who had successfully been able to prevent her from reading his intentions. He had chilled her blood the very first time she clapped eyes on him, the way he had looked at her, as if *he* had been able to read *her* mind.

She cut the motor and let the dust settle. The scratch kiteport, and the garden surrounding it, was deserted. The bar itself was unlit and silent. Even the strange moon had disappeared from the sky. It was eerie. The Police had departed and the Zappers — those in the air to watch the Fall — had scattered immediately. Minutes after the two kites had begun their descent — their alternately coloured light-streamers visible half-way across the County — the SkyPol had arrived on the scene. The bar had emptied. She had been left alone to watch from the nearest hill while the ambulance medics pulled the body clear of the wreckage of the Black Shadow. The sky had been full of fast Police kites and the sound of their lethal fission-canons popping the Zapper kites like human skulls inside a furnace. It was eerie to be back again, almost immediately, as the dawn of another day broke calmly over the memory.

The bar lights came on. By the time they reached the door they could hear the sound of bolts sliding and then they were looking down the half-sawnoff barrel of an old Navy Colt revolver. Sam lowered the Colt and, without any other indication, stepped back into the bar. She followed him and the old man in Zeb's jacket followed her.

Already the saloon was swept clean and polished as if it were on the point of opening for business. Glasses glistened in the rack over the sink. Along the length of the bar stools stood at an equal distance from each other. The chairs were positioned symmetrically around the card-tables and in the centre of each table there was a neat face-down deck of cards. The air tasted fresh. On the pool table the white cue-ball rested on the spot, defying the solid phalanx of the colours. They reminded Zelda of herself and the odds stacked against her. As if nothing had happened the previous evening, Sam's bar was primed for the next eventuality.

THE SPACIOUS old-fashioned bar-room was empty, as cool and peaceful as a place of prayer. Wall-mirrors spanned the polished wood saloon, reflecting each other, silver and exact, as if to remind the congregation that nothing is ever as straightforward as it seems.

He stood next to the girl, savouring the atmosphere while the old barkeep – who was almost as old as himself – replaced the pistol in the holster strapped to his leg under his robe. He obviously slept armed.

'You need a drink,' he informed them and then disappeared, like Alice, into the mirror behind the bar.

Sollyheim eyed the ancient Zapper staring at him until the barkeep reappeared holding a bottle that had a plain white label with a spidery script across it. Without dusting the bottle he broke the bondseal and filled four whiskey glasses.

'This is the last bottle,' he said. 'In the world, probably. I bought a case when Old Forrester went bust. Twenty years ago?'

They each picked up a glass, leaving the fourth glass alone on the bartop. Sollyheim, nosing the liquor, had to shut his eyes to stem the heavy mist of regret for a lost epoch it conjured, evidence of a time when the authentic had made a stand against the substitute that they had all gotten used to. When he couldn't stand it any longer he poured the bourbon down his throat. It raced through him like a lighted fuse and he saw stars.

Nobody spoke. The barkeep divided the fourth glass equally between the three of them. And then it was done.

'That loner who Zeb got tangled with,' the barkeep said. 'Came back round after the SkyPol hauled ass. He was looking for you, Zelda. You wasn't none of his business, I figured, so I let him think you left with Zorab. Zorab will help him conclude any outstanding business the dude has.'

'Thanks Sam,' Zelda said. 'He gives me the heebies.' Then she took hold of Sollyheim's hand and, in her other hand, one of Sam's. 'This is Sol. I gave him Zeb's jacket. He stood by me at the fucking Clinic. He don't have no place to go neither.'

Sollyheim and Sam looked each other over, each submitting the other to the unspoken mutual appraisal that takes place when old men meet each other for the first time, which young people are often unaware of.

'Don't I know you from some place?' Sam said.

'Could be,' Sollyheim told him. 'Could well be.'

'You was . . . kind of well-known. A few years back?'

'Quite a few back.'

'About the time Old Forrester went bust. They said you was crazy.'

'They were crazy.'

Both men momentarily shared the same memories.

'Then they said you was dead.'

'They said everyone was dead.'

Sam finished the whiskey in his glass and urged the others to do the same.

'Let me get this straight,' he said. 'We was thinking you was dead when all the time you are alive, and when we thought you was alive, you thought we were dead?'

Sollyheim shrugged. What could he say?

'What is this?' Zelda looked from one to the other. 'You two already know each other, or what?'

Sam shook his head.

'Nope. You couldn't say that.' He stood up.

'Let's go find you both someplace to sleep. It's so late it's getting early.' He looked at Zelda. 'Are you . . .?'

'Yes,' she said. 'We are.'

WHEN THE the small SONY next to the bed bleeped Joe King was in the middle of a delicious dream starring a beautiful high-status woman in a cream-and-blue chevron-ned silk dress. The woman — at that precise moment — was in the process of unbuttoning the front of the dress, on the point of stepping out of it into his arms. She was taking her time, though, loosening the buttons one by one. She seemed to have been doing this all night. The SONY continued to bleep until Joe woke up and reluctantly told it to go ahead. He turned over. There in front of him, framed in the little screen, was the face of the woman of his dreams. He knew this because she was wearing the same cream-and-blue patterned dress, all the buttons of which were now done up.

'Joe, wake up will you!'

It was Cheryl Duvall. She was looking alarmed. It was an alarm call.

'Something terrible has happened! Wake up!'

Joe rubbed his eyes. He couldn't help glancing under the sheet to satisfy himself that he was alone in the bed.

'I dreamed you came over and spent the night here Cherry,' he said.

'I did!'

'You were wearing a nice cream-and-blue dress . . .'

'I was! I mean, I still am! Listen . . .'

'Why did you have to leave so early!'

'Never mind that now. I have to see you. I need to talk to you. Something terrible has happened!'

Seeing how alarmed Cherry was looking, Joe decided not to ask her why she had left his bed to find a public payphone to call him up to tell him she had to talk to him – the only thing you could do from a public payphone.

'Well, go ahead. What is it?' he said.

'I can't tell you over the public link.' Cherry was looking over her shoulder as if she too was making sure that she was alone.

'Where are you? Whyn't you here?'

'I can't tell you that either.'

Cherry had called him up to say she couldn't talk to him.

'You in some kind of jam?'

'You could say so!'

'What d'you want me to do?'

'I don't know what you can do! You have to help me!'

'How? What can I do?'

108

CHERYL DUVALL left the payphone booth and returned to the waiting taxi. She didn't need to be apprehensive. There was nobody about. The eatery alongside which the payphone was situated had not opened yet. As far as the rest of the city was concerned it was still night although dawn was looming behind the ocean mist which lay across the Bay Area. Inside the kite she sat watching the grey light drag itself over the horizon with the alacrity of an early-shift service-worker on his way to perform some thankless necessary task. At least there were no people around. Soon there would be plenty and she would not be able to tell which of them were going to be after her. As long as she occupied the whole landscape, alone and awake, she was safe and the city innocent of the things she knew. She had about thirty, forty minutes.

She glanced at the clock on the dash but the time showing was three months out of date. Like nearly all the Metroplex Transit Authority cabs this one was due for a re-fit. She could smell the body fluids of its recent occupants in the worn and faded upholstery. Depressed, she directed the cab to transport her back to the condo-block from whence it had recently ferried her.

She had to reach Joe's before every cab in the city had her number. She had nowhere else to go. If she reported that her prisoner had escaped her employers would find her and hurt her. Probably they would not need to hurt her physically but they would find some humiliation. They had always encouraged her to expect so much from herself that failure on such a scale as this was beyond her worst fears. She would never work again. Did they hope she would finish herself off with her own issue pistol, save them the embarrassment of doing the job themselves? Whatever they hoped, her skin, when they found her, was not going to be worth being in.

But she was not the only one who was vulnerable. Sollyheim was out there somewhere, alone and without friends. A walking time-bomb for the Protocol. She unfolded in her mind's eye the piece of paper she had read on Sollyheim's typewriter. It read:

'*Mein Liebeskind* – Gone to Righi's to buy me a donut. *Ich kann nicht mehr hier bleiben. Tschüss* – Gottlieb.'

She couldn't help smiling at his fondness for Righi's doughnuts. It was just like him to leave a goddamn sentiment, no information, no clue to how he had gotten clear of the security systems. The old fox. If the Nazis hadn't been able to break him how could the Protocol hope to?

What did she care what the Protocol hoped? Gottlieb had escaped and she was glad! She wished him luck. It meant the end for her, of course, but so what? It meant another chance for Sollyheim. His escape had released her. At least she was freed from the burden of lying to him, screening him from the world, drugging his nightcap. And also from the fear of failure. After this she would never need to worry on that score again.

But if she was in a jam – as Joe King had put it – Sollyheim was the reason. As soon as her boss was informed that the most famous man in recent history had risen from his niche in the Lincoln Memorial and was at large in Northern California she would be finished. Ben Cznetsov was genial and, most of the time, charming – the one time she had slept with him had not been unpleasurable. She liked him. Like everyone else who worked for him she found it hard not to. But there was not an officer inside the CIA-wing of the Protocol whose ass did not tighten up in his presence. His charm was terrifying, immobilizing a person the way the dance of certain reptiles paralyses their prey by hypnotic fascination before the fatal sting. There was an ambiguity about Cznetsov's

110

smile. Like a length of piano wire, it left it to you to imagine the uses it could be put to – murder or a sonata. Being a man sensitive to the feelings of others, like all masters of political terror, he understood the nuances between love, pain and humiliation.

For no obvious reason, a spasm of fear tore through her. Her heart pounded and her palms began to sweat. Cznetsov was far away. The old taxi-kite was skating safely high up over the fog and the pinnacles of Sanfran's pyramids. The sky was clear. Something about the smell of the worn upholstery unnerved her. It was increasing in intensity. Her hand slid into her purse and fished around until it clasped the butt of her standard-issue pistol, which Cznetsov had made her promise she would always carry, despite her objections. 'I'm never going to have to use one of these, Benny, let's face it,' she had tried to assure him. 'Maybe not. I hope you're right,' he had said, smiling his smile. 'That's not the reason I want you to carry it. One day maybe you'll understand. A gun is a lethal weapon. It kills people, Cherry. Where you point it is up to you. I'm giving it to you to keep your mind on the business you're in. You're not a cop until you have a gun, every hoodlum knows that.'

She kept her eyes on the stopped clock in front of her as her liver pumped epinephrine into her bloodstream. Without any doubt this was the day Cznetsov had been talking about. She released the safety catch with the thumb of the hand holding the gun. Then, having made a split second calculation of the odds, slowly turned in her seat and pointed the light-weight Walther .38 at a human being for the first time in her career. She had to hold the gun with both hands, it was shaking so much.

The wide-open eyes in the face of the person crouching in the rear luggage-area of the cab blinked slowly.

She had never seen a face like it, an old and gnarled gargoyle that had been worn away by the forces of nature into a half dozen conflicting expressions. She had no idea

111

what lay behind any of them. An uncut white beard poked through the skin from the neck to the ears – or, rather, to the flaps of the red-checked woollen cap the gargoyle was wearing. It was a wino's face, the eyes blinking with an old wino's confusion.

'Who the fuck are you?'

The wino grinned toothlessly.

'Spight.'

'Is that your *name*?'

He nodded.

'What are you doing sitting in my cab? How did you get in here?'

In a broken falsetto he piped: 'In my head is my only house unless it rains!'

It occurred to her that he might be singing.

'You spend the night here?'

'Ma'am.'

She lowered the gun, realizing as she did that it was no longer shaking. That was something. She could see that the taxi was descending towards the communal kite-port of the block containing Joe King's tiny apartment. The situation was ridiculous. She had lost one old man and somehow picked up another!

She replaced her pistol into her purse.

The old wino Spight farted quietly again to himself.

IT WAS a horrible sight first thing in the morning. She, fresh and nice as a peeled fruit. He in the final stages of entropy. A cautionary conjunction.

Joe dumbly gestured them to step inside, which they did, following him into the small kitchen. He started for the coffee-maker, determined not to ask what was going on until he had had a cup. Before he reached it the arms of Cheryl Duvall encircled him and held him tight.

'Darling,' she said into his kimono. 'Whyn't you fix me

and Spight some breakfast?'

He turned in her arms. 'You and *who*?'

'Spight. That's his name. I found him in my cab this morning – well, *your* cab, the one you had wait outside the ABBACCA last night. I think he must have spent the night in it.'

Over her shoulder he watched the man she called Spight gnawing a smile in the doorway, his hands fidgeting as he waited for whatever was going to happen.

'Hello, Spight. Pleased to make your acquaintance. Take a seat. How d'you like your coffee?' Joe said.

'Don't be sarcastic!'

She pushed him aside and set to work on the coffee-maker. 'First of all, this has nothing to do with Spight. When I called you I didn't know about him. I only found him after I got back in the cab.'

'I see. Spight just came along for the ride.'

'Very funny.'

She shook cornflakes into three bowls.

'You want some cornflakes Spight?'

The old man grinned.

'Take a look inside my purse, Joe.'

Joe picked up the woman's purse and slid his hands in. When he took the hand out there was an automatic pistol in it. He had a good look at it. It interested him. He had never been this close to, not to say handled, a genuine firearm before.

'Well?' Cheryl Duvall said over her shoulder. 'What do you see?'

'I see you have a gun.'

'Is that all? Do all your girlfriends carry .38 single-action parabellum pistols in their purses?'

'I guess it puts you in breach of the government's firearm legislation.'

'I'm not in breach of it though, Joe. I have a licence.'

'I see.'

'Do you?'

'I see you're a cop.'

'You don't sound surprised.'

'I'm not,' Joe lied. 'How else could you have been able to check out my CD alias so easy?'

'Don't you mind? I mean, does it make any difference – to you and me?'

'*I'm* the status-evader. You tell me.'

'I'm not that kind of cop. I had a special assignment. I certainly never used that thing you're holding, except just now when I waved it at Spight. By the way don't touch the safety-release. It has a hair trigger. You'll blow me through the wall.'

Joe glanced at Spight who was watching the gun the way a cat watches a dog.

'You *had* an assignment,' he said. 'Don't you have it anymore?'

'I don't know how to explain. Or where to begin. I have to tell you something you won't find easy to believe but before I can do that I have to tell you something you'll find impossible to believe.'

His colleague, Jerry Kittow, would have hated the sound of this but all the years Joe had spent devouring illicit pharmaceuticals and ancient pulp fiction paperback books had prepared him for this moment. At least, he hoped they had.

He laid the pistol aside. He didn't need a pistol, he needed a cup of strong coffee.

'When you know what I'm about to tell you, Joe, you'll be different. I'm warning you. Knowing it will change you for ever. You'll never be able to see things the way you do now.'

Joe sipped his coffee and waited. He had to report for work in three hours.

'My assignment was high up in security. In order to carry it out I had access to classified material. Very few people know what I know – even inside the CIA-wing. I can tell you this now because it doesn't matter anymore –

or it won't matter when my boss finds out . . .'

'You're thinking aloud. Just tell it straight.'

'For chrissake! It's about as straight as a homerun! First you ought to know I was detailed to look after someone very important – very old, very VIP. My job was to keep him company and make sure he had what he wanted. There were others around to make sure he didn't start wandering the corridors. The Protocol had reasons for wanting him kept out of circulation. He knew . . . things. Things the Protocol didn't want him to communicate. He disagreed with it on a couple of points . . .'

SPIGHT FINISHED his cornflakes and the woman immediately re-filled his bowl again. She never quit yammering while she did. Either she was or he was. Still, it was a good breakfast. He took a slug of real instant coffee.

Neither the woman nor the man was speaking to him. They were acting like he wasn't there. They just went on yammering. This was the way it always was. Spight knew there were probably reasons for everything that went on around him but for many years now he had given up trying to figure out what they were. People had gotten so strange.

'Why d'you say *was*?' the man said. 'Isn't he around no more?'

'Oh sure. He's around. But he's an old man who should be at home in bed, not pounding the pavement like Spight here.'

Spight heard his name. So they were talking about *him*. He listened slyly, careful not to show that he was. He ate his cornflakes.

'I said *was* because officially he is – as he would say – *dead*,' the woman said. 'Has been for years.'

'Haven't we all?' the man said.

'Yes. But he thinks he isn't dead.'

'And he isn't.'

115

They were going round in circles.

'No. Not dead in the sense *he* means it. That's one of the things the Government disagrees with him about.'

'Hold on. Do I have it right? He thinks that everyone thinks he's dead, but he thinks he isn't?'

'We're getting there.'

'He has some mental disability?'

Spight's head started to hurt.

'Not that I noticed. Fact he has the sharpest brain I ever encountered. But he's very old. He finds it hard to give up the habit of thinking he's *alive*.'

There followed a long silence. Suddenly nobody was speaking. This worried Spight. Had they caught on that he was listening to what they were saying about him?

'I see,' the man said. 'He knows that everyone in his terms, thinks he's dead – which he isn't – when in fact we all think, in our terms, that he isn't dead at all, he's been Returned.'

'Right!'

'And all the time he was dead or alive, whichever, he was enjoying the hospitality of the Protocol?'

Spight gulped down more coffee. His hand was shaking so bad he could hardly hold the cup. In order that the young feller and his girl would not see that he was listening he stopped listening. His head hurt anyway, like it nearly always did when he tuned into other people. Folks had gotten so strange. Ever since they had begun talking this way, trying to convince him he was *dead* for chrissake, he had acted the part of a crazy old man. He wondered how these two had gotten his number so quick. If they started to work on him, he was going to play even extra crazy.

CHERYL WATCHED the man she had made love with the previous night, surprised – and relieved – how calmly he was taking the hot piece of information she was giving him. When he understood it fully, its significance, however, would he want to make love with her again?

'You see, the old Dover Administration needed him – they needed his ideas – to help them establish an ideology for their power-base. This was before the Protocol got big and the alliance of international companies began buying up the Soviet currencies. He didn't want to help them so they attempted to strongarm him. When he still wouldn't be their patsy they put about he had Alzheimer's – and then that he was dead. Which he wasn't. And – this is the point – *neither are we!*'

She waited but Joe just looked at her. The old wino sucked his coffee noisily.

'Well, say something!'

He didn't say a word.

'I don't want to have to spell it out for you, who he is, Joe. Figure it out for yourself. So at least I can say it wasn't me told you.'

'If . . . Look, if he's who I think he is,' he started.

'He is. My assignment was to look after him. We have . . . well, become pretty close. I had a room in his apartment. The place was meant to be escape-proof but when I got home this morning he had gone! Somehow the old guy has found a way out . . .!'

'You mean to say Gottlieb Sollyheim is . . .?'

'Yes!' she cried. 'And soon the whole of the CIA-wing will want to know how! You have to help me Joe! What am I going to do?'

Instead of offering her some particle of hope or any practical suggestion, Joe King said, 'You helped hold Sollyheim against his will for the Protocol Organization?'

'Yes.' She had no choice.

'You knew what the government was doing all along?'

Again. 'Yes.'

'Well why? Why did you do something like that?'

Joe King waited.

Lieutenant Duvall, turning her back on the question, said nothing. It seemed the only honest answer.

117

10

Investigator: Rick Stator
File Code: RS/7
Report: 13

Last night I returned to the Zapper tavern I mentioned in my last report. As soon as I walked through the door Zeb saw me and beckoned me over. I followed him down the length of the bar to a table in a back room where a game of poker was in progress – stud, it looked like. Two vacant chairs conveniently awaited our arrival. None of the players made any comment when we sat down except the one holding the deck.

'You want in?'

'Are we bought in?' I said.

He dealt each of us one card, face down.

'You're here is collateral,' he said.

I peeked at my hole card. It was an eight of clubs. Normally I would not have bet a button on an eight in any suit but I bought against the odds to warm me into the game.

We were six, the best number for a game of stud played with a stripped deck in order that every player would think he – or she – was holding a winner. Zelda sat sidewise to the action, one leg hooked over the arm of her chair, handrolling a cigarette. A current of warm air was coming off the desert through a pair of open glass doors. Someone on the back porch was flatpicking a steel guitar.

I finished up with another eight and a pair of aces which, at the showdown, raised a smile. Zelda had bet on her hole card without even looking at it. She didn't smile.

I realized a conversation was underway, one of those pointless pokerplayers' conversations. What was the correct attitude to be adopted by the participants in a Double Helix Fall? In this illegal manoeuvre the controls of two kites are hooked up to each other. The crystal-grids inside the circuits of both sonar systems are coordinated, such that each pilot is in control of half of his own machine – and, of course, half of his companion's. There was some disagreement on points of strategy. The proposition under discussion was that the beauty of the Double Helix relied on the harmony of two minds working together, any failure in empathy was measured on the short scale between life and death. This is the kind of talk that makes Zappers so different from other social groups. They toss around illegal terminology with the relish of outlaws chewing the King's venison.

Zeb dealt the next hand. Zelda won it just on what she had showing.

'You sentimental whore . . .!'

The new dealer was an ox-like Zapper on my right whom I knew enough to nod to. Zorab. He was doing his best to rile the woman on the other side of me. His wife, as a matter of fact. I was caught between the pair of them.

'When you give someone a half-stake in your anti-inertia drive system, your payoff is a half-stake in his!'

'Or hers.'

'You don't want some dumb shit up there having the heebies on you. What keeps the Helix from falling apart is fear, Zanthe. Plain and simple. Lose your fear of a machine – a kite or a can-opener – you're gonna fuck up. Likely get hurt.'

I tossed my cards on the table. So far Zelda had played every hand without looking at her hole card unless she was

119

paid to. She had a pair of aces showing when she had folded. No one said anything but I had never seen poker played how she was playing it. Zeb caught my eye and batted an eyelid.

'She always plays this way, Rick,' he said. 'Claims she hates all card games.'

'Does she win money?'

'That depends on how mean she's feeling.'

It was my turn to deal the cards.

'That's only half of it,' Zanthe said.

'Damn right it is!' Zorab handed me the deck without looking my way. 'It's the half of your kite your partner has by the balls!'

I scooped the dead cards from the table myself. No one raised any objection so I shuffled them into the deck and offered it to Zeb to cut.

Zanthe said: 'You're kidding yourself, if you think that. What keeps a Double Helix together is we don't let that fact interfere with our judgement. We can't afford to. Zorab, you and me have Helixed plenty. We treat each other's machine with respect, right? Like it was our own. No different than we do each other's body when we fuck. I wouldn't Helix with you, I thought you thought I was afraid of you.'

I dealt the hole cards and deliberately gave Zelda the same card she had been dealt in the previous hand. I didn't know what it was but I wanted to see what difference it made.

'That's what you find out when you're up there, Sweetheart,' Zorab said. 'Ain't nothing to beat co-ording the two halves your brain with the opposite halves of another person's, to get to know them.'

I dealt the second card, face up, and then we placed bets and I dealt the third card. I had a pretty good hand in spades: the Jack and the Queen, but I had sweet zero in the hole. A red nine. Whoever needed a red nine?

'Sure, Honey. But if you're afraid your partner is afraid,

you already found out everything you need to know.'

'If your Helix partner *trusts* you. No sense doing it – same as fucking – with a person you don't have total trust in.'

Zorab guffawed.

'Well, I'll be dipped in shit, there's any point doing it with someone you do!'

By now I was showing the King in suit but Zelda's hand was straightening too. So far she had a King Queen Jack which my flush – assuming I had the ace – would beat. Only I didn't have the ace. No one else came near us. There was a pair up which the hole card could turn into three-of-a-kind so I bet hard and the pair quit and there was just my flush which I didn't have against her straight. The conversation paused while the other players pretended not to be interested in how I was going to handle it.

With the ten of spades I dealt myself I had a gambler's hand. I was – at least on the face of it – holding a straight flush. Zelda looked bored. It didn't make any difference to her what I was holding. Her cards lay untouched in front of her. She had not looked at any of them. Of course, it made no difference to me either. I just wanted to have a look at what she had in the hole.

It was Zelda's bet and she raised it to the table maximum, which was the right thing to do with the cards I had showing. Without the ace I couldn't allow her to see me. It was just possible that my own straight would beat hers. So I met her and raised.

'You're wasting your money, Stator,' she sneered. 'Or somebody else's. You got shit down there.'

I told her to call or pass. It was a tense moment, beautiful in its way. The very heart of poker. Outside on the porch the guitar player was listening to an owl hooting.

Zelda paid to see my nine-to-king straight. It was still a damn good hand. Then, without looking at it, she tossed her hole card onto my lap. The ace of spades that busted my flush.

121

While she took my money I found myself wondering why she had folded the previous hand when she was holding an ace. Three aces is a good hand to pass in five-card stud. But she hadn't looked at it. This meant she played randomly. On the other hand if a player won consistently that way sooner or later any poker table would know she was either cheating or a telepath, which at a certain point amounts to the same thing. No cheat would allow herself to win all the time.

While Zanthe dealt, Zorab began to gnaw at the bone again. He wasn't going to let it go. Nobody expected him to. The Zappers were keying each other up for the opportunity to put the question under discussion to the test. I had not said anything but I could see that there was a balance to be tipped. The poker game was just honing their nerve.

Zeb spoke.

'I think you're both right. Both half right. Fear and faith – what keeps any marriage together – are entwined as close as the twin paths of the kites in a Double Helix, which is as close as any two people can get.'

But the two points of view refused to be reconciled. The Zappers had psychologically aligned themselves into the twin states of mind, fear and faith, the polarity of opposites which cohere together during the Zappers' dangerous ritual rehearsal of the structure of the DNA molecule during gestation. When they climbed into the totemic representation of the double helix, mimicking the arrangement of the strands of polynucleotides in the structure of deoxyribonucleic acid, the two Zappers would not just be taking on the fission guns of the SkyPol. They would be confronting, literally and symbolically, the determinacy of Protocol society.

'What none of you don't understand,' Zelda said. 'Is that it can *never* be reconciled. Never should be. That's why we're Zappers.'

Zeb nodded.

'Sweetheart, I love you. You put your finger on it! The kick the Helix gives us is never because fear and faith are reconciled. It's a fucking disaster when they are! The important thing is that two people risk death disobeying the fixed laws of the structure of the chromosome. We have to fear and trust each other in the right proportion, sure. But that's something humans face all the time. What we're talking about here is chance versus causality. The Zappers versus the Protocol. Out of contradiction comes forth understanding.'

It was fighting talk. The Double Helix is not some irresponsible caper the Zappers undertake to amuse themselves. It's a perilous enterprise that asks everything of the couple who undertake it. Not all Zappers try it. Not all who try it survive it. To understand the manoeuvre you have to have seen two kites falling out of the night sky like a pair of luminous love birds having a tiff in public, trailing their brilliant coloured interlinked helicals after them. The ritual defines the Zappers' off limits reason for being. When two Zappers link their fate with each other, they harness chance to the determinism of the chromosome, whose law the Government has embodied – through the Protocol – into the State.

'Let's put it to the test,' Zeb said.

Zeb and Zelda had a reputation for the elegant balance of their Falls. Obviously they feared and trusted each other in the right proportion.

Zelda said, 'I'll pass, thanks.'

'I didn't have you and me in mind, Honey. That would be no test. We're lovers, same as Zanthe and Zorab. No, I was thinking about Rick here. Him and me. We hardly know each other. Fear and faith don't enter.'

Zelda bit her lower lip. If she had changed her mind she didn't say. She knew you are not allowed to change your mind when you're playing poker. Zeb had placed his bet. I had no choice. If I wanted to stay in the game, I had to call or pass.

123

'It's a great night for it,' I said.

The tension around the table snapped. Chairs scraped on the floor as Zorab and Zanthe and the fifth Zapper whose name I did not know stood up, scooped their money and headed for the bar . . .

'LISTEN SZMIDT . . .! Lemme tell you something . . .'

The booming voice of Larry McAlister remonstrating with Szmidt preceded both men into the workshop where Osip Pelig was watching a video screen and, at the same time, making a series of elaborate folds in a sheet of paper. The moment he heard the approaching voice of his partner, Osip spun his wheelchair through thirty-five degrees and killed the video.

'. . . Those bastards can close us down for not wearing neckties! They don't need a fucking *reason*!'

Rick Stator's report was something Osip wanted to keep to himself for the time being. Rick was largely his own creation, from its somewhat old-fashioned value-system to how it played a hand of poker. There were a quarter million micro-crystals integrated into the circuits guiding the K model's cognitive and motor faculties and the molecular structure of each one carried information and experience to keep it successfully operating as a competent social individual. The bulk of this information had originated from Osip because the assembly team had used him, for want of any other volunteer, as the generative matrix from which the hominoid's own personality had been printed off. Stator embodied Osip's idea of how a private eye should behave. There was a bond between them. But Osip felt certain that Larry McAlister would want to wind up the project the moment he found out how close Rick had come to his quarry.

Osip pressed down the final folds into the sheet of paper. He had better let this one lay. If ever Szmidt allowed

McAlister to take the K out of his hand he would never get it back. It would get turned into some racket to make money. Rick Stator, after all, could easily be modified into something less personable.

The tall broad frame of McAlister swept into the workshop closely followed by the round, smaller figure of Szmidt. In Osip's opinion Szmidt's down-to-earth ballast kept McAlister from sailing away altogether.

'Say, Osip. Listen here to what Szmidt has to tell you!'

'Hello, Szmidt,' Osip said.

The paper kite he had been working on all morning left his hand and described an elegant Innerman loop, soared upwards and then, losing momentum, banked and dove to the ground, coming to rest at the feet of his two partners.

'Pretty,' Szmidt said. 'Very pretty. Can we sell it?'

Osip and Szmidt grinned at each other.

'Tell Osip what you just told me,' McAlister said.

Osip had a lot of time for Szmidt, the wily company lawyer who somehow kept QUASAR out of the hands of the public receiver. Szmidt was so different from himself that they were able to be friends. And although Szmidt also disapproved of the private investigator role the K model had been given, Osip knew he would not try to close it down without a reason. Szmidt's arguments against it were more solid than McAlister's gut emotional aversion. He wanted to see the company's new hominoid marketed more seriously, that is, more profitably, rather than used in such frivolous exercises as the one Rick Stator was currently engaged in. So far, fortunately, Szmidt had not been able to come up with anything better.

'Spit it out, Szmidt,' Osip said.

'The Protocol,' Szmidt bent down and picked up the paper kite lying at his feet, 'have been in touch with me.'

'Yeah? What they want?'

'They say they want to give us a routine house check.'

'Didn't we have one of those recently, about eighteen months ago?'

'Fourteen. That's what I told them – or rather him.'

'Who was it?'

'Dalgano,' Szmidt said.

The three men looked at each other in silence. The name of the City Protocol Chief caused them all to ask themselves the same question.

'What does he want with a small fish like QUASAR?' Osip asked Szmidt.

'He didn't say.'

'What *did* he say?'

'He told me it was some kind of new check. I dunno, seems they're trying to track down status-evaders.'

'There are no status-evaders here.'

'You'd think he'd have better things to do!' McAlister growled.

'He wants to come up, see us sometime.'

'Well, I guess we can't stop him.

'That's not all, Osip. It's what he wants to discuss that makes me feel uneasy. Our contract with the State to provide it with a homeoactive fire service.'

Osip looked from Szmidt to McAlister and then back to Szmidt.

'So?'

'*So!*' McAlister's voice rose an octave. 'So it's none of the fucking Protocol's business who we have contracts with!'

'I got the impression from Captain Dalgano,' Szmidt continued, 'he was trying to lean on me. He was friendly enough, I guess. He apologized for the trouble he was putting us to, all that crap. But I didn't trust him.'

'You don't trust anyone,' Osip joked. Nobody laughed.

'He said he wants to go over some details before we proceed.'

'Sounds to me like Dalgano has got hold of something,' Osip said. 'He wants an excuse to come nose around.'

'Right!' McAlister nodded.

'I guess we'll find out what it is when he decides to tell

126

us,' Szmidt said.

'QUASAR is operating inside the licence the Protocol issues us . . .' Osip started to say.

'Except illegally opening a private investigation service!' McAlister fired. If they opened the window Dalgano could probably hear from where he was.

'But there is nothing in the Fire Service contract which is outside it. On the other hand there's plenty in our line of work which a big surveillance organization would be interested in. I say we keep from Dalgano the research we've put into high effect artificial intelligence constructs. It's not just the private eye angle "Rick Stator" is involved in – I agree, Larry, the Protocol isn't going to like that – it's the technology we've developed. We are ahead of the field, no one comes near us. I don't think we should just hand it to Dalgano on a plate.'

'They find out about "Rick Stator",' McAlister said, 'they're going to take our trading licence away on the spot.'

Szmidt shrugged. 'We sank our assets into developing the Joesy into the K Model. If we lose control of how it's marketed we're never going to see the return which that investment represents.'

Rather to their surprise, Osip, Szmidt and McAlister, for their own different reasons, found themselves in complete agreement with each other. Details of the K Model prototype would be withheld from the Sanfran Protocol Chief when he made his visit.

'Are we agreed?' McAlister asked.

Osip and Szmidt nodded. The ad hoc board meeting was over.

'By the way, Osip,' Szmidt said. He tossed the paper rocket through the air toward the inventor. 'Heard anything from that plasmatic gumshoe of yours?'

Osip grinned as his latest heavier-than-air design circled and banked exactly as it had done previously. McAlister – he had obviously given up trying to keep tabs on the movements of Rick Stator — left the workshop without saying anything.

'Nope,' Osip lied through his teeth. 'Not yet. I guess it won't be long.'

Szmidt looked at him with the eyes of a lawyer.

'Don't worry, Szmidt! Rick knows what he's doing. He's smart.'

'You could be right,' Szmidt said. He moved towards the door. 'After all, we made him in your image.'

As soon as he was alone again Osip spun his wheelchair back thirty-five degrees and re-activated the VDU. Rick Stator's report advanced from the point at which it had been halted.

. . .THE BAR had filled up some while we'd been playing. There were Zappers of all shapes and ages, wide tattooed men, fine-boned women, angel-faced boys and girls, children. Everyone was acquainted. There was the good-humoured hum of folk who share the same purpose taking their ease, as of a nomadic tribe temporarily at rest. You realize, when you've been around Zappers a while, just how much shit is talked about them.

We made our way through the crowd toward the bar. Sam noticed Zeb and passed a couple of beers along to him, one of which was destined for me.

'I hope I didn't shoot you in the back there, Rick,' Zeb said. 'You know how it is. We coulda been yammering all night.'

'I had aces and eights. What could I expect?'

He laughed.

'But what makes you want to Helix with me?' I asked him. I wanted to know.

'I like your poker game, Rick. It's not easy playing against Zelda's blind card. You done good.'

I asked myself why he used my name every time he spoke to me as if he thought I suspected he didn't know who I was.

We hung around drinking beer while the Zapper mechanics co-orded my Silver Wing with Zeb's Black Shadow. When they were through it would be as if my kite was being directed by one lobe of his brain and Zeb's by one lobe of mine. Zeb handrolled a cigarette and lit it while I examined the sky. It was a clear breezy night. Delicate cirrocumulus clouds streaked across the face of the moon. He handed me the cigarette.

'What you want me to do with this?'

'Smoke it. 'll help you relax, focus your head.'

'On what?'

'That's what we're gonna find out.'

Zelda approached us from the bar. The heavy leather Zapper jacket she was wearing over her torso made her look attractively vulnerable.

'Don't go up, Zeb. Please! Not tonight.' To me she sneered: 'Lurk off, Creep!'

'Hey . . .!' Zeb laid a hand on her shoulder. 'Why you so edgy? I done this plenty times. You know that.'

'Just don't tonight.'

'Why not? Rick here's looking forward to it.'

'Because if you do I won't see you again.'

'You always say that,' Zeb laughed.

'This time it's true! I know what will happen.'

'No one knows what will happen, Zelda.'

He gave me a wink over the top of her head and walked her away from me. I watched him speaking softly to her, trying to calm her. I was standing alone. No one spoke to me. I took a pull from the cigarette and waited. The warm breeze brushed over the small hairs on the back of my neck. So far I had done everything I could to get close to the Zappers in order to establish a basis for my involvement with the subject. Now I was about to crawl into a kite and plug my brain into the brain of one of them in order to undertake the perilous ritual of the Double Helix Fall. A sudden weariness of spirit came over me. Was this

129

what I was getting paid to do? I took another pull of Zeb's narcotic cigarette and then threw it away. It was depressing me.

When the time came we climbed into our kites and took off, shaking hands first, the way Zappers do.

'Here, we go,' Zeb said over the inter-kite video-link. 'Don't think of your mother, Rick.'

Our two kites rose as one. Both machines soaring in a steady loop. It was like dancing a really sexy dance like a tango, sharing another person's momentum in order to challenge your own inertia. I breathed in. I could feel Zeb's strong hand leaning on the course my Silver Wing was taking. Then I remembered to breathe out. I had to keep reminding myself that I was only in control of half of reality.

'I don't have a mother,' I said.

Zeb glanced across the video-link. His cardiac and respiratory activity was being monitored on a small scanner next to the screen. The face grinned. The ECG tremored regularly. Similar information was being transmitted to the Black Shadow.

'How's that, Rick? Most everyone has a Ma and a Pa.'

Yes. Most everyone does. But not me. I never knew my mother. At least, I have no recollection of her. I often try to recall something about her. Nothing. Nothing, that is, except one small fragment in which I am a little feller opening the door of an apartment – the old kind that had a worked-iron communal elevator shaft down a central stairwell. In this memory I'm opening a door and a woman has her back to me, doing something with her hands, cooking maybe, and I say: "Ma, can I go slide down the stairrail?" Without looking round she says, "Ossie, didn't I tell you to stay away from that stairwell?" I don't know what "Ossie" means but in the only recollection of my mother I possess that's the name she calls me by. Then I remember sliding down the polished stairrail, round and round, racing the elevator down, my heart beating so fast because I can't stop.

The cigarette of Zeb's seemed to be working . . .

OSIP PELIG paused the tape. His heart beating fast. He recollected perfectly the memory as soon as Rick Stator began recounting it, which wasn't surprising since it was one of his own. His mother had always called him 'Ossie'. They had rented in an old-style apartment block that had an iron-work elevator and he was for ever asking her permission to ride the stairrail, which she had always refused to give. He had ridden it anyway, racing the elevator until the occasion he had lost control and gone into free fall, a momentarily wonderful sensation, permanently damaging his spine on impact with ground zero. He had never walked unaided since. Sure he remembered it.

Somehow this trauma had shorted over from Osip to the K Model while they were ingramming Rick Stator's personality. It had been captured and retained. Clearly there was more to Rick than QUASAR imagined. The accidental transfer of deep memories could, theoretically, impair the efficiency of the hominoid. At a critical point it could become confused and, like any human, suffer a nervous breakdown.

Osip, his heart still hammering, keyed on the tape-replay to see how it was going to work out. Or, rather, how it had worked out.

. . .I SHOULDN'T have told Zeb I never had a mother. The intrusion of the memory fragment was a distraction I didn't need. We were high up over the range of peaks that overlook Sam's bar. We could see the shoreline all the way from the Bay to Carmel like a section from a relief map. Lights winked in the ocean-side real estate. To the east we

131

could see the urban sprawl of Fresno, mile after mile of mid-status condos where folks were settling down for the latest White House episode. Cloud shadows were rippling across the Diablo Hills below us like shoals of black-backed fish.

At 50,000 we levelled out and prepared for the Fall, circling each other like condors. The difficult part of the Double Helix is accepting that the other feller is travelling in a counter direction to yourself and you have to correct his flight-path accordingly, which is not as easy as you might think. You get the sensation your right- and left-hand skills have been reversed. This is because the sonar of both kites has been co-ordinated, half of it scanning the position of the other kite as if it were itself, the other half scanning itself as if it were an alien object in the sky. Naturally, if both machines were allowed to proceed on this basis they would automatically collide. The skill, I discovered, lay in judging how far to let your Helix-partner have it all his own way and how hard to resist him. There's a strong temptation to handle both halves of the two kites as though they were the same, let them become one and be done with it. I began to appreciate the point of the argument that had taken place around the poker table. Fear of your partner screwing up alternates with your confidence in his ability. The spark alternating between these opposites accelerates as you fall, like dynamo electricity.

We ignited our streamers, the brilliantly coloured trails which, from a distance, give the Helix its spectacular appearance. These are simply the afterglow of gamma-activated particles which hang about in the air and trace the paths the two kites take. The vermilion of my own would wind in and out of the pale green of Zeb's to form a double helical of light which the cops for miles would be able to see. As soon as we came out of the Fall there would be a cordon of SkyPol kites to penetrate.

'Rick?' Zeb said. 'How d'you feel?'

'Good. Let's go!'

We kept the kites to almost the helm-circle of their turning-axis. For as long as they shared an equal velocity one kite would be crossing pretty close to the point which the other had just vacated. Any alteration in acceleration, therefore, must be co-ordinated simultaneously in both vehicles. My Silver Wing was handling sluggishly, much less manoeuvrably, it seemed to me, than Zeb's Shadow, which was turning nice and tight. This could be due to the natural imbalance of the two machines or else to the fact that Zeb, unused to mine, was leaning too hard into it. I knew my own kite, however, and was able to compensate for him.

We passed each other easily. Zeb's Shadow was becoming familiar and lighter, whereas my own was acting mean. It was like trying to get a cow through a gate. I had to wrestle with it to make it cleave to the tighter axis which the slighter kite was forcing on it.

'OK, Stator,' Zeb spoke over the vidlink. 'Let's have it.'

'What are you talking about?'

'Just what are you in this for?'

'To come out of it in my skin,' I said.

By now I was having to push hard. I began to suspect why this was. Zeb was not just leaning into my kite. He was leaning into me.

'Listen to . . .' he said.

'Don't fuck around, Zeb!'

We passed.

'. . . I can kill you!'

The face in the screen was no longer the easy-going Zapper's who had bought me drinks in Sam's bar.

'We can kill each other,' I reminded him.

'Just tell me what you're after. Or put it this way, where d'you learn to cheat at poker so good?'

I tried to laugh it off. Evidently Zeb had noticed the switch I made on Zelda's cards. The dealer never picks up. Every poker player knows that.

'You mean the hole-card I dealt back to Zelda?'

'Yeah. Why d'you do it? You didn't stand to gain nothing.'

'I was just fooling. Every poker player can cheat some.'

'But not all do.'

We passed – close. I felt I was looking down a rifle barrel – which is just another kind of Double Helix.

'You don't add up. Or else you add up too good. I never met anyone with an alpha-rate regular as yours.'

We passed – closer. I didn't know what he was talking about.

'You want Zelda. Say it.'

Zeb was burning down my trail with as much friendliness as he was pushing me through the Helix.

'I don't lay my pipe across another man's land,' I said.

'Don't shit me, Stator! You ain't all you say!'

We passed.

'. . . You want something! Only thing I have anyone would want enough to send a man after is Zelda. You want *her*, right?'

The grip Zeb had on my Silver Wing tightened. I couldn't prize him off. He was edging me into the path of his own kite. I didn't want to lie to Zeb – I liked him, I liked Zelda. On the other hand I had a client, even if he was a rich asshole I had no reason to respect. The identity of the person I was hired to find was between the client and me. Whatever allegiance I felt for Zeb and Zelda was between me and me.

'I don't want to lie to you, Zeb.'

'I thought so . . .'

We passed.

'. . . you're some kind of dick.'

'Not Police. Nor Protocol. If that makes any difference.'

'It don't.'

The game would be raw from now. From the alpha scanner I could see that our rates were no longer synchronous. We were just two guys falling through the

134

sky, one of whom was doing his best to destroy the other.

'Zelda's Mom and Dad hired you to bring back their li'le girl so she can marry some fucking queer from her own status.'

'She's no ordinary runaway, Zeb.'

'They never are.'

'The girl you know as Zelda . . .'

As succinctly as I could in the circumstances I disclosed the identity of the subject. I thought he had a right to know. I thought if I hit him with the truth I might claw back some of the initiative I had lost.

'That don't change a thing! I have nothing 'gainst you, Rick Stator — if that's your name — but I'm Zelda's feller . . .'

We passed — just.

'. . . she expects me to look after her interests. That includes holding off cold-hearted cops who come snooping round her. I'm going to do my best to kill you.'

'Listen . . .'

'Listen shit! You had a choice. You made it. Now we're on different sides. You're going to have to kill me . . .'

'I don't . . .'

Our two kites passed . . .

'. . . want to kill you.'

. . . like bullets from a pair of duelling pistols, each aimed at the heart.

'You better start trying!'

His voice and picture cut out from the screen along with the information relating to his psycho-motor progress. Zeb had pulled the plug. We were out of communication with each other.

It was becoming almost impossible to helm both kites at the same time. Each of them was accelerating towards an imaginary point just in front of the other in order to be high enough off the ground to pull out ahead. When the time came, there would only be space for one. Our corkscrew was approaching the Diablo Range of mountains

135

at Mach. Zeb had the nerve but in that kind of two-step my heavier Silver Wing had the muscle. His stripped machine lacked the torque which he had earlier derided mine for possessing. When the time came I didn't give him an angel in Hell's chance. I had been here before. I was shinning down the stairrail round the elevator shaft of an old apartment block, going into free fall. It was easy. As soon as the opportunity presented itself I pulled out and tried to pull Zeb out also. Too late. His kite struck Mount Hamilton like a match head against the heel of a boot. My own kite immediately spiralled upwards, out of control.

But in the last moment before impact the vidscreen flashed Zeb's face. The old smile.

'*Stator*!' he said. 'The stationary part in a moving machine! Of course!'

Then nothing.

Then his kite exploded.

Then nothing again.

11

O n the enormous TV screen the attractive features of the Staff Nurse at the Bethlehem Clinic, Galina Hope, were displayed. Her lips were moving. She was trying to tell him something. He watched them form the words: *Where are you?*

'I'm on my way, Sister,' he told her.

The face, however, refused to go away.

'I'm on my way,' he tried to reassure her.

This exchange repeated itself so many times it began to feel as if it had been going on for ever, as in a dream, and therefore he must be asleep. He opened his eyes.

Galina Hope, gazing down at him, said nothing.

'I'm on my way, Sister . . .!' he said.

He lowered his eyelids. Obviously he was still asleep. But when they re-opened a moment later she was still there.

'Hello, Mr Wyman, how d'you feel?'

'Where am I?'

'You're in the Clinic.'

'Already?'

'You passed out in the kitebay last night and spent the night in the Accident Wing. We, I'm sorry Mr Wyman, but we didn't know . . .'

She faltered. Something had gone wrong.

'Val . . . Is she OK?'

'She's doing fine. And Theo died perfectly normally.

Nothing to worry about. I'm just sorry you couldn't be present for the death. We, I didn't know you were here.'

'Nor did I. I don't recall much what happened last night. I was loaded, I guess.'

The lovely Staff Nurse said nothing. She wasn't going to reproach him.

'I have to see her and . . .' He raised his head from the pillow. Boy, did it hurt! 'Theo!'

'Hey, slow down!'

She laid a cool hand onto his hot forehead. Vergil lay back and wished it could stay there for ever. He had fucked up, whichever way you looked at it.

'What time is it?'

She glanced down at the upsidedown watch pinned to the front of her uniform.

'7.18.'

He was going to be late for work.

'Can I see them?'

'Val's sleeping momentarily. But you can visit Theo. Why not? You take an anti-V ray douche.'

Vergil dressed and followed the Duty Sister to the main wing of the Clinic, where the babies died. His head throbbed. He had the sensation that he was being drawn into the wake of some tragic event. A catastrophe had just preceded him which the ambulance siren in his ears was slowly catching up with. He entered the cubicle in which his wife lay. He took hold of her hand. On her chiffonier the jaws of the little wooden dog that he hated but which she never travelled without howled mutely while its luminous eyes, the clock's digits, glowed green. The walls of the room were smooth and white and brittle as the shell of an egg that would soon crack. The dog's eyes winked: 7.31. He was going to be late for work.

Since Vergil did not have time to take the douche, the Staff Nurse had an AI orderly hold up the dead baby for him to inspect. The little feller took one look at him across the glass pane and crumpled his face into a howl which he could not hear and reminded Vergil of Val's travelling watchdog. Mumbling his thanks to the Staff Nurse, he departed down the deserted corridors in search of the exit which he had no recollection of having ever passed through. He had missed his own son's death. Now he was about to be late for work. What a mess! He jumped into the nearest cab and gave it the address of his workplace. Obviously there was no time to go home and change. He had been inside the pair of underpants he was wearing for two days already. What difference did one more day make?

Fortunately it was only a short distance from the Clinic on Potrero Hill to the high-status residency on Hunter's Point. In a matter of minutes the kite had docked at the Security Suite, the highest in the building. Stacked below were the luxury residences of high-ranking Protocol personnel, cartel executives, TV people and a few sports personalities. The only thing higher than the Security Suite was the penthouse which his boss occupied.

'Hi, Vince!' he called out.

There was no reply. The Suite was quiet. Too damn quiet in Vergil's opinion. Vince Wazckinski, the officer it was his duty to replace, had already departed. This had never happened before – but then Vergil had never been late before.

Without pausing to change into his uniform, he completed the security checks it was his first duty to perform, even though he had come to suspect that they were not necessary. The instruments were capable of carrying out the checks themselves and they probably did. On the other hand, if his tasks were not essential, what would happen if he were not there to carry them out?

He poured himself a cup of coffee and sat down at the security communications unit. Later he would put on his uniform and take a stroll through the building in order to show his face to the residents. He knew it gave them a feeling of confidence to meet and greet their security guard. It was probably the reason the Management did not have an AI perform his duties. They liked to ask after his wife – and now, of course, his son – and invite him to drop by sometime for a drink, trusting he would have the good sense not to take them at their word. Sipping the coffee, he put through the call his boss was waiting for. He waited. She would wish him good morning, say how glad she was he had everything under control, as she always did. She would thank him, whatever he said, and log his report. When there was no acknowledgement of his call, he played back the Unit's memory to locate her message. But there was no message. Lieutenant Duvall had left no instructions, something which had never happened before.

If there was a routine to follow in the event of a communication failure such as this Vergil made no attempt at recalling what it was. His head hurt. He couldn't rid his mind of the image of his wife and son. Val, fragile, asleep inside the egg-like white room in the Clinic. Theo framed behind the plate-glass screen. He himself cut off from the process, unable to communicate with them. He was going through the motions. He might as well have been an Artificial Intelligence.

Taking with him his tool-belt, Vergil left and locked the Security Suite. He watched himself in the mirror of his boss's private elevator while he rode it up to her office, something he had never done before. He was curious to see his own reactions to the event. He had stepped outside his routine. He wanted to observe himself as if he were someone else. Which, he was beginning to realize, he was.

The current security procedure in his possession gave him access to every inch of the Schryer Building. The area he was headed for, however, was not included in the Security Officer's list of responsibilities so it came as no surprise to discover that the procedure would not trigger the entrance to Cheryl Duvall's apartment. He would have to use his tools to remove the terminal. When he had done this he held a screwdriver across the current-switch and shorted the locking mechanism. The doors slid open.

Removing the screwdriver, Vergil entered the unlit apartment. The doors closed after him. He headed towards a splinter of light which failed to illuminate the gloom. His fingers pushed aside the drapes. Sunlight blinded him. He blinked.

Upholstered furnishings. Painted canvasses. Wood and leather. The place was stocked with objects constructed from materials whose properties he barely knew how to perceive. Like most people he distrusted the unstable nature of organic substances. They gave him goose pimples. Here they predominated in unhealthy profusion. There were books everywhere, the pages of which looked as if they were made of real paper. On a carved polished bureau they were stacked, open and shut, on top of each other. An ancient black enamelled iron typewriter with mechanical keys squatted among the confusion.

Vergil made a tour of the empty apartment. Having opened one door which he should not have opened he found it easy to open any number. He entered the private chamber of a high-status young woman, just as he had expected. The bed had not been recently slept in. On the other side of the apartment he came across a room belonging to someone who wore faded denim coveralls, brushed cotton plaid shirts with attachable collars and colourful bowties, which he had not expected. In a frame among the books on the table next to the bed – also undisturbed – there was a photograph of a girl in a blue dress taken about fifty years ago. The occupant, it was reasonable to infer, was a man, no longer young. Vergil found himself surmising whether his superiors in the Protocol were aware of the existence of this person who was not, as far as he knew, on the official resident list. But the question was absurd. The apartment was the home of Cheryl Duvall who was his superior in the Protocol. A second question posed itself. Where was Cheryl Duvall, the only person who could answer the first question?

Returning to the library, Vergil discovered that he was not alone. He had company. A pair of eyes belonging to a black cat scrutinized him from its upright sphinx position on top of the old black typewriter. Vergil seated himself in the leather-padded wooden swivel chair in front of the animal.

'Hello, Felix. Mind if I join you?'

The cat continued to watch him without blinking, calm amid the confusion of books spread around it, covering every inch of the bureau. Vergil had never seen so many books and it had been a while since he had seen any at all. They were open flat, folded back, piled one on top of the other. It made him feel giddy to look at them. Holding one book flat was a large china ashtray filled with half-smoked cigar butts. Vergil picked out the largest butt and lit it from a worn silver petrol-fuelled lighter and inhaled the smoke, something he had never done before. He removed the ashtray in order to read the words underneath it, some of which had been underlined in pencil:

'*He who sees Infinity in All Things, sees God.*
He who sees the Ratio only, sees only himself.'

Felix stepped from the typewriter onto the page of the volume in Vergil's hand. The cat gazed into his eyes for a long time, then climbed delicately between the precariously stacked tomes, accidentally on purpose, it seemed knocking over the whole pile onto Vergil's lap. The page that fell uppermost had words underlined in the same soft pencil:

'*. . . If a man will be a philosopher without going astray he must lay the foundations of his philosophy by making heaven and earth a microcosm, and not be wrong by a hair's breadth. Therefore he who will lay the foundations of medicine must also guard against the slightest error and must make from the microcosm the revolutions of heaven and earth so that the philosopher does not find anything in heaven and*

142

earth which he does not find in Man, and the physician does not find in Man anything which heaven and earth do not have. And these two differ only in outward form, and yet the form on both sides is understood as pertaining to one thing. As above, so below . . .'

Vergil continued his leisurely random perusal. He had the impression – perhaps it was the cigar – that everything he read made sense of everything he had just read before. Having stepped outside the round of his routine, he had become trapped in a sequence of unpredetermined occurrences. It made him giddy. The sense the words made confused him.

He read and smoked until his confusion was interrupted by a slow whiplashing roar, as of a steel spring uncoiling. The cat, wide awake, leapt from the table. Vergil started. On the typewriter, flat where the cat had sat, he noticed for the first time a sheet of paper. He attempted to read the words but they were not in his language.

'Mein Liebeskind . . .'

Vergil removed the typed sheet as the thump and stomp of boots and metal burst into the apartment. He had time to screw the paper into the dime pocket of his slacks before pale blue uniformed arms grabbed him from behind.

THE VIEW from the kitchen window of Joe King's condo consisted of all the other condos which made up the John Kennedy complex. As a view it wasn't much. It was monotonous, to say the least, but for a person on the run from a Government law enforcement agency it had a certain charm. The monotonous midlow-status condominia would conceal her, Cheryl Duvall liked to think as she followed the imperceptible progress a grey tanker chain was making out of the night towards a destination

143

marginally less grey than itself. Under normal circumstances these obese transport vessels depressed the hell out of her but today, this morning, while her lover questioned her integrity in front of a stranger, she saw them in a different light. Their ponderous udderlike aspect was a comfort. They were slow and necessarily ugly, crossing the horizon with an ordinariness of purpose she coveted.

'What made you do it?'

For Joe it was straightforward. His hard question was easy to ask. A sharp knife that cut both ways. It wouldn't make any difference what answer she gave. It would become isolated from her. A target. He was not asking her what made her do it – be Sollyheim's nurse, companion, keeper. He was asking her who she was.

'I don't know. I mean, I know what made me do it, sure – but not what else I could have done. In the circumstances.'

'You were trapped . . .'

'No.'

'. . . Is that why you're here? Because you have no choice?'

The knife was entering the target.

'I came because I wanted your . . .'

She wanted his love.

'. . . help.'

'I been waiting years to meet you, Cherry. Not someone like you – *you*. You make sense of all the crazy shit I had to go through. You want me to help you, I will. Before I can, you're going to have to tell me what made you want to deceive a billion people and lock up an old man who never hurt anyone.'

She turned to face her persecutor.

'Why is that so important – for *us*?'

'I have to know what's going on up here . . .' He tapped his skull. '. . . In the woman I'm running with.'

They stood opposite each other in the little kitchen, very close but also separated by the moral canyon which had

144

opened between them.

'Try and understand it's impossible to say I did it for this or for that reason,' she said. 'I didn't do it. It happened. Slowly. Over the years. Ever since I was a kid. Some of it I even enjoyed. The bits I didn't enjoy I got paid for . . .'

'I'm a little pimp with my hair greased back,
Pair of khaki pants with my shoes shined black . . .'

Spight sang.
'You're saying you couldn't have helped it?' Joe said.
'Yes . . . No . . .!'

'Got a little lady, she walks that street,
Telling all the boys that she can't be beat . . .'

'Joe, I couldn't have acted differently. Not then. Later maybe. Now, sure. But then I was part of something so enormous I couldn't see the edge of it. The people I mixed with were Bs and Cs and Ds, at least. We lived in nice apartments in AB/DC states. Natal. California. Provence. All I knew about the other statuses was what we were told. According to my Chart I was an educated exec-type CD. Didn't say anything about who processed the sewage or picked the peanuts. About being on the run from the CIA. Meeting you. Spight. Didn't say anything about doing something I could avoid!'

'You're the injured party, the way you talk.'

'Isn't that the point? Everything we do is more or less inevitable. Our SollyChart determines . . .'

'Don't tell me! I write the fucking things!'

A canyon divided them. Joe was a midlow-status Technician. His work was built around the fiction which the Government had made of Gottlieb's work, the fiction she herself had been instrumental in maintaining.

'We see things differently,' she said, weary.

'You mean, because you've been Sollyheim's sleeping partner?'

145

At least he had said it, if he hadn't actually called her a whore.

'Sure. Best thing ever happened to me, you really want to know! He broke the mould. He got behind that Protocol crap inside my head. Talking to him, making love to him, freed me from the past I didn't realize I was carrying around in front of me like a mirror wherever I went!'

'His jailor!'

The growl of Spight's music echoed off the wall:

'Mirror Man, mirror me.
Mirror Man, mirror me.'

'I wasn't his jailor! I looked after him. There were tougher cops than me making sure he kept in nights. I was his only friend. As, until I met you, he was mine! I couldn't leave him. I thought he couldn't do without me. When he obviously can.'

'He's out. And you're here.'

'I told you you'd be different, when you knew.'

'You're forgetting where we met.'

'The ABBACCA room.'

'Right. I was making my own way through the Protocol shit.'

Joe stepped across the canyon. He took her into his arms. He kissed her nose.

'It's like waking up after a dream which you knew was a dream even while you were asleep.'

Spight laughed.

'A squid eating dough
In a polystyrene bag
Is fast and bulbous – got me?'

'Is he OK?' Joe said. 'Is he trying to say something?'

'Whyn't you ask him?'

'Hey, Spight – what's on your mind?'

'Fast and bulbous!'

'The poor bastard's cracked.'

'Don't say that!'

She approached the table and sat down next to the wino and laid a hand on his arm. Spight grinned at her.

'Her eyes are a blue million miles.'

he sang. He looked in Joe's direction.

'Nowadays a woman's gotta hit a man.'

Spight's lyrics, if you didn't try to make sense of them, made a sense of their own. They countered the straight reasoning of Joe's questions. They were bizarre and poetic. You could take from them whatever sense you wanted and it didn't make any difference to Spight which sense you took.

Spight withdrew from his pocket an object Cheryl had never seen before, a polished silver thing with neat toothlike serrations along the side. To her surprise he put the object to his mouth. Weird high-low noises came out of it as he blew. Then sang.

'Her eyes are a blue million miles . . .'

He put the instrument back into his mouth, singing and blowing alternately.

'I look at her and she looks at me,
And in her eyes I see the sea.
Far – As – I – Can – See
She loves me.
I can't see what she sees in a man like me,
Yet she says she loves me!'

No one spoke. Joe because he had just crossed the canyon. Cherry because she was in Joe's arms and she knew they were still standing on the edge of it. Spight because he was picking pieces of cornflakes from his teeth with a splinter of wood which he had taken from his pocket for the purpose.

147

'What we're left with,' Joe said, 'is that old man Sollyheim is walking round out there same as Spight here – with a secret that could blow the Protocol off the map?'

She nodded.

Finally he was looking at the situation from a point of view that was not his own. The problem was no longer between him and her. It was between them and everybody else. She was sure he would help her find a way to keep the CIA from discovering the flight of their important captive. He was clever. She needed him. Spight was a crazy old poet they needed, it seemed, to keep them in touch with each other. He wasn't there for any particular reason. Joe she had come looking for.

'Obviously we have to find a way to let the world know he's here, walking around the earth! Not dead. Alive. Oh boy! Soon's people realize he isn't *dead*, they'll understand that they aren't either! They aren't stupid! We tell everybody to watch out, he's the old-timer on streetlevel with a head full of sorrow. We have to find him before the Protocol . . .'

'Hold on a minute . . .'

'. . . Not easy. The Protocol franchises all the news agencies. Owns the TV networks. We wouldn't get far. They'd think it was some stupid hoax . . .'

'What are you saying? We advertise Sollyheim has escaped, we alert Cznetsov. He'll be looking for him with all the Government resources. You won't be doing him a favour. They'll find him and fix him good.'

'Who's Cznetsov?' Joe said.

'Head of CIA. My boss. You don't know him.'

'And he don't know me! Listen, Lovely. This Cznetsov will find him anyway. Probably already did.'

'What's Sollyheim going to gain from us telling the folks out there he went missing?'

'This. The Protocol is a powerful machine you can't fuck with. They'll find Sollyheim and, sooner or later, us. We can't change that. All we have is we know there's a screw loose in the machine. We have to loosen it some more. Start some kind of rumour that the Protocol has a skeleton in the cupboard. Or rather hasn't.'

'How do you aim telling people? The only place to put news across is the TV networks which the AB families practically own?'

'Right. But we can send messages over the public link, same as anyone else.'

'You mean, put out private calls?'

'Why not? We call folks up. Explain the situation . . .'

'Joe. There are a billion private numbers. We can't contact them all!'

'We call as many as we can. Your acquaintances. Mine. The people we work with. The public agencies. Feed in the directory if necessary. As a CD you must be good for a few restricted codes. We print them all out and block dial a single pre-taped message on the public vidlink. Folks'll turn on their TV. Find it on the screen. Send one to your pal, Cznetsov. Go on the offensive!'

She nuzzled the front of her dress against his chest.

'We'll have to print a one-off message. The Company would never put out a continuous loop.'

'Then we get the fuck out of here before the Police arrive.'

'Do you think anyone will believe us? We can't prove a damn thing. It's not as if we have Sollyheim to show them.'

Spight, his head nodding to silent music, sang out in his cracked voice:

'*Distant cousins, there's a limited supply.*
And we're down to the dozens, and this is why:
BIG EYED BEANS FROM VENUS! Oh my, oh my!
Boys and girls, Earth people around the circle.
BIG EYED BEANS FROM VENUS!
Don't let anything come in between us.
Beam in on me baby and we can beam in together!'

'I got it!

149

Joe grabbed the old wino to his feet, grinning. 'We vid them old Spight here. *They'll never know the difference!'*

SHE HATED to be alone. The apartment was too damn quiet. There was nothing in it except herself and the minute sounds she made as she moved from one part of it to another. She went first to her bedroom where she disrobed with the gentle hands of a nurse undressing a patient, folding away the uniform which she had been inside throughout the night. She stood under the shower and let the hot downpour wash away the particles of tension which clung to her after her shift. Without dressing, she padded barefoot to the kitchen where the white laminate flooring chilled the soles of her feet. She listened to the sounds she made while she prepared her vegetable drink, although it was not so much the sounds she was listening to as the silence surrounding them, the absence of any other presence.

She was in no special hurry to go to bed. It was only 8.42 in the morning. The sun was rising. Her neighbours were eating cornflakes in front of their TVs. She didn't have to start recharging herself immediately. She could relax. Unwind slowly. Take her time over her drink. She could check her mail. Watch some TV. Play with Joesy.

Galina Hope shivered. The thought had escaped, as it did when she was tired and at her most vulnerable. She might think of something else – she might succeed – but it would return again to be decided on. The thought of playing with Joesy pressed no harder than anything else in her mind. It was she herself who would not leave it alone. She didn't want to play with Joesy. On the other hand, she wouldn't be able to do anything else until she had.

On the white laminate stool, her cool drink balanced on her bare knee, she regarded her own unclothed body, conscious of the sharp boundary between it and the world outside it. She ran the tips of her fingers over the surface of her skin, the curve of her breast, feeling brave and brazen, a child caressing the unfamiliar pelt of a strange animal, exploring the awe in which she held it. Obviously her body did not belong to anyone else, yet there were only brief occasions when she trusted her own possession of it. It was hers in the sense that the uniform she had just removed and folded away belonged to her. She washed it. She looked after it. She felt nothing for it. But if she closed her eyes while her finger tips caressed her skin she had the momentary sensation that they belonged to some other person. She was an object as well as a subject in the world. It was a delusion, of course. The fingers were just as much a part of her body as they were apart from the person she wanted to belong to. It was a childish delusion to make use of one piece of herself in order to verify the rest of her.

She called the homehelp which she rented from the agency Joesy because it did not seem right to refer to it as the J-Model self-servicing artificial intelligence as the repairmen from QUASAR Electronics did. Ever since she had first watched Joesy carry out the instructions she had given it, she had been unable to think of it as just a mechanical household aid. Its mannequin's features, the image of servitude, touched her. She had begun by addressing the hominoid directly, kidding herself that it understood what she said. Later she had expanded the range of assignments which the QUASAR Technicians had assured her the device could perform. They had played games of intellect: chess, go, poker. Mumble-the-peg and crack-the-whip. When she lost, as she almost always did, they ended up horsing around the empty apartment. One game had led to another.

It had become a habit which she craved and simultaneously dreaded – after her work, after her shower and her veg drink – to have Joesy bring her to a level of climax which she had never experienced before. Each time she consigned her body into her homehelp's embrace she found, to her surprise, that she was capable of a far greater degree of disinhibition than she had previously known. She let go all the way. Joesy's lack of sense or sensitivity meant she had no reason to hold anything back. To be fucked by a machine was an exquisite self-abasement which, paradoxically, she had complete control over. The paradox excited her. She was able to increase or diminish Joesy's grip according to her mood and the needs of her biology. When she came in the unselfconscious embrace of the hominoid's hands the boundary between her body and the world disintegrated. Her skin belonged to her again.

Afterwards she would sleep. She would wake up and go to work. She would smile professionally at low-status women like Val Wyman, who depended on her, who never saw her. Who only ever saw her uniform.

Placing her empty glass on the kitchen surface, Lina Hope accepted the inevitable. She would go through it again. She would play with Joesy. Almost sick with anticipation she allowed the urge to pull her towards the TV room. The TV promptly went into its introductory routine – greeting, news flashes, the morning's episode of the Show. She didn't especially want to see or hear this stuff but she didn't especially mind either. The latestgoings-on inside the White House would put some noise into the silent apartment. She had to catch up on it sooner or later.

The violet eyes and golden hair of Annie Bernier filled the screen. Lina vaguely recalled the previous episode in which Annie, dressed in tennis clothes, had left to play tennis with that mutt Adrian Buckingham. At the Clinic there was a lot of talk about where it could end. Some said Annie was going to marry him for sure. Others, Lina among them, found it hard to believe that the cartel dummy was the man for Annie. On the screen Annie was horseback-riding across green hills that looked like the grounds of their château in Provence. She was attired in equestrian dress so she must have changed her mind at the last minute. Hooves were pounding over the marled earth.

The roan belonging to Annie noisily inhaled and exhaled clumps of air like a man shovelling sand, bringing to mind the reason why Lina had come into the TV room in the first place.

While the Show proceeded she fetched the homehelp from the closet where she kept it. At a touch Joesy swept her off her feet. It carried her over to the grosgrain bench sofa with the confidence of a man who knew exactly what he wanted. He laid her down on the sofa as, on the TV screen, Annie Bernier's yellow hair flew in the wind. Annie was laughing, showing her throat to, well it didn't look like Adrian Buckingham, Lina thought just before she stopped thinking.

Already the J-Model's strange and familiar fingers had begun to trace over the surface of her naked body, fixing inside its memory the volume she occupied in space. After this stage in their ritual she would be a three dimensional object in Joesy's repertoire of automotive functions. Joesy would be able to calculate to within a hair's breadth the disposition of her limbs. Lina closed her eyes as Joesy proceeded to investigate her further. Over the TV Annie Bernier was shouting into the wind but what she shouted blew away like a hat. Lina could hear nothing except her own blood stumbling lumpily through the vessels in her middle ear. When Joesy penetrated her she ceased being Galina Hope, neat competent Staff Nurse at the Bethlehem Clinic. She became a colossus, a vast pagan goddess inside which her worshippers, the numerous electrons stirring up, detonated slow rolling waves of ecstasy.

Afterwards – as usual – she fell into a deep sleep while Joesy cleaned up the apartment. The ordeal was over. She could relax. When she opened her eyes the Bernier Saga was over, the horses had galloped away over the hill. The apartment was empty and clean and for the time being she didn't feel so lonesome inside it. While she had been sleeping warm midday sun had made itself at home around her like an old friend who had the run of the place. Over on the TV screen some face was yapping at her, getting her to purchase some lousy product.

'. . . who revolutionized our understanding of Death and Life back in the last years of the first Dover Administration. You know all about the work he did into perinatal experiences and their influence on the developing proclivities of the individual in later life – the so-called afterlife. It was he who discovered the principles of cell-organization during gastulation which determine those proclivities. You know of the famous disagreement between Sollyheim and the Government on whether his research, in particular the use of the uteroscope, should be made compulsory – and the outcome of that disagreement. About the same time, so the story goes, Professor Sollyheim began to lose his grip. It was put about that he was senile. According to the official history of the period, he was Returned and we have a legal holiday on September 3 to remember the event. You know all that. With your permission I would like to tell you something you don't know . . .'

The woman's face on the screen was replaced by that of a very old man. Her voice over continued:

'This is the face of Gottlieb Sollyheim. He is still with us. He never went insane. He was never Returned – he did not die! He fought the Administration because he believed that what it was doing was wrong. They were perverting his ideas. The only way they could convince us that we were *dead* was by convincing us that *he* was. He isn't. We aren't. You aren't. Gottlieb Sollyheim has been a prisoner inside a luxury apartment block in Sanfran, California, known as the Schryer Building. The news is he has escaped. Here he is.'

The face of the old gentleman – what you could see of it behind the growth of facial hair – blinked and the mouth grinned uneasily. Eventually it was replaced by that of the young woman.

'My name is Cheryl Duvall. I am employed by the CIA-wing of the Protocol to supervise the incarceration of

Professor Sollyheim . . .'

While she spoke the woman's hands toyed with a silver-barrelled Police hand gun.

'Now, you might ask, why should you believe me? No reason at all. Whether or not you do believe us won't change the facts. This old man is on the run from the Authorities so if you see him stop and ask yourself if you shouldn't lend him a hand.'

The screen closed onto the old man whom the young woman claimed was Sollyheim. Her voice continued:

'Don't try to make a decision — your decisions are all wired into the Protocol Centre computer. *Take a chance*!'

The old-timer grinned slyly. One of his eyes blinked — winked maybe.

'WELL . . .?'

'Is that it?'

'What d'ya mean?' Captain Dalgano growled. 'Ain't it enough?'

Benny Cznetsov chuckled. He shook his head.

'Aw, c'mon, Dalgano! These people are crazy!'

He felt relieved. The situation was not nearly so desperate as Dalgano had made it sound up on the kitedeck twenty minutes before. It was not the best news to be greeted with, that old Sollyheim was on the lam, but this pirate tape in circulation on the public communications channel was a joke.

'They go to the trouble of springing Sollyheim, then vid out some old bastard wouldn't fool an educated person more'n two minutes. It's a joke!'

'It's not the educated persons you want to worry about.' Dalgano said. 'If it's a joke, I ain't laughing. No one don't make jokes on my beat what I don't see the humour in!'

The beefy Protocol Captain, Cznetsov was pleased to see, was taking the business personally. Somebody had spat in his eye. A crime had been committed in his sector. He would sweat blood – preferably someone else's – to clear it up. He was a good cop despite – or maybe because of – his bad grammar.

'What time was this first put out?'

''Bout midday.'

Cznetsov consulted his watch. 'It's 13.47 now. Not too bad. Can we throw a cloak over it?'

'Some of it we can.'

'How extensive was the distribution?'

Dalgano picked up a printout from his desk.

'It was a block-dialled tape, the kind anyone can make, they got the dough. Most public service agencies received one. Every tollfree number in the book. Then every terminal in the Schryer and the John Kennedy complex. Some of them we can erase. But there're a number of private individuals as well, workers at the Bethlehem Clinic and . . .' Dalgano frowned, '. . . some numbers this Joe King feller could never of gotten hold of . . .'

'You don't have to be so coy, Captain!'

This was the part that hurt. Cherry Duvall was one of his best people. If anyone was to blame for her turning it was himself. He had chosen her. He had liked her. And he had been wrong.

'She fed in every classified CIA number she had access to,' Dalgano said.

'That's not so good.'

'If it was just the JK the damage wouldn't of been near so bad.'

'This Joe King, did you put a line out on him?'

'We hit his place like a fucking steamhammer! The Schryer too. They had already cut out, natch. Two people – three, you want to count the Professor – won't get far. Sooner or later they going to have to use the System.'

'One thing's bothering me, Dalgano. It was them alerted us. Does that make sense to you? Apart from we ought to have known anyway. Why would they do that?'

'That's top of the list of things I'm hoping this VW can tell us. We caught him going through Sollyheim's papers. If he knows, he'll tell us.'

'Did you TM him yet?'

'Any moment now.'

Cznetsov sauntered to the window. Outside it was a sunny summer day like any other. From Dalgano's diurnally rotating office on top of the Protocol Centre in Union Square he got a good view of the quakeproof pyramids of the Business Section. The Centre was connected to every one of them. The commercial activity of the City, its amusement facilities, transport and accommodation requirements were all responses to the policy-making process that was taking place in the computers inside the Centre. If events followed an orderly course this was because the Protocol devised solutions to problems before they became problems. Elevators never jammed. Babies never died on legal holidays. Stress-fractures in tall buildings were identified. The transit-shuttle operated in response to population movement. Sewage, heating, air-conditioning, nutrition-balance, kite traffic-control, you name it, the Centre had it under control. It co-ordinated a complex modern society's simple requirements. Citizens were not actually spied on – it was a free country, everyone knew that – but their activities could be deduced. No citizen could escape the extensive planning that was necessary to keep a city like Sanfran going. There could be no room for error. If nothing was ever to go wrong accidents should never happen.

He felt confident that the Protocol had eliminated the trauma of chance interfering with history, just as medicine had eliminated the smallpox bacillus. Trusting to luck had become an anti-social activity, like pissing in the street. Sollyheim's escape, therefore, was not simply a political embarrassment to the Administration, it was a challenge to the ethical basis of society. To have escaped in the first place Sollyheim may have needed, as Dalgano maintained,

157

the help of accomplices, but to survive long free of the determinacy of Protocol society he would need more than friends. He would need luck, and plenty of it. A rare commodity these days.

'We made a mistake, you don't mind me saying so, when we didn't destroy Sollyheim back when we could of,' Dalgano, behind him, said whether he minded or not.

Cznetsov faced his lieutenant. 'We can only learn from our mistakes,' he said.

Dalgano nodded. He understood perfectly.

'When we're through with this Wyman we'll know him better than he knows himself. Soon as we TM him there won't be an hour of his recent a-life we don't got a picture of. Meantime, Sollyheim's pals won't be able to move, take taxis, use the public link, nothing, without we aren't there tapping them on the shoulder!'

Cznetsov couldn't help grinning. Dalgano's double negatives expressed the man himself, the equivocal psychology of the cop: there would be nothing he would not do.

'That will leave me to finish the business that brought me out here,' he said.

'You mean the Berniers' girl. You ask me . . .'

'Nobody's asking anybody,' Cznetsov cut in. 'I don't want her name breathed even. You have the file on QUASAR?'

Dalgano picked a slender cartridge of microfiches from his desktop. 'I was planning to go over there sometime, blow some smoke in their eyes.'

'Leave this to me, Captain. You have your hands full already.' He took the fiches out of Dalgano's hand. He grinned. 'There's no smoke without fire. We got to start the fire first. C'mon. Let's go say hi to the VW.'

Cznetsov and Dalgano descended through the bowels of the Protocol Centre to the green room where the VW in question sat alone on a comfortably upholstered green chair waiting to have his brain hoovered by the Protocol computer, his thoughts over the last seventy-six hours matched with its projection of them.

12

Kicking off his beach-sandals on the wooden deck at the ocean-side of his house, Osip Pelig stepped barefoot up the short plank stairway into his kitchen. He wriggled the expensive toes at the end of his new QUASAR-designed and -constructed legs so that grits of sand dropped onto the polished tile flooring. With unhurried automatic movements – as if the ideas occupying his mind were some brittle, easily destroyed flotsam he had picked up from the beach – he assembled the laid-out steel parts of the pressure-filter coffee-machine, measuring the water, screwing the filter into the base, scooping the necessary amount of grains into the aluminium compartment. It was something he had done a thousand times. He did not need to think about it. He put the machine on to heat and waited.

'Good morning, Osip,' a soft female voice said. 'Did you have a good walk?'

'Yes, thanks, Roxana.' Osip said automatically. 'How 'bout you? You sleep well?'

The advanced Validator giggled. It was an old gag between them which they both enjoyed.

'Couldn't sleep a wink!'

Osip had never thought of Roxana simply as a security unit, a Validator with a communications facility which he had installed to stop himself going crazy. Their relationship was more complicated than that. She – as he preferred to think of it – was more of a friend, an intelligent conversationalist to whom he could say anything he liked. Naturally, considering the amount of time they spent in each other's company they had grown used to one another. It was the ultimate platonic relationship.

'Any mail?'

'Only one call, Osip. And that was for me. Mr McAlister called to tell me to make sure you got to the office this afternoon in time for the colloquy with the City Protocol Chief, Captain Dalgano.'

'*Colloquy* . . . ?' Osip queried while he poured out the coffee. 'What the fuck kind of word is that?'

'It was the term Mr McAlister used himself.'

'Yeah, I bet. But what does it *mean*?'

'A talking together, a conversation, a conference. Also a written dialogue, as in *Erasmus's Colloquies*. A verbal exchange. Byron used it in this sense in 1818: "*Shunning all further colloquy* . . ." A secondary meaning – the one I think Mr McAlister had in mind – a highlevel serious discussion. As a verb . . .'

'Stop showing off! What else he have to say?'

'He said you were to wear a necktie.'

'What! I don't even possess a goddamn necktie! Do I?'

'I think you'll find your old blue one, the one with those awful yellow spots on it, in the bottom left corner of the sock-drawer in your closet.'

'You know everything, Roxana!' Osip said. It was the truth.

'I know,' the Validator verified.

Osip carried the coffee through to his workroom and seated himself at the bench before he allowed himself to taste it. Only then did he feel in a position to consider the problem which had occupied his mind throughout his morning walk: the two-way sensory receptor of the K Model hominoid, the terminal of which was spread in pieces on the bench.

He had deliberately disassembled the receptor at the

160

QUASAR shop and transferred it piecemeal to his work-room at home. For a time bits of it had been in both places. He had wanted to be sure that the Repairmen at QUASAR were prevented from tooling the thing back into commission. He knew what they were like. It was the only way he could guarantee that the K would carry out its assignment without anyone, for example Larry McAlister, fussing over its every turn. The difference between Rick Stator and earlier models was that it had not been built to perform a determined set of tasks. It was capable of determining its own tasks. Where was the logic in designing a machine to simulate the cognitive behaviour of a human being and then treating it as if it were a machine?

Nevertheless Rick Stator *was* a machine, and Osip did not have to look far for the person responsible for its actions, having shaped its primary endopsychic functions himself. Although there were certain acts which Rick would always be incapable of performing – such as destroying another human being – Osip would have to answer for the consequences of the decisions it actually made. If only to himself.

It was a delicate situation. Osip did not want the performance of the K Model screwed up by the manipulations of a remote operator – the K had to work things out for itself – but events had taken an unexpected turn. The QUASAR hominoid had been responsible for the destruction of a human being – three human beings if you wanted to count the pair of Zappers shot up by the SkyPol. It opened up the question – a real can of worms – of whether moral responsibility was a notion which could be applied to an artificial intelligence. The human being in question, it was true, had done his darndest to destroy Rick first because Rick was getting close to the girl Zelda. The Zapper, on the other – or was it the same? – hand, had given Rick a chance. The game had been equal. So it didn't seem fair that Zeb had been destroyed without knowing that he hadn't stood a chance in a battle of nerves against the advanced QUASAR construct. Rick Stator, at the still point of the turning world, neither flesh nor fleshless, did not possess any nerves.

At least, that was the theory. The fact that a poignant recollection of the past – one of Osip's own traumatic memories – had become trapped inside the K Model's sense of itself, suggested that there might be more to Rick Stator than QUASAR was aware of. Could other typically human characteristics, feelings and intuitive power, have also been transferred?

Then – according to Rick Stator's most recent report – it had come close to wiping out another human, the outlaw known as Zorab. It had recounted how Rick, in pursuit of the girl in the aftermath of the Double Helix fiasco, had been sent on a turkey chase, set upon by a quartet of ace Zapper kiters with which it had been obliged to engage in combat. Nobody, it said, had been hurt. There was even a hint that some Zappers were looking to Rick Stator as a leader, replacing Zeb. Things were getting out of hand. The idea of a tribe of social deviants uniting together under the influence of an artificial intelligence made Osip nervous, though he suspected there were plenty of individuals much less well-adjusted than Rick Stator walking around out there. He had come to the conclusion – on the beach this morning – that it was time to bring the receptor back into commission and re-establish a direct monitor on the K's activity. Once the terminals had been reconnected to the receptor it would be possible to have instantaneous access to what was taking place inside the K's head. Osip would see and hear what Rick Stator saw and heard. He would be party to Rick's innermost thoughts. What choice did he have? Rick Stator, the finest self-regulating AI ever assembled, wasn't worth the destruction of even the worst human being. Whoever that was.

*   *   *

THE LAST to arrive at the colloquy with the City Protocol Chief, Osip wheeled through the almost deserted workshop in his awful blue and yellow spotted necktie. The place was unnervingly tidy. And quiet. A handful of workers were at their benches and Osip could tell that their minds weren't on the tasks in front of them. They probably sensed the importance to the firm of the meeting about to take place. He guided his old wheelchair through the door into McAlister's office.

They were all there. Szmidt, seated apart, and McAlister in conversation with the Protocol Officer, a powerfully-built white-haired cop in a stylish civilian suit. He looked to Osip like a retired Army general, a man who had seen everything, done everything, heard the punchline to every joke. He may have been a Protocol Officer but he sure's Hell wasn't Captain Dalgano.

'Good! . . . Here's Osip, he can tell you himself.' McAlister interrupted himself. 'Osip, this is Ben Cznetsov. You, ah, know why he's here.'

'I'm not sure I do,' Osip murmured.

The man called Ben Cznetsov held out his hand and took hold of Osip's in one of those military handshakes that civilians find so offensive. He had clear blue eyes.

'Relax, Osip!' he said, grinning. One of his blue eyes winked. 'This isn't meant to be a shakedown!'

For just a moment Osip almost believed him. The man's manner suggested that he knew all about McAlister's bluff and blunder and he wanted Osip to share in this knowledge. The meeting had not even started and he had created the illusion that he was able to divide the directors of QUASAR one from the other.

'How about we get down to business?' Szmidt said. He was seated behind McAlister's desk, his hands resting palm down on it as if to demonstrate that there were no loose cards or firearms concealed in them. 'You asked for this interview, Mr Cznetsov, so maybe you wouldn't mind explaining what it's about.'

Szmidt didn't know much about magnetic-rivers or the principles of gamma vision but he knew how to handle the government stiffs who tried to screw QUASAR. Osip was glad they had him on their side.

Everyone sat down. Cznetsov slid a hand into his cut silk suit jacket and drew out a neat clip of microfiches which he flushed on the desk top as though they were a deck of cards. The three QUASAR partners watched him, waiting for him to deal them each a hand.

'This here is the QUASAR file,' he said. 'Let me immediately put your minds at rest, gentlemen. There's nothing in it you need to sweat over. You're building up quite a nice reputation for yourselves here at QUASAR. I notice that your finances are not in such a healthy state as you might like but I understand the calibre of tech you're developing. It's not something you would want to skimp on. I understand that. You don't need me to come here and tell you you're spending way over the ceiling of your Federal loan.'

'Does that . . .' Szmidt nodded towards the microfiches, 'include our current order book?'

'Oh sure. I anticipate you'll want to point to the Fire Department contract you just landed with the State Auxiliary Services Account, and you could do with more of that kind of business. Right. I didn't come here to discuss your current short-term cash-flow problems. Matter of fact you might find us – the Protocol – prepared to underwrite QUASAR. We could make a further back-up loan to cover your initial development outlay on the Fire Department project. We're not talking nickels and dimes here.'

Osip glanced at Szmidt.

'Why,' Szmidt said, 'would the Protocol take such a big interest in a small electronics company?'

'Don't undersell yourself, Mr Szmidt! QUASAR is building a reputation in this field. It's time you stopped being small and got big. You're putting some excellent

164

products onto the market and the Protocol, naturally, is getting to hear about them. We are a potential market you can't afford to ignore. We could give you specifications direct, for example, without you have to tender. As you can imagine, such an arrangement would practically guarantee indefinitely the financial stability of QUASAR . . .'

Osip braced himself. Cznetsov had softened up their defences in just the area where they were most vulnerable. He had held out the carrot but – even Osip knew – a promise of credit was not money in the bank. The cash itself would hang on the nature of the work the Protocol might have in mind. To draw him – and to save Szmidt from having to – Osip asked the sucker question.

'This sounds great, Mr Cznetsov. Mind if I ask what all this Protocol money will buy?'

'You're a suspicious bunch!' Cznetsov chuckled. 'I don't blame you, I guess. But let's try and get one thing straight. I'm not here to discuss money. You can work out the details through your local Centre. I'm here on another matter entirely.'

Cznetsov evidently belonged to a higher echelon of the Protocol than Dalgano. Osip knew exactly what he was going to say next. The money-talk was simply to spell out the stakes. The Protocol had come to hear of the K Model project.

'. . . I'm here to look into certain business activities which QUASAR has gotten itself involved in. Activities which are outside *this*.' He tapped the file of fiches against the table top. 'Unlicenced – and therefore illegal – activities.'

'There's been some kind of mistake . . .' McAlister said, rather too earnestly, Osip thought.

'I'm sure you're right. You see, it's come to our attention that QUASAR is running a private investigator agency from its registered premises.'

Osip stared at the well-dressed smooth-mannered Government official who embodied everything about the

Protocol, its stylish efficiency, its veiled threat of coercion beneath a mask of benevolent charm, hating him.

When no one offered to refute the allegation Cznetsov continued: 'QUASAR is licenced to operate an engineering outfit.' He quoted from memory the exact wording on their licence certificate. '". . . For the purpose of designing, constructing and marketing self-regulo equipment, sonar-orientation gearing, molecular crystal circuits . . ."' He grimaced, a cop out of his depth. 'Whatever they are. Don't say anything 'bout running a gumshoe agency. What the fuck you boys playing at?'

None of the directors wanted to say anything. There was, besides, nothing to be said. The high-ranking Protocol Officer knew all about the one area of their business which they had decided to throw a cloak over. Szmidt finally opened his mouth.

'Your information is inaccurate. We're engineers. We employ biophysicists of the highest calibre, none less than a PhD. You can take a look at our salary sheet if you don't believe me. We can account for all of them, their individual research field, how they spend every hour we pay them for . . .'

Szmidt had made a valid point. One thing about Rick Stator, it didn't exist on any Protocol computer. But if this were the case, how had the Protocol become aware that it existed at all? It was unlikely they had found out through QUASAR. The only other source, Osip realized, was Rick Stator's client. Only the client — whoever that was — had access to Rick's operating base.

'Would you care to give us the source of your information?' he said.

Cznetsov looked Osip in the eye. A horrible experience.

'How we know is not important and, frankly, none of your goddam business.' He made a despairing gesture. 'C'mon fellers, gimme a break! You couldn't expect to keep something like this from us for long. We do have some experience in the detection business ourselves!'

He knew all about the client. Perhaps even the identity of the person whom the client had hired Rick to find. What he knew was what QUASAR did not know. On the other hand, he didn't know what QUASAR did: the investigator's identity, what the investigator had found out. He certainly didn't know that the investigator was a product of QUASAR Electronics!

'Well, of course,' Szmidt bullshitted, 'you're going to have to prove these allegations.'

'Please don't embarrass yourself, Szmidt! I know what you're doing. You know I do. Let's talk . . .'

'In court . . .'

'In exchange for a breakdown of your legal activities I'll guarantee the State Fire Department contract and even . . .'

McAlister exploded. 'You can't do that! It's already signed and warranted!'

The Senior Protocol Officer shot McAlister a pitying look.

'I can't? The contract can easily be *un*signed and *un*warranted. You'd better believe me, Larry!'

Could this man break QUASAR with just a couple of phone calls? Osip didn't doubt it.

'Why would you want to destroy us?'

'Why do you say that?' Cznetsov showed the palms of his hands. 'I was the one had the Fire Department contract put QUASAR's way in the first place!'

A lengthy silence followed. A chair creaked.

Szmidt said: 'You want we give you information concerning an infringement of Protocol we don't admit to committing in exchange for you don't piss on our company?'

'Most elegantly put, Szmidt!'

Cznetsov beamed at all three of them. He stood up. The office was his and it was time for his visitors to leave.

'Now you understand the situation, I'll leave you to talk it over. Call me soon as you reach a decision. You can get

167

me on Captain Dalgano's number.'

'And if we don't?' Szmidt said.

'If you don't, you'll put me in a difficult position.' Cznetsov tucked the file of fiches into the pocket of his jacket. 'I guess the boys in uniform will pay your factory a visit. They'll be in the hair under your armpits. Please don't risk it. Any secrets you have stashed they'll find. But I can't believe you'd be so unwise.'

Cznetsov turned toward the door.

'I'll expect your call before noon tomorrow!'

'That's blackmail!' Larry McAlister hurled after him.

'No gentlemen. That's business!'

Osip, sweating, pulled loose his necktie.

It was like a jigsaw game to which they each possessed a different piece and the one Cznetsov needed to win was in the possession of QUASAR – or, rather, of QUASAR's latest prototype hominoid.

He sat at his workbench deliberately not watching the beautiful kinetic sun framed in the open window in front of him. One part of his mind was absorbed in the tricky exercise of realigning the intricate circuitry of the sensory-receptor of the K Model. His fingers, by trial and error, manipulated back into position the tiny autobolts around the echo-plates which he had once – far more easily – purposely removed. While he sweated and the sun dipped lower into the sea Roxana, without saying a word, adjusted the lighting inside the studio in order that Osip could see what he was doing.

In another part of his mind Osip played back his recollection of the day's events. First the meeting with the Protocol Officer and the unpleasant blackmail threat he had made to QUASAR. Then – almost as unpleasant – the argument between McAlister and Szmidt and himself over the course of action they should take. McAlister, naturally, hadn't seen any advantage in holding out against Cznet-sov. The idea of showing the finger to a powerful member of the Protocol filled him with despair. It went against the grain. 'You can't beat these bastards!' he had said. 'They'll take what they want in the end. Shit, we're not here to beat them! Or to make private investigations!'

He had been right. But so what? McAlister was always right. That was what was wrong with him.

Szmidt: 'I don't love Cznetsov any more'n you do, Larry, but nor do I think he's out to break us. I don't think he even cares about the private eye angle. What he want's is Rick Stator. Or – what's even more likely – whatever it is Rick Stator has found out.'

McAlister: 'So we hand over the information without he has to take it. That way he needn't hear about the K Model.'

Szmidt: 'He can't prove a thing unless he reveals the name of Rick Stator's client!'

McAlister had pointed out that a Protocol team would soon turn something up. Right again. 'We give him the information and undertake to lay off sleuthing.'

Osip had been forced to inform them that this was not possible. The only direct access to the information was through the receptor, which would plug Cznetsov straight into the K Model. And even if they could keep it from him, the receptor was currently out of service. QUASAR didn't have the information. Rick did. They could try and persuade the K to hand over the file to the Protocol Officer, something which went against its entire ethical programme, and – though he had not said so – against Osip's as well.

Larry McAlister had cussed Osip blind. Said he was prepared to ditch Rick's client without a qualm. They didn't have a contract with that person. They didn't even know who the person was. QUASAR wasn't under any obligation to protect him – or her.

Well it was something, Osip had argued, when an

engineering firm chooses to ignore the ethical parameters it had engineered into one of its own products.

McAlister had almost burst into tears. 'For chrissake, Osip! You're beginning to treat the thing as if it was fucking human!'

He had been right. He was.

Szmidt had said: 'Listen, Cznetsov wants something that we have, and bad. Only we don't know what it is. Until we can fish up something through the receptor we aren't in a position where we can bargain. What do we have to lose? Do we want to become a Protocol subsid? We all want to keep the tech involved in our latest prototype to ourselves. None of us want to put QUASAR into Cznetsov's pocket. Before we do that, I quit!'

McAlister had been right in everything he said but Szmidt and Osip together had forced the issue. Osip would fix up the receptor. Szmidt would try and stall Cznetsov. McAlister would try and live with the decision of his two partners.

As daylight faded and the light in the workshop modulated accordingly, the logical part of Osip's brain sweated over the receptor's terminals. He was running into some problems – reassembling microtech systems had never been his forte – but only when the problems had been solved could he find out what Cznetsov wanted to know.

'*Osip!*'

'Roxana . . .' Osip murmured.

'What are you doing? I called you a couple of times, you didn't answer.'

'Sorry, Hon. I'm trying to figure out how to fix this goddam K Model receptor, you really want to know. It ain't easy.'

'Can I help?'

'Only if you can tell me which way up I should align the crystal-processors in the echo-plates. I tried everything.'

'Always in the direction of the information flow, Osip,

and that will depend on the molecular structure of the specific crystals involved. You'll have to look each one up in the manual. You'll need to determine the structures for every set of tasks and align them accordingly, taking into account that they will all eventually have to function interdependently.'

'Like a jigsaw?'

'A jigsaw, yes. A very good analogy! An arrangement consisting of small intricate and irregular pieces that interlock together to form a picture. 1833. An interlocking child's puzzle. 1919 . . .'

13

Following the dogfight that had taken place the night Zeb's kite had failed to pull out of its illegal manoeuvre and a member of the SkyPol, as well as two Zappers, had been killed, Sam's bar was closed down by order of the Protocol. The closure didn't seem to bother Sam any. He knew that the Police had his place marked down as a Zapper haunt. They had just been waiting for an excuse to fix him good, he said – to nobody in particular. He had pulled down the blinds and put up the shutters. The Zs had moved on to some other, worse bar. He would reopen later maybe, when the dust settled, build up a new clientèle. A few of his old customers would drift back. He wasn't bothered. That was the way with bars. Always had been. It was a sign of a good one, he claimed, when the authorities had to close you down.

It didn't bother Sollyheim either. As long as he had a garden to cultivate he was happy. He put on one of Sam's old aprons and set to work on the vegetable patch at the back of the tavern while Zelda cracked eggs and jokes and cooked the potatoes he brought in for her. Sam made inventories of liquor he hadn't sold and wiped over glasses no one had drunk out of.

In the evening Sollyheim and Zelda and Sam's cat took their ease in the Charleston chairs on the back porch overlooking the garden. Zelda picked uncertainly at an old steel string guitar. Sollyheim, careful not to think too hard about another garden, another woman and – most painful of all – another cat, smoked his cigar while the sun set in its own sweet time. A pair of jays flapped off and on the ridge-poles that ran up and down Sam's patch of string beans. Off and on. Off and on. At intervals one of the two jays would fly away out of sight and the other would up and follow it. Then the first would return, its mate close behind.

'They can't wait for Sam's beans,' Sollyheim murmured.

'Me too.'

She was just fooling. She couldn't really play the guitar. She didn't understand, he could tell, the layout of the fretboard of the instrument, but she had a good ear and a great sense of rhythm so it didn't matter. It didn't matter anyway. He had always loved listening to a person learning to play a musical instrument. Zelda's alternating 6ths and 7ths – perversely missing out the notes of the octave – caught the uncertainty of the moment, their own relationship and that of the blue jays playing tag around Sam's beans as the sun went down.

They sat quiet for long periods. He was getting used to her ever-changing moods – silence, laughter, tears, again silence – a reaction that was not inappropriate to a period of mourning. Like a child or an animal she absorbed the mood which predominated around her. She shone if the sun came out, dimmed when it went in, as if everything, life, death, joy and despair, was all somehow her responsibility. He knew, only too well, the clinical name for such a condition.

'Did you speak to him yet?' she said.

'Speak to who?'

'*Sam!*'

She turned her face toward him. He watched the shadow of doubt flicker across it. One of the bluejays, perhaps, had flown between her and the distant fission of the desert sunset.

'I . . . kinda got the impression you did,' she said.

'You don't need to talk to Sam, Zelda. He lets you know. He's a barman. A good barman is like a mirror. He reflects what people want, unmisted by hate or desire.'

The day before, while Sam had been giving him a guided tour of the vegetable fields, he had said: 'You don't want to worry, Sollyheim.' He had said this from the other side of the row of beans when neither of them was in a position to see the other. 'You can stick around here for's long's you want, you know that.' Sollyheim had thanked him. He wasn't, anyway, planning on going anyplace. 'No one'll disturb you here,' Sam added. And that was it. Sam revealed the small ripening seed-sacks among the vermilion flowers and they never referred to the question of his identity again.

'I got this feeling,' Zelda continued, 'you two are in cahoots.'

'Why d'you say that?'

'I dunno. You never talk to each other but you both seem to know what the other is going to do next.'

'You're suspicious . . .'

'You bet I am.'

'. . . because you don't trust things as they are. You rely on your feelings.'

'Who says my feelings are wrong?'

'Not me, Zelda!'

He smiled at her frowning face.

'Except I'm not in cahoots with Sam!'

At least, he didn't think he was.

Zelda looked away.

THE TWO jays, first the one, then the other, upped and flew from the beanpoles. The blue evening became an even more heart-breaking shade of blue, the warm air a degree less warm. While she waited for the return of the birds, unwilling to acknowledge to herself that this time their departure was final, the world modulated into a fractionally less benign place. A moment ago she had known where she was, who she was, who she was with. Now she was not so sure. As each day passed, she noticed, she was becoming less and less sure. More and more certain that she was going crazy.

She had done her best to keep her identity secret – from herself as much as from anyone else. She had cut and dyed her hair, smoked, swore, wore a leather jacket. But her relationship with a man, his knowledge of her, his death, had changed her more than she had been able to change herself. The personality she had invented for herself was more authentic than the one she had disavowed. Nonetheless, she had to face the fact, it had proved impossible to disavow her essential nature completely. The secret information she possessed about herself had become a deadness in her heart, a physical pain – particularly in the evening. Her distant past and her recent past denied the existence of each other. For the first time in her life she had no future. She lived in a continual present, at the mercy of her fears and intuitions, unable to prevent herself suffering the horrible pointless beauty of the world. Her feelings, he called them.

But she called them the Blues.

'Look – you see Sam's beans?'

She looked but in the fading light she didn't see them all that good.

'Sure.'

'They'd strangle themselves if we didn't do their thinking for them. They don't understand that it's themselves they're clinging onto. Same with your feelings. Urgent, irresponsible, they are unable to tell each other apart. Your anger, your sadness, your happiness, don't recognize that they all belong to the same person – which is *you*. Sam's beans are beautiful – but *dumb*.'

'Or crazy.'

He shrugged.

'Illogical maybe. What we like to call craziness is something only adult *homo sapiens* is capable of. Insects, plants, children, animals – cats excepted, of course – have no intellectual faculties. You could say they are fortunate in that respect.'

In that respect! For an old bagperson he sure had a way with words! It hadn't taken him long to talk himself into her life!

'Which category d'you put me in?' she said.

'I don't make a habit of putting people into categories. But, since you ask, I'd say you haven't made up your mind yourself. A child and obviously no longer a child. It's true your reliance on your emotional connectiveness to events is abnormal – but not dangerously so. Seems to me you've turned your back on intellectual systems because in some way they've failed you. You're not incapable of ordering your instinctual and emotional responses. You just don't want to. Psychosis is nearly always a rational attempt to come to terms with an irrational situation.'

'I'm a Zapper. What do expect?'

He drew on his cigar. He exhaled the smoke.

'Are you?'

She looked away.

High up – higher than the bluejays, an almost stationary speck hung in the sky. It might have been an eagle cruising a thermal but she knew it wasn't. For a while her eyes followed the kite as it slowly traversed the evening on its private solitary errand, idly envying its purposeful progress. It was on its way someplace, whereas she herself had reached her destination, which was the edge of the map. From here there could be no retreat, no surrender.

'What's eating you, Zelda,' he continued, cool as you like, 'is you don't think what you do will make any difference. You're stuck in the delusion – fairly common among adolescents and the terminally ill – that events have already been pre-determined, you can't escape your fate. But history is forever being fertilized by chance.'

She listened to the murmur of his words and at the same time watched the progress of the kite overhead, as if the one made sense of the other.

'. . . Think of any occasion something happened to you that changed your life. Then try and recall the small unimportant event it came out of.'

'Meeting you in the Bethlehem Clinic,' she said.

'Good example! Yes. Wasn't that like a seed – for *now*?'

'Why *did* you talk to me?'

'I wanted a light for my cigar! Had I not, well, we might not be sitting here watching Sam's beans grow.'

The speck in the sky was becoming, with every second, less of a speck. It hovered uncertainly, silhouetted against the last of the daylight.

'I used to think I could see the future,' she said.

'I know.'

The kite had dropped to within earshot. From being small it had become large enough for her to see what it was, a lightweight single-pilot vehicle, unmarked. As the machine drew closer the pitch of its mass-driver rose. It was going to land. From being something on the horizon of her thoughts it was settling into the dirt of Sam's kite-port. Like a seed taking root. A warm breeze fanned over to where they were sitting as the pilot released the speed halo. They watched the kite in silence and then the kite was silent also.

'As above . . . So below.'

The old man gestured with his cigar toward the machine as if it was something he had conjured up to illustrate some point he wished to make.

A DESCRIPTION of the movement of the celestial bodies, it was Paracelsus's assertion, should always be concordant with a description of the smallest workings within the body of Man – and Woman. Cosmology and Medicine were one. The stars in the sky moved according to the same laws as the cells in the heart. But the separateness of Other and Self was the necessary delusion of consciousness that children, to become adults, needed to be convinced of. It was a fiction, of course, which the more intelligent, the more perverse among them – such as the high-status child-woman sitting next to him – were quick to spot. The kite had left its serene course through the heavens. It was settling onto the dirt strip horseshoeing Sam's vegetable garden. Other was fortuitously transmuting into Self before their eyes. A timely apt intervention of outside events into the dilemma of the young para-psychotic sitting next to him. He hoped.

'As Above, so Below.'

The machine – silent, its lights burning – stood in the half-light like some splendid immobile tropical beetle. Sollyheim waited with some interest to see who would step out of it.

Zelda – he caught her quick intake of breath – was shrinking into her chair, her mouth and her eyes open, her knuckles gripping the neck of the guitar as if she intended to hit someone with it.

'I feel so cold,' she said.

A tall helmeted figure stepped clear of the stationary kite and walked, taking his time, across the deserted dirt track toward where they were sitting. As he walked he began to release the lock of his helmet. He lifted the protective shell from his head with both hands as though it were a delicate amphora. With the helmet under his arm the kite-pilot approached the garden.

IN THE time it had taken the sun to set Osip had completed each of the tests on the separate functions of the reassembled receptor. The echo-plates, with Roxana's assistance, were back in position. It only remained to see if the inter-dependent terminals of the unit worked together. The headset would re-evoke the world and decision-making processes which the K Model was experiencing at the moment of their occurrence. That, at least, was the theory. Once he had subjected his own senses to the data that were being relayed through the receptor he would see everything Rick Stator saw, hear the sounds Rick heard, comprehend the mental activity travelling through Rick's cognitive fenestra. He would be inside the K Model's head.

This did not mean, however, that he would be in a position to interfere with the decisions which the hominoid was making, to control its actions. In order to proceed to that stage Osip would need to co-ordinate his own physiological progress with the micro-crystal versions of Rick Stator that had been encoded into the receptor. Before he did that it would be prudent to make an exploratory examination of Rick's performance and assess the situation.

'Well, here goes, Roxana . . .' he called out to his Validator, 'I hope you were right, about the echo-plates!'

'Was I ever wrong?'

'Never! Wish me luck, sweetheart!'

'You know that's illegal!' the sweet-voiced security unit chided. 'But *good luck!*'

Osip, lowered the instrument over his head, which immediately self-activated.

SHIT, IT'S dark! Dim after being in bright lights so long, not noticing that the sun has set. I need air!

When I've taken this pod off . . .

That's better. I can see what's going on. The air – a warm breeze – tastes good. I can smell honeysuckle – or is it night jasmine?

On the back porch of the building two people are

looking in my direction. One of them is an old-timer with a white beard, a good ol' boy in faded denim. The other, holding the guitar, is the girl. What a classic tableau, an Emmy Lou Harris LP record sleeve.

This ain't going to be easy. Here they are, shooting the breeze out on the back stoop, watching the sun go down. What the rest the world's doing don't matter more'n a row of beans. They're going to love me, I butt in, say different.

Take your time, Stator. Walk through the garden real slow. Appreciate the horticulture. Eggplant, asparagus, squash. String beans look good, smell fine. Give them one more week, be ready to eat. At a second storey window a white face peeps. Sam, watching. Act like you didn't see him. Watch your step. There are cracks in the old stone flags, yellow saxifrage flowering between them. You don't want to put your foot on one. The face in the window has disappeared, like the moon behind a cloud. And now the fragrance around the old wooden veranda, of white jasmine. Try not to break the spell.

'Sure's a beautiful evening.'

Spencer Tracy· — his white hair, thick and wild, electricity running through it — gives me a kind smile like I was a son returning from a stroll around the garden — or the world, waiting for me to lie.

The girl . . .

Speak to her!

'Hello, Zelda. How ya doing?'

. . . looks at me as if I block her view, there's something behind me she can't see. Tell her the truth.

'I came to talk to you.'

'Pff! What can *you* want to talk to *me* about?'

She is beautiful like the evening. The fragrance of jasmine is damn near overpowering. The old-timer sitting beside her like Spencer Tracy, waiting for my offer for her hand. He knows that no one can have her without he loses something, and not just anything but the thing he values most, a bully his power, a thinker his mind. Me — what?

Tell her:

'I want you . . .'

I do. I never felt this way before – a cage with some nearly extinct plains-roaming creature inside it.

'. . . to know I'm real sorry about what happened to Zeb. I didn't want to Helix with him in the first place. You know that. It wasn't my idea. There was a fault in the co-ording, I guess.'

Her eyes know I'm not telling the truth. They can see through me. To have her I must lose everything.

'What's your angle, Stator? Something 'bout you makes my head hurt. Always did.'

Tell her why you came.

'I want to level with you, Zelda . . .'

She laughs in my face. She has such a beautiful laugh.

'. . . because I like you.'

'Tell me why. Entertain me!'

'What d'you mean? Why I want to level with you or why I like you?'

She shrugs. 'I don't care.'

Two people talking to each other, neither knowing what the other is feeling. Words coming out of their mouths like animals escaping from a zoo, first tigers, then eagles, next vultures, last snakes. She opens her mouth and glass-winged lepidoptera fly out, settle on me, leave their sting, depart. Her breasts under her plaid shirt are like waves rising, never breaking. Something incomplete, forever just about to happen. Fight her.

'That's one reason why I like you.'

Make her fight you until she cares.

Old Spencer Tracy rises, slow as smoke. Leaves his seat like a pharaoh. We both wait for what he's going to say.

'Young fellow. Why don't you sit down so you two can bitch with each other like civilized people.'

The cat already seated in the third chair gracefully steps out it. It can take a hint. Walks away with supreme dignity.

Through the porch door a pistol barrel, teasing it open. Sam, a tray with three glasses on it in one hand, steps through the door. In his other hand his antique Navy Colt hanging by his side. He stands there for a moment as if undecided which of them to use. Zelda, her head upside-down, looks for him over the back of her chair. Sees him. Laughs.

'Shoot him, Sam!'

Her throat white like a truce flag.

'Time for a beer,' he declares.

None of us want to make an issue out of it. We each take a glass and I sit down.

'Did you find Zorab?' Sam says.

'He tried to kill me.'

He nods.

'What happened?' Zelda, no longer laughing, wants to know what happened.

Well, here I am in the tableau, on the ol' back porch, a cold beer in my fist and a story to tell, the pretty girl holding the guitar is waiting for me to tell it, how I got jumped by Zappers, had to fight, got damn near killed.

'They came at me from four angles, what they call a clawhammer – which I believe is a guitar playing term. I had to take them on. Had no choice. Zorab came this close to colliding into Zia. I'm glad to say they didn't. He signalled he wanted to smoke the pipe so we grounded and that's what we did. The Zappers are in bad shape, they have zero morale. The SkyPol is burning their asses wherever they set down along this part of the coast. They haven't worked out a way to evade these new fission guns the SkyPol have fitted. They, well they say, they want me to put in with them. Seem to think I can help them work something out.'

'What d'ya say?'

'What I'd found out – after Helixing with Zeb. A strategy. How to fly against the SkyPol. But I couldn't put in with them. I'm not a Zapper.'

Sam turns his back, heads back through the porch door. He's heard all this before.

'If you're not a Zapper, what the fuck are you?'

Take your time, Stator. Don't let her rush you. If you tell her you know who she is before you tell her how you feel about her she'll never believe you. She'll only be loved as Zelda – as Annie Bernier never. If you tell her how you feel about her before you say who she is she'll think you're only in it for the payoff.

'You know, you need someone to look after your interests, Zelda.'

'I don't need no nursemaid, thanks. Anyway, I got old Sol here!'

Fight her. She wants you to.

'Not – with due respect to old Sol here – with half the CIA-wing of the Protocol on your tail.'

She holds her tongue – between her teeth as if she is considering whether to bite it in two.

'Leave my tail out of it.'

The fight is fizzing. She has to see my hole-card, even though she's holding shit. A funny feeling is in the air, the hard humourless feeling that poker-players live and die for.

Spencer Tracy – Old Sol – he can't stand it any longer – says: 'If you two want me to leave? I imagine you would prefer to do this in private.'

Polite old buzzard.

'Stick around, Pal. I might need you,' she says without looking at him. Then, to me: 'So that's your business, Stator. You're a snooper.'

'Why don't you call me Rick?'

She looks away into the fading azure of the black sky as if she hopes to find some small ray of hope out there. But it's too late, the sun has already set.

'Rick? I always knew there was something funny 'bout you!'

'Don't let it worry you.'

'You know who I am?'

'Sure. Who you are. Where you came from. Your Mom and Dad . . .'

'Marie sent you.'

She's scared, as she must be if she wants to stay being Zelda, if she wants me to help her. If I know what it is she's running away from, I have power over her. When she trusts me she'll know I'll use it to help her.

'Your father.'

'Same thing. What about . . .'

She throws a glance at the old-timer but he's lifting his beer, pretending he isn't listening.

'. . . What about Cznetsov? I can't believe he's in this. He would never fuck with a chickenshit gumshoe.'

The old-timer has spilt his beer all down his front. She pushes the guitar aside to get to him, wipes his shirt front.

'I'm fine, fine. Getting that old I can't find my mouth.'

'Cznetsov has kept in the background. So far as I can tell.'

'Benny'll be around someplace. Bet your ass! Look . . .' She hesitates. She wants to know what I intend doing. Or, as she will put it, what's in it for me. 'I don't have any money!'

'Nor do I.'

'Stator . . . Rick . . . Don't, please, don't play games with me! I have to fuck you just say so.'

'You don't have to fuck me.'

'So what do you want?'

'I want you to stop feeling so damn sorry for yourself. You're not the first runaway in history. You left home to find a place you could feel real in, be free to make your own mistakes. Naturally you chose California. But you seem to have forgotten that. All you remember is the habit of running, of not trusting. You're acting like the spoilt brat you didn't want to be. Stop turning away! Trust someone. You can't make it on your own!'

She turns away from me into the lap of the old-timer,

184

lays her head there, crying tears. They'd never believe it, the TV viewers of the world, they saw her now.

'Rick's right, Zelda . . .' he says. He strokes her hair. 'You can't beat Cznetsov on your own. I know. I tried it.'

Zelda isn't crying anymore. She's listening. I'm listening. The beans are listening. The man in the moon is listening.

'. . . If you're who I think you are, you're going to need all the friends you can lay your hands on.'

The old-timer has stepped into the picture. Cecil B. De Mille is readjusting the cast, making some alterations to the script. It's not what you know, it's how you know it. I must call, to see what he has in the hole. Or else pass.

'Who do *you* think she is?'

He bats an eye at me over her head. Her head on his lap like a cat. He's loving this.

'If she has Benny Cznetsov after her and her mother is Ammarie, there *is* only one person she can be.'

He manages to say everything he knows without giving away any more than we have told him.

'And if this young person is Annie Bernier . . .'

Spencer Tracy . . .

'. . . it's been thirteen years since I held her like this, a babe in my arms.'

. . . *is Gottlieb Sollyheim.*

OSIP'S EYES focused on the half-empty coffee cup on his workbench. He must have fallen asleep. The workroom was very quiet although, through the open window, he could hear the familiar distant sighing of the ocean colliding with the coast. The sun had set, it was night out there. He must have fallen asleep in front of the TV. It must have been an old movie he had already seen before because he experienced that guilty nausea of having just slept through someone else's dream which you only have after waking up in front of an old movie on TV.

185

He lifted the cup to his lips and swallowed the dregs. The poignant taste of cold coffee caused him to recall something which he had overlooked. There was no TV in the workroom. Never had been.

'Roxana?'

'Yes, Osip?'

'Where are my cigarettes?'

'You're not supposed to smoke. It's against the Surgeon General's Advice. And mine.'

'Where are they?'

'You made me promise, last time I told you, not to tell you next time you asked me that question.'

'Roxana, I need a cigarette. Please tell me where they are.'

Or was it the coast colliding with the ocean?

'There's a pack of Luckies,' Roxana said eventually and with obvious reluctance, 'under the photograph of your mother.'

He stretched forward to the plastic drawer containing the teak box marked 'SMALL TERMINALS', the only thing of his father's he possessed. Every time he opened the lid of the teak box he got a hit of his dad, how he was. A crazy old guy who collected small terminals – blue ones, red ones, terminals salvaged from machines before they had been thrown away, terminals you could never use in a million years. He fished out the pack of Luckies, careful not to look at either his dad's terminals or the photograph of his mother.

'Thanks.'

He tapped out one of the cigarettes. There was the acrid taste in his mouth from coffee which had been made about twenty years ago, before he had begun reassembling the receptor, before the meeting at QUASAR during which a smooth bastard called Cznetsov had tried to blackmail them into handing over Rick Stator. He had witnessed – through the receptor – the arrival of the K Model at what looked like a remote country tavern where there had been a girl with a guitar and a man smoking a cigar, apparently expecting him. An old bartender had brought everyone a beer. They had discussed what Rick was doing there. The girl had broken down and the old man had spilt his beer. Now the ocean and the coast were quietly colliding against each other in the darkness.

The girl with the guitar, it had been revealed, was the same girl he had seen on TV only yesterday in a white lace tennis dress.

Rick Stator was messed up with Government people. Cznetsov was head of the CIA-wing of the Protocol Organization. The missing person of his assignment was the star of the White House Show, daughter of the President, Annie Bernier, no less, who – as far as Osip was aware – was not even missing. And, as if that weren't enough, Rick had gone and fallen in love with her! How much more can an Artificial Intelligence mess up?

Plenty more, apparently. The reason Osip knew the identity of the young runaway whom Rick had been hired to find was because the old man had revealed it, the old man whose identity was even more improbable than hers. Gottlieb Sollyheim had not, as the Government claimed, been Returned. He was still *dead*!

'Roxana?'

'Osip?'

'We're in deep shit.'

'Anything I can do?'

'Not unless you know how to pray.'

'To address one's Maker in humility and adoration? Sure, I do it everyday, O Lord and Master.'

'Very funny.'

Abandoning the K Model receptor, he stepped out of his wheelchair and left the workroom.

'I'm going for a walk, sweetheart,' he said. 'I got mental indigestion.'

'OK. But watch your step out there. It's already pretty dark. Those legs of yours are good but they were never made to climb up and down the side of a rockface in the middle of the night!'

Osip Pelig left the house and descended the stairway hewn out of the rock from the cliff's edge to the beach below. He moved his prosthetic legs with extreme caution over the slippery steps. Roxana knew what she was talking about.

14

It was a flight from themselves. Behind them lay warm apartments, cornflakes, TV, friends and purpose. Every step they took forward closed their way back. Like a pawl inside a ratchet mechanism, they could progress in only one direction, away from everything they belonged to and that belonged to them.

Joe King, as he jogged through the darkness on the heels of the old man, Cheryl Duvall behind him, did not consider he had any cause for regret, however. He had everything he needed, his tool satchel and the two people who, between them, had keyed open the closed circuitry of his socially engineered condition. He had no need of an apartment in the JFK Building, a job he required narcotics to hold down, a mid-status routine. He was going to miss – no denying it – his collection of antique genre paperback books. On the other hand, wasn't it more exciting to have the sensation that he was actually inside one?

'Where the fuck are we, Spight?' he called in a loud enough whisper for the old man to hear.

Spight growled. Ulloa, it sounded like. So they were in Parkside, a fairly fashionable neighbourhood, heading south. Joe was fascinated. He had never been to Ulloa before. He had never been on streetlevel before and the queer landscape of fantastical masonry did not coincide with his TV picture of it. Unwatching towers, inert and silent, stretched like desert mountains under moonlight.

189

An aluminium winter light fixed brief origami structures in a perpetual stationary tantrum. Barbaric, classical, solemn. Joe's sideways glances snatched crazy incomplete scenes, debris jettisoned from the legal daytime world above, rusting wheel hubs, abandoned autoderricks, wrecked skeletons of transport mechanisms. A poignant collage of error. The consequences of mistakes. A surgeon's nightmare.

He looked over his shoulder for Cheryl, momentarily unable to place her among the uneven shadows. He was on the point of calling out her name when Spight backed into him. The old man hissed. Shit, it sounded like.

'What's the problem, Spight?' he said aloud.

Spight said nothing but made quick gestures with his hands that they should turn around and head back in the direction from which they had just come. Which, of course, was impossible.

IT WAS like a nightmare in which she was required to run, naked, down foreign black-walled streets, her future pursuing her like a spurned lover. Nothing was familiar except the person she herself was pursuing, Joe King – he for whom the lover had been spurned – and he was running away from her as if it were his intention to leave her alone. She might just as well have been alone. And naked. Darting unpredictable gusts of wind, like prurient men's fingers, teased under her thin silk evening dress. The shimmering fuchsia pink dacron jerkin which she was wearing over the dress and her high-heeled fuchsia-blue peep-toe shoes – just perfect for the ABBACCA Room – served no useful purpose here. She was a species mis-adapted to its environment. Running, panting, to keep up with the two men, her poise shredding on the jagged path they were striking, she did not know where she was nor where she was going, only that she was moving further away from the ABBACCA Room with every step she took.

She halted to catch her breath, gulping down mouthfuls of the dirty air. Was she drowning or falling? Her fingers clutched dust, unable to find any purchase among the decay. Soft mortar crumbled under them. She coughed and walls laughed or else tumbled distantly. She was lost on streetlevel. Joe King had abandoned her. She held her breath and listened to the blood pounding – damn damn damn damn – through the veins inside her head. Shadows, the departed souls of a million street-people, flitted about her, touching and tugging at her dress with pointless urgency. She ignored them – they were harmless. In front of her loomed the real danger. What she was running from. Huge, luminescent, approaching her with the brilliance of its knowledge of her. The fate she had so recently eluded had already caught up with her.

'CHERYL DUVALL . . .'

A calm rational voice boomed through the night. The sound of her name wrapped her like a rug. It was cogent and sincere, the voice of her parents, of her friends and teachers, of Benny Cznetsov. The voice she had never failed to listen to, reminding her how much she owed, which side she was on, what she should do, who she was. Everything about her that was known. Surrendering herself to her instinctual fears, she fumbled for the one thing she possessed which marked her authority, loading it with all the hatred she could muster from her years of obedience, and hurled a fine splinter of rage into the belly of her adversary.

Spight sensed the presence of the CES before he saw it. The couple behind him were pushing too hard and fast, like they had some kind of destination, an appointment to keep. Their singlemindedness was giving their movements a steady pattern, which the scanners of the Curfew

Department would find easy to fix onto. This was not Spight's own preferred method of travelling on streetlevel. He had not had a destination in years, let alone an appointment. He never moved in straight lines. In so far as he made decisions at all, he made them by the metre, choosing direction at each intersection. That way the Curfew Evasion Seekers had no opportunity to run a scan on him and predict his position. It meant that Spight never travelled with any purpose and had to rely on happenstance to come up with something – which it usually did. It had kept him off the auto-tracking screens of the Curfew Department.

But these two young folk who walked as fast as they talked, who had gotten him to take them down to streetlevel – he had already forgotten why – seemed, the way they acted, to *want* the scanners to pick them up. Spight, well as he liked them, they had been good to him and he wanted to help them if he could, sure's hell couldn't figure them out.

More than anything he hated the scanners – the sight of them, the sound of their droning sensors. They gave him no peace and forced him into the darkest corners of the labyrinth of streetlevel. Bulkier than your average kite, and not especially fast, they never gave up. They just kept a-coming.

As soon as he heard the dreaded drone, Spight signalled to the feller in back of him to slow up but it was probably too late. They would do everything the scanner expected them to. Evasive action would lead it straight to them.

'What's the problem, Spight?' the man said.

Spight said nothing. If this young feller wanted to put his voice-print over to the scanner that was his business. The whirring of the autopilot, the searching beam of light which swept the street, were cutting through the darkness toward them, a goal they would have to make for. They had no choice. Spight indicated that they should turn round. Go back. Get the fuck out of there.

The man wanted explanations. Spight was about ready to give up. The scanner's power-halo ground dully on, the searching beam of light was vanquishing the darkness, shadows darted and collided into each other, then it was all over, not a single penumbra for fear to crawl under.

'Shiny Beast!' Spight whispered, throwing caution to the wind.

The beast shone like a sliver of daylight, the searching finger of the Protocol. Legal, righteous, all-powerful. It hove to over them, too bright to be seen, a small sun whose orbit they were now in.

A voice issued from the pilotless Government vehicle.

'CHERYL DUVALL, JOE KING, I DON'T HAVE TO INFORM YOU THAT YOU ARE IN VIOLATION OF CURFEW LAW. YOU ALREADY KNOW THAT. FOR YOUR OWN SAFETY YOU WILL BE TAKEN INTO CUSTODY. PLEASE DO NOT RESIST OR ATTEMPT ESCAPE . . .'

Spight sucked his teeth. Shit! He had kept out of reach of the Protocol for more years than he could recall, living like a rat in the roots of the earth with only chance befriending him. Now . . .

A girl – *the* girl – brushed past Spight. She walked upright, her arms at her sides, her pretty dress fluttering in the downdraft of the CES. She didn't look fazed at all. With the light on her and all she looked like a million dollars, graceful and beautiful. A spring flower blowing in the wind.   She stood inside the light as if she was its reason for being there, her dress giving it shape and purpose. The girl – well, young woman, really – raised her arm, calm as you like, and fired her fission pistol into the belly of the scanner – Bamb! – into the heart of its brightness.

The CES ignited. Pieces of light began falling from it like flaming rags. It became a fireball tumbling to the earth, disintegrating. Shadows darted out of the darkness, tearing to pieces the glowing mass like a mob taking revenge on the master it had always hated.

Spight – pulling the girl – ran.

AND NOW the darkness was total. Their hands occasionally knocked against each other as they each placed pieces of broken lumber onto a common heap which they could not see in front of them. They crouched in silence around the heap, praying for something to happen to it. Cro-Magnons longing for the miracle of dawn, cold, fearful and ignorant. The habit of consciousness, a luxury of civilization which could not be sustained outside air-conditioned apartments, had narrowed into a single beam of hope, that this pile of junk would combust. All they needed was a single spark.

Joe King trusted his mental picture of the laid out parts of the disassembled capacitor from which he was endeavouring to bleed sufficient juice to touch off the kindling. If his hand mistook one part for another they might have to stay cold until morning.

Spight and Cheryl Duvall said nothing. Spight was still stunned from what he had just witnessed out on the street. Cherry was getting accustomed to the state of mind which the transition from her own world to her present circumstances was forcing on her. She was a derelict, a hobo, huddled round a heap of junk in some hole underground which another derelict had led her through a maze of tunnels into.

'It'll be easier when we are outside city limits,' she said.

'We should leave the city?' Joe murmured.

He continued with his task, applying his mind to their present predicament. Cheryl could worry about the future.

Spight – his contribution to the conversation – began blowing music through his mouth harp. Whatever he had to say they needed to hear. Their lives probably depended on it.

194

'. . . *Bulbs shoot from its snoot 'n' vanish in darkness*
It whistles like a root snatched from dry earth,
Sods bust'n rake like grey dust claws,
Announces its coming into morning,
This train with grey tubes that houses people's
    Very thoughts and belongings,
Bat-chain puller,
    Their very remains and belongings,
Bat-chain-puller, puller. . .'

In the silence after Spight's song, Cheryl said: 'We need
Spight. He's one of us. But we also need a strategy. I mean,
one of the two sides is going to pick us up sooner or later,
for sure . . .'

'What are you talking about?'

'Well . . . Either the Protocol or its enemies will . . .'

'The Protocol has *enemies*?'

'Of course! There're people the Government never
succeeded in convincing.'

Joe — it was like feeling for razorblades in the dark —
groped for her meaning.

'*Zappers*! They'd crucify us!'

'Maybe. Least we wouldn't be giving Benny Cznetsov
the pleasure.'

'They hate status people! They're just . . . *animals!*'

'Listen, Joe. All you know about Zappers is what the
TV told you. You still want to believe the TV — *now*?
We're in the same tub of shit as they are. We have the same
mob chasing us. Plus we have a lot that the Zappers would
be very interested in?'

'Yeah? What do we have?'

'We have all the CIA classified material inside my head
— I have a broad idea of Government strategy regarding
Zappers. We have your tech skills, your knowledge of the
uteroscope. And, not least, we have Spight here and his
music. A poet must be useful for something. Most
important of all, we have the dirt on the Bernier clan. We

can lift the lid on the whole trashcan. They'll *love* us!'

'You reckon the Zees are going to be interested in any of that? Only thing on their minds is drinking and flying kites. They're mean bastards!'

'Mean enough to keep the SkyPol watching behind every bush. With what we have to offer they'll become more than that. They'll have a reason to be mean!'

'Since how long did Zappers listen to reason?'

'They won't have a choice. Like I told you, as soon as the story on Sollyheim is out it'll change everything in their heads. It'll make sense to Zappers easier than anyone else!'

Joe had the same aversion for the no-status group as everyone else but there was no denying Cheryl's point.

'They'll become a *political* force to be reckoned with. When they have the truth!' he said.

'You got it.'

'Bat chain puller, puller. . . !'

There was a spark in the dark. The circuits had shorted, and then another spark. The kindling took, flaring quickly. Joe wasted no time. He fed it from the main stash until the dry litter was crackling. A dull glow warmed them.

'Well done, sweetheart!' Cheryl said, moving closer to him.

'Just one spark,' he said, putting his arm around her, 'was all it needed.'

They kissed.

Light licked around the refuge which Spight had brought them to. They could see now that it was some spacious underground cellar with an opening near the ceiling through which the smoke was leaving. The place was empty. Yet they were not alone. Eyes stared at the fire as if it were a TV screen.

'Rats . . .'

Spight chuckled.

'. . . Live on no evil star!'

*   *   *

196

THE DARK light of dawn entered the electronically-adjusted jalousie screened into the enormous silver wall-windows, crossed the carpet of the sparsely-furnished suite until it reached the pupil of someone seated inside the gloom watching the misty city loom patchily before him like an image appearing on photographic paper. Only the tallest office pyramids South of Market and – when he rotated his chair – in the Western Addition so far rode above the ocean mist. The condo-blocks over in Richmond and Sunset were, mercifully, not visible at all. The man surveyed the panorama without emotion, it might have been a non-terran crystalline landscape. He was waiting for the day to get on with its business, for the good citizens inside the office pyramids and the condo-blocks to yawn into activity. When they did, when the sun struck the haciendas on Pacific Heights, they would find Benny Cznetsov already in the saddle, one step ahead.

The Sanfran City skyline was unique, different from any other in the world. Cznetsov hated it, as he did differences of any nature. He preferred reality to be more or less uniform – because, he reasoned, it was much more difficult for language to gain purchase among similarities. Irregularity and the baroque only made people fidgety and aspire to understanding. Smooth away incongruities and there was nothing to be understood. He preferred Atlanta, and the blandness of the Protocol suites which he customarily stayed in. In every city there was one where he could hang his hat. You couldn't say anything about the suite he currently occupied which would not be true of any other – except that damned view. The suites were standard, the furnishings not particularly interesting to behold. They were free of any sign of the handful of high-ranking Protocol personnel who sometimes stayed in them. This suited Cznetsov fine. Having eschewed the comforts of a family home for the thankless spartan service of engineering the ethics of society, he enjoyed the impersonality of a world without contours through which he could pass and leave no mark.

In addition to its pyramid skyline the city was unique in another respect, its historical connection with the movement which formed the basis of his own organization. For it had been right here, out of the original Bethlehem Clinic on Potrero Hill – Cznetsov kept his back turned to it – that Sollyheimism first emerged. It had been in Sanfran that Sollyheim had fought his belated rearguard action against the New Orthodoxy which his own ideas had engendered. It was here that the old bastard, at his own request, had been detained, out of sight and out of mind, in the Schryer Building.

Sollyheim's escape – it peeved Cznetsov to admit – was not in the script. It was something he had not accounted for. Sequestering the Doctor had been his own idea but he regretted, as soon as old man Dover had gone, not having had him quietly put under the fancy marble vault on Capitol Hill where everyone thought he was anyway. But it had not been his decision. Archer Bernier had vetoed the proposal.

The vidscreen at his elbow interrupted his reverie. There was a call stacked, waiting to be accepted. Cznetsov swivelled about and watched the face of the caller waiting for him to give the go-ahead. It wasn't the face of a man who had just awakened from a restful night's sleep.

Larry McAlister looked beat. It did not surprise Cznetsov to see the Senior Partner of the electronics firm. If anyone at QUASAR was going to crack it would be McAlister. Neither the far-too-young legless autonomic-systems expert, Osip Pelig, nor the hardboiled attorney Szmidt would consider making a deal, he could see that. But McAlister, an obvious hysteric, invested too much of his own ego into the firm. Cznetsov knew the type well. It was a syndrome he encouraged among his own employees. Personal identification with the aims of the organization guaranteed a degree of loyalty. It was an admirable quality in an employee, less admirable in an employer faced with

198

the destruction of his company. McAllister – Cznetsov could tell just by looking at him – would panic into any line of action which he thought might save his crummy little outfit.

Cznetsov touched the go-on key.

'Good morning, McAlister. You start nice and early. I didn't expect to hear from you so soon,' he lied. 'I guess you saw the sense in my proposal.'

McAlister hesitated, no doubt holding back from saying the words which would set him on the road to betraying his two partners. If he was acting without their knowledge it was because, like Cznetsov, he knew they would never approve a deal which would make the company beholden to the Protocol Organization for its survival.

'Proposal?' he said without attempting to conceal his contempt. 'I don't recall any proposal, Mr Cznetsov. What I recall is you hardassing us with you can pull our wings off one at a time, we don't give you the information you want!'

McAlister, having swallowed the bait, was tasting the hook. All Cznetsov had to do was feed him enough line, break his will, gaff, and creel him.

'Slow up there, McAlister,' he said. 'Let me recapitulate my position. One, you're operating an illegal service way outside your licence. An investigation agency has nothing to do with turning out high-effect labour-saving devices. I could have a court revoke your licence just on that count. Two, you're in a very competitive market and, I don't have to tell you, you're running broke. That's a situation QUASAR got itself into. You can't blame it on *me*! I don't control the market in auto-gadgets! The level of technology necessary for your systems costs more than a single private company can afford. You're going to have to face the fact you can't maintain the quality of your products without a backer. We need your systems, you need our cash. Three, I'm not out to bust QUASAR, but you can't expect us to put money into an organization without we run a check on its activities.'

McAlister said: 'I don't need this horseshit. I made up my mind.'

'Whyn't we get together?' Cznetsov suggested. It was time to haul the poor bastard in. He looked beat. 'Come over here for breakfast – yeah? We can talk this through.'

McAlister nodded. The screen blanked.

Forty-three minutes later the Director of QUASAR Electronics was seated inside Ben Cznetsov's undistinctive suite inside the Protocol Centre. He was shaved, sipping coffee in his best suit. He looked like someone waiting to be interviewed for a job. As far as Cznetsov was concerned, that was precisely the situation.

'First of all, McAlister, let me say we have confidence in your firm. We're going to be watching how you handle the Fire Department contract. There must be hundreds of uses your systems can be modified to perform that would interest the Protocol. Hell, we have labour problems just like any other big organization. And don't forget the security forces. Let's face it, Larry, you been targeting their application very down-market, when you consider the sophistication of the tech that goes into them. Homehelps? Streetcleaners? Where's that at?'

McAlister's expression did not change. He glared with the dumb comprehension of an aphasiac.

'I can't fight you,' he said eventually. 'You can flush us down the toilet with a few vidcalls. Your river flows through our land. We want to work it, we going to pay you anything you ask. We have no choice. But, please, Cznetsov, spare me the horseshit. What do you want?'

'You have an operative tailing a highplaced AB kid,' Cznetsov said. 'I happen to know he has picked up her trail.'

McAlister raised an eyebrow.

'How do you know that? Our "operative", as you put it, is in contact with us and, of course, the client.'

'But you have no idea who that is.'

'We don't. Do you?'

Cznetsov shrugged.

'Let's say I have friends in high places who need my patronage. Don't expect me to exchange the identity of the runaway for the information your investigator has because you don't need that information. It's no use to you. You level with me, I'll guarantee that QUASAR won't collapse. We'll overlook the illegal irregularity also.'

'QUASAR isn't doing anything illegal,' McAlister said with slow emphasis as if speaking to a child.

Cznetsov shuddered. He had the sensation, now only too familiar, that he knew exactly what was going to happen next. For a moment he saw himself and his interlocutor objectively, as if from a great height. They were actors in a play which he, the author, was watching from a balcony. Something in McAlister's voice had triggered the first *déjà vu* attack of the day.

'C'mon, Larry,' he stalled. 'It's too late for that shit! You know I know what QUASAR is doing. You just admitted you have unlicenced personnel . . .'

'You're mistaken. We do not have any *personnel* working in the area you are referring to.'

McAlister stared at Cznetsov calmly, unhysterically.

'I know you have! I have *proof*!'

'Produce your proof.'

They both knew he could not do this without exposing his source of information – the client who hired the QUASAR operative in the first place.

Nettled, struggling to hold off the *déjà vu* attack, Cznetsov said: 'I don't need proof to break you. I can do that any time I want.'

It irritated Cznetsov that McAlister had gotten him to lose his poise.

'Then what I say or don't say makes no difference?'

'Nossir.'

McAlister put down the coffee cup. He stood up and prepared to leave. Perhaps Cznetsov had underestimated his man.

'Sit down Mac! That was a nice try. I respect the fight you're putting up. But it isn't necessary! I'll give you written guarantees nothing will happen to your firm. In return, you'll quit screening your investigating activities from us and hand over your files.' He grinned. 'Dammit, you're poaching our business!'

'QUASAR Electronics, Company Registration Number SF/9689961 manufactures and markets high quality homeoactive systems.' McAlister said flatly. 'None of our employees is involved in any illegal activity.'

'You still deny it!'

This could go on for ever. Cznetsov was beginning to weary of the position McAlister was holding to. Somehow their situations had reversed. The *déjà vu* attack was not going away. A sensation of familiarity haunted the conversation, the flavour, no more, of having had it before, the certainty that he knew – without really knowing – what was about to be said.

'What I just told you,' McAlister said, 'is the truth. I didn't deny the truth of your allegation. Put two truths together, you can usually figure out a third. The scientific method. Then you'll understand why we're not involved in any illegal activity.'

No QUASAR personnel were involved in the gumshoe operation. QUASAR had an operative on the trail of Annie Bernier.

Cznetsov and McAlister watched each other in silence, as if the solution to the conundrum was going to jump unaided from one mind to the other, a spark shorting between two terminals.

'Your operative . . .'

The false sense of familiarity with the situation peaked. Cznetsov knew what he was about to find out – before he understood it. Shit, it was so fucking obvious!

'. . . *is a selfregulating machine!*'

McAlister looked at him, expressionless.

202

'A one-off prototype of our latest model,' he said. 'We call it a hominoid. It's unique. You won't find anything like it in the world. Operates under the name of Rick Stator.'

Cznetsov opened his mouth to speak.

McAlister turned.

'Where is he . . . it?' Cznetsov called after him. 'What's he found out?'

'I'm not prepared to say any more.' But at the exit McAlister turned and, with some dignity, added: 'I didn't tell you anything. You worked it out for yourself. You can hose our ass if you want to – or you can try. But not through the courts. Far as any court would hold, Rick Stator does not exist. He's a machine.' He smiled at the thought. 'A damn fine machine.'

And then he left.

15

Huge wild hills loom against the horizon. A piece of unfinished business of epic proportions, too daunting to consider. Sam's Tavern, tucked into a fold in them, the small conscience whose task it is to consider it.

With the blinds rolled down the long bar is quiet and spooky, a ship in the doldrums abandoned by its crew. Only the captain remains. Sam, his face blank as snow, forever washing and wiping glasses and surfaces that don't need washing or wiping, so far as I can see, hasn't spoken a word all morning. In the back room the card tables are covered with white sheets as if the last ever game of poker that gamblers dream of but never speak about has finally been played, the last bets finally raised and called, lost and won. Zelda is out in the garden inspecting Sam's beans, moving slowly between the poles, stooping and stretching to examine the pods as if they hold the secret to a safe course of action. As they may well do. A pair of bluejays, perched on the bean-frames, observe her as if they think so too. I watch her through the square window pane she is framed by, as she is framed by what I know of her.

The morning is sprung together like the molecules inside a dew drop. The light is tensile and delicate. Beyond the back porch, where last night we drank beer and exchanged the pieces of information which have made a conspiracy of us, is Sam's vegetable garden. Zelda, in a blue dress borrowed from Sam's past, works her way among the bean-frames with the fragile movements of a patient on the mend. The card-room is criss-crossed with a lattice of shadows from the panes in the glass doors, as if the sunlight is a laid out deck of cards. The whole garden is delineated. The big jack pines way over at the end of it, every leaf, are detailed. Zelda is framed in a pane of glass like a picture in a book, a woman in a poem. I watch her like the author of it. She walks among the beans, oblivious of me, as if I don't exist. It makes no difference to her that Rick Stator, the agent her parents hired to catch her, is watching her from the card-room, doing her thinking for her. She looks happy, testing the pods between her fingers, the star of the TV show most families watch most nights crouched in the dirt like an old squaw Indian. Rick Stator is a worm beneath her contempt.

Stand. Open the glass door. Step out onto the porch. Breathe the fragrance of jasmine. The flaked painted wood of the old balustrade already feels warm under my palm. I am not alone out here. Sam's black cat is crouching on one of the three Charleston chairs, a small panther about to spring, its head pushed out low, eyes fixed on the two jays.

Walk down towards her — easy, not eager. The lioness is at the waterhole, a stillness surrounding her. A light breeze crimps the edges of the bean leaves over my head. The two jays flap off together as I approach. Zelda makes no acknowledgement of my arrival.

Crouch beside her. Watch her run her fingers through the red soil as if it is valuable seed corn.

'Good morning, Rick Stator,' she says without looking at me. Black ants are racing over the back of her hand. The front of her blue dress hangs open. 'These little fellas can't stop still for one minute!'

She is a sphinx. Her breasts, half-hidden, half-glimpsed, are cleft like the answer to the riddle her body puts to me. She keeps her shoulder toward me, reluctant to face the reality I personify. I am the finger at the end of the long arm of her father's power. I can reconcile opposites. I complete the circuit.

'We need to talk, Zelda.'

'I guess they think I'm some kind of earthquake. Or do they? I mean, think? Maybe they just think they do. Just look at them! Did you know that ants can move objects eight point seven times their own bodyweight?'

She isn't listening to me. She's eyeing the margin, like a psychotic.

'The funny thing about ants is they are so full of purpose. Almost human in that respect. Always on the move, busy. We only act like them when the house is on fire. And the funniest thing of all is they don't know a damn thing about what it's like out here – ships to Mars, peanut bars, TV, music . . . They don't even know the landscape they're crawling over belongs to someone, a person, or that humans make movies about them with microscopic lenses to vid into a billion human homes on the Wednesday Nature spot. So business-like, so dumb!'

'Zelda, listen to me, will you?'

'They act like they know what's going on, the world is just made for them. Fuck, they don't know it's round even, rotates on its own axis around the sun. Or that our solar system is just a speck of dust on the edge of infinity!'

She takes a handful of soil, flings it across the ground. I'm going to touch her. Then, perhaps, this feeling of separateness will end.

'Do we make the same mistake?' she says. 'I mean, we fight and fuck and feed ourselves like they do, like it's really important. Maybe we're no different than ants on the palm of someone's hand.'

She is focusing on the enormous and the minute, planets and insects, realms in which she does not have to make any decisions, in order to avoid facing the obvious size of the fix she's in here and now. She's drifting into apathy in order to ignore the urgency of my concern for her.

My hand reaches across the distance between us – I watch it as if it belongs to someone else. It rests on the nape of her neck, warm like wood left in the sun.

'There's something about you, Rick Stator . . .'

She lifts my hand from her neck. Gently turns it over in her palm. Examines it as if she expects to find some message. A single black ant runs across from her own hand onto mine.

'Y'know, I used to be quite good at reading futures. But there's nothing about you I can fathom. Look, your hand, your palm, so perfectly formed, as if nothing ever happened to you and you don't have a future.'

With the tip of her finger she traces the lines engraved in the skin of my palm. My hand in hers.

'I don't get it. Maybe my ability to see what's going to happen is just a high-status psychotic delusion, like Gottlieb says, but, fuck, I dunno . . .'

She tosses away my hand as if it were an old glove.

'. . . You spook me. I don't know what you're thinking. What you're like. What you intend doing about me.'

The bean plants rustle over our heads. She takes another handful of soil and tosses it after the first. Tell her.

'You won't know until you trust me. You've acquired the expensive habit of looking into other people's heads. Now you're one of us you'll have to learn to trust people. It's what *we* do all the time.'

'You're blaming me for being the Baby Bernier!'

'That's who you are.'

'It's who I *was*!'

'It's time to turn and fight!'

'You think you can con me into going back?'

I'm getting nowhere.

A bluejay squawks behind us, a single stifled cry. Zelda's eyes jerk up, fix on something over my shoulder. Turning, I see a single bird sheer off like a piece of shrapnel from the direction of the building, careen through the air as if fighting to the surface of water. It brings to mind the terrible angle at which the earth fell toward me during the spin which Zeb threw my kite into, the lurch out of it against his murderous weight.

'For once,' she says, watching me through narrowed eyes, 'I think I know what you're thinking.'

'Zeb tried to murder me, Zelda. I couldn't have done any different. It was him or me.'

'I know . . .' her eyes close completely, '. . . what Zeb was like. I knew the moment he stepped into the Shadow he was going to try and work on you. He didn't trust you either – for his own reasons. I can guess what happened up there. It was no accident. He wanted you to tell him the truth. Fuck, that's what Double Helixing is all about! He guessed you were going to put the bite on me and he tried to get you to admit it. In the arm-wrestling contest he came second, which does surprise me because he was a lot stronger than you are.'

Her eyes, neither blue, nor grey – like an horizon just before dawn. Violet.

'I'm sorry. I liked him.'

'Don't be sorry, Rick Stator . . .' Her voice like paper tearing. We are characters in a book and she is tearing out an unsatisfactory page of dialogue. 'I knew from the start how it was going to end up. Some people can only change their circumstances by doing the same thing over and over, making the same mistake. Like it's inside them.'

'I didn't know Zeb one way or the other, but I watched him die. He didn't want to. He wanted *me* to.'

'Zeb hated the Protocol, hated having his fate printed out on some prick's computer. And there's the paradox he was trapped in. The fate he chose for himself was all the Protocol left him to choose. That's the joke! He had to keep going up in that fucking kite until they either shot him down or . . . what happened. He never believed he was *dead* or part of the status system. But in order to stay alive – to experience life in the sense he understood it, he had no choice except to be a kite-crazy dumb Zapper!'

'I couldn't prevent it.'

'Neither could I.'

She looks through me as if she is watching through glass an age-old necessary disaster, one lifeform preying on another.

'If you was ever in love, Rick Stator, you'd understand the fuck I'm talking about!'

I'm an ant in the palm of her hand.

'Love is just a word, a name for an emotion some people get. We don't even know if they're talking about the same emotion.'

'Oh yeah . . .?' When she grins she looks so pretty. 'And what name do you give for the emotion you get off me?'

'Words are public property and the Government owns the public. You want me to entrust my innermost feelings to them? I'd be crazy!'

'You love someone means you're ready to take that risk. That's what love is, you dope!'

'Let's say, then, something happens to me when I'm near you. My pulse-rate rises. I perspire. I get the shakes. I don't know if that's what every other dope calls *love* — and frankly I don't care. When I'm with you I become confused. It's like there's a whole bunch of electricity building up inside me. I need to put it some place.'

'There, that wasn't so painful! But no way for a private detective to talk to the person he was hired to bring in.'

'I just quit being one.'

She separates one of the pods from the plant and slits open the seam with her nail to reveal the livid seeds inside. She offers them to me.

'Try one. They're ready to eat. Don't even need to cook them.'

In my mouth they taste crisp, full of light. The ungarnished truth.

'There's more to you than you say, Rick Stator. Or maybe less. I dunno. Maybe you don't know yourself.'

She turns her head. Our eyes simultaneously snag on the

same quick movement, an animal darting across a corner of our field of vision. Under the bean plants only a frame away from where we are crouched a black cat jogs past. An inert weight is hanging from its jaws, dangling like a rag bundle, huge in relation to the size of the cat. A flash of blue. Two wings trail the dirt like sleeves. A brilliant eye strikes back at us. The cat sees us and freezes. The dead bird's head gimbals in its jaws. It hesitates, watching us, then quickly trots off in the direction of the big jack pines where the garden meets the hill. The cat, envious of the flight of the bird, has put a stop to it.

We continue to crouch side by side in the dirt, listening to the silence and the grasshoppers stitching their little ladders through it. Zelda lays her head on my arm.

'What d'you want me to do?'

FOR SOME time after the departure of Larry McAlister, Cznetsov followed the dawn's progress through the window while he accustomed himself to the light which McAlister's information had thrown onto his investigation. The spurious guarantee he had given McAlister for the survival of his company had bought a great deal. Rick Stator, the shamus in contact with the girl, was made of tin and straw. He was, in McAlister's vocabulary, a hominoid. But this information, interesting as it was, did not bring him any nearer to finding Annie. Swivelling his chair, turning his back on the stubborn disaster-prone city, he tapped out a number on the console. Soon he was looking into a sleepy pair of eyes.

'Good morning, Catherine,' he said.

The eyes opened, alarmed.

'Mr Cznetsov . . . ! Oh, good morning.'

Cznetsov let her have his best old-friend-of-the-family smile. He waited for her to get over the fact that her husband's boss was on the line. He had taken her by

210

surprise. She was still in her robe. Her pretty auburn curls were uncombed. Cathy Dalgano, he recalled, was taken by surprise by almost everything that happened to her. She was sensitive and vulnerable as a cop's wife should be. Whereas the cop whose wife she was, the person he wished to speak to, was tough as algebra.

Behind her Cznetsov could hear the kind of noises a standard CD family makes around the breakfast table. The TV, the kids yapping, Dad trying to make himself heard.

'Who is it, honey?'

'I'm sorry to call you so early, Catherine. I need to consult with your husband. You know how it is. How're the kids?'

'The kids are fine.'

She was terrified of him, for no better reason than that he was her husband's boss. She was terrified of her husband, as she was of all cops, as citizens who have never dreamed of committing a crime often are.

'I'll . . . put him on, Mr Cznetsov.'

The once-handsome features of the Sanfran Protocol Chief filled the screen. His necktie hung loose inside the pressed collar of his uniform. 'I was just,' his mouth was full of breakfast cereal, 'about to call you, sir.'

'Have you made any progress?'

'Yes . . .'

Dalgano straightened his necktie in his reflection on the screen.

'And no. The Doctor, Duvall and the JK are still in city limits. They went down to streetlevel – about the dumbest thing they could of done, you ask me. I guess . . .'

'I don't want your guesses, Dalgano. How do you know this? One of your scanners get them?'

Dalgano hesitated.

'They got one of our scanners.'

'What are you talking about?'

'They destroyed a CES. Cheryl Duvall shot it out the sky with her issue parabellum .38. The lightest firearm any of

211

our personnel is permitted to carry.'

Cznetsov could not suppress a smile. He remembered issuing the weapon to Cheryl personally, the same model that he carried himself, persuading her to carry it at all times. He couldn't help feeling proud that it was going to take more than a dumb scanner to bring in one of his best agents.

'Well, at least we know they're not in Wap Wap.'

'Sure. We'll soon net 'em.'

Cznetsov did not share his lieutenant's confidence.

'What about this Security Guard?'

'Vergil Wyman? We drycleaned his brain for him. He's pretty fucked up, you want to know the truth. But he don't know nothing. And he has an alibi.'

Cznetsov, while Dalgano tried to deny that the situation was not improving, allowed himself to consider the possibility that he had made a mistake in withholding information about Sollyheim's escape from Archer Bernier. He had gambled on a early recapture. The opportunity to finish off the Doctor for good was slipping away.

'This private tape circulating on the public channel, did you put a block on it?'

'The public ones, sure. But it went out on the private link. Be difficult closing them down without walking in even more shit. It's being passed along from one user to another. Exponentially, they tell me. Not easy to stamp out. Short of a total blackout.'

'It won't come to that,' Cznetsov said. There was no point being defeatist. Dalgano nodded. He wasn't going to argue.

'Joe King is the key to this. I'd like you to get over to the JFK, dig out his story. Sleuth it.'

Dalgano nodded again.

Cznetsov, relieved to be initiating action, said goodbye and cut the link. He took pleasure in relaying these pointless requests to the Protocol Captain. This was his territory. He knew it like the back of his hand. As soon as the *déjà vu* attack passed, he called up the kiteport and left instructions for his kite to be made ready. By the time the port clerk called him back the Protocol suite he had occupied was ready for the next guest.

Solitary on the tarmac in the breezeless morning his kite hummed. A young apprentice was seated inside it, gently revving the powerhalo, appraising the instrument panel. Cznetsov's kite, no regulation Government vehicle, bore more resemblance to a Zapper hog than anything legally permitted to fly.

'This is the finest machine, Mr Cznetsov,' the apprentice – just a teenager – commented as she jumped clear, 'I ever saw.'

She caught his eye and smiled. Cznetsov's heart almost broke. Here she was. At last. Just when it was too late. The woman he should have married – the girl at the gas station who thumbed you up and you never saw again. As the kite rose he watched the kumquat of her coveralls, her smile, her arm waving, become smaller and smaller until she was just a speck in his imagination.

As the kite crossed over the broken back of Golden Gate Bridge on course for Osip Pelig's residence, Cznetsov recalled how everyone had wept, Archer Bernier included, the day the most beautiful bridge in the world collapsed into the ocean. Everyone except Benny Cznetsov. The great feat of engineering reduced to rubble said everything he wanted to hear about the Old Order, the shattered spine of a generation. His recollection of the time perfectly suited his present mood. He gunned the kite towards the Point Reyes seacoast. He was ahead. He had an edge. He possessed the least reducible fact about Rick Stator. Every aspect of the illegal detective, from the righteous way it had twisted Archer Bernier's arm to its taste in Lewis Leather jackets, was a fiction composed and assembled by Osip Pelig and the QUASAR team. Cznetsov was going to join the team.

The kite located a solitary cliffside edifice. Pelig's

eccentric residence had been constructed on the sheer edge of the rock. A single kite was already parked on the landside of the building. It did not require a CIA training to arrive at the conclusion that somebody was at home. Seeing no reason to conceal his arrival, he had the kite park alongside the one already on the ground.

He crossed the old marbled terrace. The water-filled air tasted like a fine cold sweat. A spiral of white flagged steps coiling into the house instantly anticipated his reaction to what he knew was about to happen. He halted – as he knew he would do – and experienced the texture of the situation which had not yet happened. He recalled each step as though he had already taken it, almost a hundred per cent certain that he never had. The shape of the stairway spiralling into itself was identical to the shape of his recent attacks of *déjà vu*. This was the second today. They were increasing in frequency. And intensity. He descended the stairs, determined to follow them to the conclusion they were drawing him towards.

He emerged in a kitchen that opened onto a wooden deck overlooking the ocean.

'*Pelig?*'

He glanced over the furnishings of the room, enjoying the opportunity of examining the character of his man from the intimate domestic signs defining him. Going through a person's pockets was his job. An opened pack of Lucky Strike cigarettes lay on the work surface next to a coffee machine. Intrigued, he picked up the pack and carried it with him on his exploration of the property.

'Good morning, sir. Osip Pelig is not at home. Please identify yourself and state the nature of your business.'

It was the voice of a young woman, calm and authoritative.

'Where's Pelig?' Cznetsov said as he entered what looked like a TV repair workshop. Tools and electronic appliances, ancient and modern, occupied every horizontal and vertical surface. He had never seen so much crap.

'For your information he just left for his morning walk. Please state the purpose of your visit.'

'Where the fuck can you walk round here?'

'I insist you identify yourself,' the voice demanded.

Cznetsov continued his examination of the workroom. On a bench in front of a view of the ocean there was a saucer with ash in it, also a matchfold bearing the inscriptions *McGoon's Restaurant – the finest Hangtown fries.* This was prequake debris. He wasn't sure he could recall what a Hangtown Fry was.

'You do not wish to entrust your identity to a security system?' the security system said.

'You'll have to excuse me. It's an old habit.'

'Please put down the pack of cigarettes. I must ask you to respect Osip Pelig's privacy.'

'In my line of work nobody's business is private.'

'I see. You are a law enforcement officer.'

Cznetsov said nothing. The apparatus alongside the matchfold attracted his attention. He sat down on the stool facing it.

'I should warn you . . .' a hint of anxiety had crept into the computer's voice, '. . . that everything you do will be recorded and is now admissible evidence in any court action brought against you. This is in line with the Supreme Court ruling in the case of . . .'

'Go fuck your mouth!' Cznetsov sneered. He remembered the case. Only too well.

The security computer, having arrived at the conclusion that rational discourse would serve no purpose, maintained a dignified silence for which Cznetsov was grateful. With one finger he touched the domed headset of the rig in front of him. It responded to the light pressure with a reciprocal lightness. A high calibre piece of engineering.

'What's this gizmo?'

The computer said nothing.

'Looks like a receiving mechanism to me.'

He hooked out one of the filterless cigarettes from the

215

pack. The taste of tobacco was a pleasure his position inside the Protocol had long ago forced him to forgo. He put the cigarette to his mouth, struck one of the matches from McGoon's Restaurant and lit it. He inhaled the distinctive Lucky's taste, recalling the caption: *It's toasted.*

Drawing on his first cigarette in twenty-seven years Cznetsov leaned forward and lowered the domed rig over his head until it rested comfortably on the bridge of his nose.

THE CONTINUOUS ratchet of grasshoppers.

A black cat, a bluejay in its teeth, has subtly tilted the situation. The fate of one has absorbed the fate of the other, as our fate has been absorbed into the fate of the Protocol. We chose to go on believing that nothing had a reason, that our future was something conferred on us at our birth, like a found glove that fits.

'I've worked out a plan.'

Smiling, this time without irony, she takes my hand in hers, so soon after having let go of it. Her breast under her dress.

'I know you have, Rick Stator! You always will. I believe you. Don't ask why. You're just different – and I can't figure out how. You win! I don't know what you're thinking. That puts me in your power – because you can betray me. I find that . . . exciting. It is, for a person who never trusted anybody.'

She takes my hand and places it on her dress, over her left breast, as if she is sealing a contract. Overhead a half-hearted cry tears the air between us like a rag. The blue jay is circling the garden, searching out its mate.

Experiencing a sudden burning sensation in his right hand, Cznetsov let the cigarette fall from his fingers.

The jagged cry of the bluejay, like a barbed hook cast

216

everywhere in despair, buries itself in Zelda's heart and my own simultaneously. Pulls us together like sewn skin. Tell her:

'We don't have all that much time. We have to try and reach your father before his goons reach you.'

'They'll have to find me first.'

'They will, don't worry.'

'Oh yeah? How'll they do that?'

Don't tell her. Let her work it out.

'You're going to have to spell it out for me.'

She must leave this place because:

'Sam's bar isn't safe. They won't be looking for you here maybe, but there's a good chance that they'll find you.'

'You mean . . .' She glances towards the house. 'The old man . . .? Right! I forgot.'

'He's your security risk.'

'What can we do about it?'

'Do a deal with Bernier.'

'You're insane! Is that your plan?'

'You're going to have to some time, sweetheart. You and he, both. It's the only way.'

'Jezus! Why do you think I ran away?'

'To become a woman. Now that you are one, you can turn and face him.'

'Oh sure! I call him up, say "Hi Dad, it's your little girl! Did you miss me?" '

'I already informed your father – last time I was in contact with him – that it was in his interest to do this quiet. He can't handle the scandal. I also got the impression he just wanted to know you were all right.'

'It isn't him I'm afraid of. It's Ammarie. Archer is just loose change in her pocket. She wouldn't stop at anything. She hates me. And you're forgetting Cznetsov.'

'That's why I think it's Archer Bernier we should do a deal with.'

'There's a lot of miles between him and me, Rick. I could never reach him. I tried to call him, the SkyPol would be slipping on the bracelets before I finished talking to him!'

'Right. So I'll do it. As a private investigator I can scramble the information enough to keep them off the scent a while.'

She gives me her sideways look.

'What kinda deal you have in mind?'

'I'll act as broker. That way they'll be no risk of anyone locating you. When you leave here I will be the only person who knows where you are.'

'I like it here!'

'I know you do. You like Sam. You want to stick around, help him harvest his beans. So do I. But it's not over yet, Zelda. You're going to have to go missing once more.'

'Fuck!'

'You want to be free to do what you want without your family or the Protocol – which in your case is the same thing – telling you different? That kind of freedom has its price. It's not, as you might think, free. You have to pay for it. To be free of the Berniers you'll have to do a deal with them. To stay in Sam's Tavern, you'll have to leave it.'

'You shoulda been a lawyer!'

'Way I see it, you still have friends, people who won't sell you for an apartment on Sunset. People who hate the Government as much as you do.'

'You're talking about the Zappers.'

Turning away, she leans her head against my chest. The hunted animal, exhausted, nuzzling the hunter's mercy.

'Right. You're still in good with them. And they need a cause to rally round. Since the SkyPol burnt them up here they've been licking their wounds down San Benito way – in a little place called Panoche Pass. Or they were, last time I talked with Zorab. You'll be safer with them than anyone else. Least they won't sit by and let the SkyPol take you. No one – except me, of course – will know you are there. Meanwhile, I'll be making the deal stick with Archer Bernier.'

'Which is?'

'I'll tell Bernier you're not coming back. He'll fuck and damn a while. Then I'll tell him you *will* go back – hold on, sweetheart, this is the price you're going to have to pay – you'll go back on certain conditions.'

'Which are?'

'You'll agree to make some episodes of the White House Show while they think of a way of writing you out of it.'

Zelda twists round so that she can laugh in my face.

'They'll never agree to *that*! Ammarie would sooner cut her throat. You aren't dealing with a *rational* person.'

'They will. They have no choice. You didn't appear in any of the shows recently and it's already starting to look funny. They can't go on clipping together archive fragments of you for ever.'

Zelda knows this to be true, says nothing.

'Anyway, we won't be dealing with Ammarie. I think I can handle Bernier. He refuses to play, I'll threaten to break the story. Start advertising who you are. Rob a few banks, blow a few minds, like Pattie Hearst, remember her?'

'No.'

'Rich man's daughter, got herself kidnapped. Next thing she was pointing guns at the people her daddy's empire was built on. Took the FBI six months to find her.'

'What happened to her?'

'That's the best bit of all. She married one of the FBI agents whose job it was to find her!'

'And lived happy ever after?'

'I guess. Point is, it don't look good, the daughters of powerful families going bad. Gives people ideas. In your case it would set kids status-evading throughout the system.'

'That might not be such a bad thing.'

'Bernier won't think so.'

'So let's get this straight. You want me to go to this Panoche Pass. For how long?'

A cloudless blue sky above. The sunlight leaking onto us through the leaves of the bean plants. Grasshoppers. Under my palm the smooth skin of her arm. What can I say that won't be a lie?

'Maybe only a couple of days. I'll kite you over today if you like, make the call from the city some place, kite back down tonight, tomorrow morning with Bernier's answer. He agrees, you might as well come back here. It won't make much difference then, where you are.'

'Aren't you forgetting Benny Cznetsov? He didn't show his hand yet don't mean he ain't holding one. You never want to underestimate Uncle Benny.'

'I won't. Don't worry. When you're in Panoche Pass you'll be one place further from him. He already had a line on you, sweetheart, you wouldn't be sat here in Sam's beanpatch making plans that include me.'

You said it, Strawman! Cznetsov growled.

Zelda, turning, adjusts her dress and her knees so that she is facing me. She leans towards me, places her lips over mine, inserts her tongue into my mouth. A key is entering a lock which it has been specifically engineering to open. The glimpse of her breasts is brief – no doubt the price I shall have to pay for her departure. Then she draws away, rises to her feet and stands over me, the sun making a brilliant corona of light behind the shadow of her head.

'You want to go immediately?'

She moves her head and I am dazzled unbearably by the light her absence casts upon me.

'Sure,' she calls over her shoulder. 'Why wait?'

She is already walking away, back through the garden. I can't let her go. Something has happened between us. As we approach the back deck of the house she takes my hand in hers. The perfume of white jasmine assails us, wild bees and butterflies busy among the flowers. In one of the two old Charlston chairs Sam's cat is asleep in the sun as if it has never moved from that position all morning.

The glass doors open . . .

A HAND grabbed Cznetsov's shoulder from behind. The receptor glided upwards away from his head. Disconcertingly the work surface and the objects on it came into sharp focus, replacing the less concrete vision of the beautiful garden and Annie Bernier walking arm-in-arm with . . .

'Cznetsov! The fuck you think you're doing?'

. . . *with a robot!*

Osip Pelig was standing over him. He recalled where he was although he had never forgotten what he was doing there.

'Stop bleating, Pelig,' he said, rising. He disliked being talked down to. 'There's no point. Your little secret is out.'

The young QUASAR inventor stood blinking and twitching in front of Cznetsov. He looked pathetic although somewhat taller standing up than he had seemed in his wheelchair. There were tears in his eyes. No doubt he was the clever whizz kid they all said he was but in this instance he had been outmanoeuvred. It was a sight to savour.

'Sorry I had to barge in. You weren't around so I made myself at home. I guess your security computer apprised you of my presence.' He gestured vaguely towards the work surface. 'I'm afraid my curiosity got the better of me.'

'You bastard!'

'Calm down, Osip . . .'

He laid a friendly hand on Pelig's shoulder.

'. . . We have one or two things to talk over, you and me. You need to keep a cool head.'

'Fuck off out of here!'

'It's too late! I already got what I came for. And even something I didn't.'

'How did you . . .?'

'How did I get to hear about the Model K hominoid? Rick Stator, the fake PI from the QUASAR workshops?'

Osip Pelig went limp, the fight went out of him. Only Cznetsov's hand kept him on his feet.

'McAlister told you!'

Cznetsov nodded.

'I don't believe it!'

'It was a wise move on his part.'

'How did you chisel him into making it?'

'He's a businessman. He understood the situation. He wants to stay in business. If you had been more candid with him yourself he might not have been so ready to trade the hominoid.'

'Rick Stator is more than a hominoid.'

Osip Pelig wasn't kidding.

'I can't disagree with you. Your product succeeded in accomplishing what the entire CIA wing failed to. That's an achievement! Cheer up, Osip. Just think of the business that'll be coming your way from us. We're partners!'

Osip groaned.

'There's no way you could have prevented your company and my organization from coming together. It was an historical necessity.'

'What are you going to do?'

'About QUASAR?'

'About . . . whatever it is you found out.'

'Just what do you think I *have* found out?'

'About Rick and . . .'

Cznetsov couldn't help laughing.

'You'd make a terrible cop, Osip! But I'll tell you, you want to know. I'll have a SkyPol patrol fly down and pick the girl up before nightfall. Don't worry, nothing's going to happen to her!'

'Whyn't you just leave her alone – or is her capture an historical necessity too?'

'It was your robot told me what I needed to know, where they plan stashing her, who her associates are! *You* made it that way! It's only a machine performing the job it was constructed to perform.'

'You don't understand Rick Stator.'

'I don't know. I like to think I have a way with machines.'

'Rick has a way with cops.'

Cznetsov began to tire of the direction the conversation was taking. Time was passing.

'Tell me something, Osip. I need the location of the place where they're at. Sam's Tavern, they called it. I can get hold of it easy enough but you could tell me, save me the time, I'd be grateful.'

Pelig, his eyes level with Cznetsov's, said nothing. A clever child playing an adult at his own game. He made no attempt to remove the hand which rested lightly on his shoulder.

'I was thinking . . .'

'Do your thinking some other time.'

'. . . Every moment I keep you here is one more moment Rick Stator and Annie Bernier have to play with.'

Cznetsov adjusted the hand so that the thumb caressed Pelig's windpipe.

'Time is a commodity we're *both* short of,' he said. 'There's something else I want to know. Stator and the girl mentioned an old man, some kind of security risk. Now who would that be?'

His thumb touched Pelig's windpipe as a concert pianist's touches the most poignant note in the *adagio*.

Pelig gagged. His eyes said nothing.

'Just tell me those two things. I don't want to hurt you. Where's the Tavern? Who's the old-timer?'

He relaxed the pressure.

Osip swallowed, then called out: '*Roxana!* Help me! Do something!'

'Osip! What *can* I do . . .?' The vocal terminal of Pelig's security system, the voice of a young woman who didn't know what to do, addressed Cznetsov: 'I must warn you,

Mr Cznetsov, your actions are being recorded. Any violation of Osip Pelig's person will go direct to the District Attorney's Office. Your position inside the Protocol will not protect you from the evidence. I advise you to loosen your grip of Mr Pelig's person and continue your discussion in a civilized manner!'

Cznetsov gave a nasty laugh.

'The local DA is a good friend of mine. Else he wouldn't ever made it to to the DA's office!'

'The Law will . . .'

'Sorry, Roxana, sweetheart,' he interrupted. 'The Law won't.' To Osip he said: 'You won't gain anything by keeping the location from me. I can find out easy enough.'

'You won't find Rick Stator so easy to push around, Cznetsov!' Pelig sneered in his face. '*Rick is in love with Annie Bernier.*'

The recent experience of Annie putting her lips onto those of the huminoid, as if onto his own, returned to Cznetsov. He watched Osip Pelig's face change colour as terror replaced the oxygen in it, helpless to halt his descent down the familiar spiral. One step after another. A cat, doomed to do what a cat has to do. To a bird. He watched the slow rictus of despair replace the terror in the face of the creator of the manthing which Annie had fallen in love with.

'*Osip . . . !!*' Roxana's voice called.

Cznetsov unclenched his fists and let the body drop to the floor. Pelig's prosthetic legs, however, continued to kick and scrape against the vinyl in a vain attempt to raise the inert weight.

'*Osip!* Oh my poor darling!'

16

'I'm real sorry 'bout our li'l misunnerstan'ing back there, Wyman . . .'

Vergil Wyman sat, limp, in back of the burly Protocol official who was operating the controls of the kite. He had been inside the pair of underpants he was wearing for three days now – or was it four? The official – some high-ranking SkyPol officer – was speaking over his shoulder to Vergil as if he had nothing against him after all. He was all smiles, spruce and clean in his sky-blue uniform. Vergil could smell how clean he was. It took an effort on Vergil's part to recall that this was the same hot-faced cop who, yesterday, had combed his brain with the minutes of the previous forty-eight hours.

'. . . Sure hope you ain't going to hold it 'gainst us,' the officer said. 'It's the drill. We can't play it different.'

The powerful police kite sped west from the Protocol Centre in the direction of the VW Dwellings on Arguello. It was a nice clear day. The sky was the colour of the Captain's uniform. It was especially nice, in Vergil's view, to be clear of the Protocol Centre.

As a matter of fact he did not hold it against them. They had bust into Cheryl Duvall's apartment and thrown him against the wall and dragged him into a kite – very like the one he was in at the moment – and hurt his arm. They had asked him a number of easy questions without showing much interest in any of the answers he had given.

Finally, late last night, they had persuaded him to sign a script authorizing them to serve a TM order on him, reminding him of his legal right to refuse and that he had a baby who had just died and a wife who would love to see him. He had signed the paper and they had said 'That's swell,' given him a tab of Mnemorex to take with his coffee and led him into a chamber with green walls. Except it had been no ordinary tab of Mnemorex. When he woke they had said 'That's swell,' again and told him he was free to go home. What he had told them under the TM process Vergil didn't know. He didn't know the questions they had asked him. He didn't even know what the letters TM stood for.

'Forget it,' he told the cop.

Soon he would be seeing his wife and his son, then he could forget it himself. He held no grudge. From the questions they had put to him it was obvious they had picked the wrong feller. He knew as much about the personal habits of Cheryl Duvall as he did about the garbulator system of the Schryer Building. When they realized this they kind of lost interest in him.

'Put it down to experience' the officer advised. 'I gotta hand it you though, Wyman. You stood up pretty good. Fact, that was one reason I was sure you could help in our 'vestigation!'

Vergil attempted a polite laugh.

'I hope you find the person you're looking for,' he said.

'It's only a matter of time. We'll get him.'

He wondered who 'him' was and in what respect he was different from himself.

'It's kind of you to lift me home like this, Captain.'

'Least I can do! Anyway, I got business in that direction. I guess you was never in the JFK complex?'

It was a rhetorical question Vergil was saved the embarrassment of having to answer by the call-tone of the kite's communications panel. A woman's face appeared on the screen. A nice face, but worried.

226

'Darling, I'm sorry to call you at work!' the face said. 'But . . .'

'You don't have to apologize, honey.' The Captain purred. 'You got something on your mind, I'm glad you called.'

Vergil discreetly sat back in his seat. The last thing a cop in conversation with his wife would want was an ex-suspect breathing down his neck. He closed his eyes. He blanked from his mind the events of the past twenty-four hours and stared at the white light behind his eyelids, consoled by the thought that it would soon be over. When the white light turned into a white page of paper with words written on it he made no attempt to decipher them. They were not in a language he knew.

'I got a message over the public video-link,' the Captain's wife said. 'And . . .'

'Some kinda bill?'

'Nothing like that. It was a taped message from people we don't know. I can't understand how they got our number . . .'

With the Officer occupied by his conversation, Vergil, finally alone, poked a finger into the small dime-pocket in his slacks and hooked out the folded-up scrap of paper which he had placed there just before the SkyPol team had busted him out of Cheryl Duvall's apartment. They had hurt his arm and persuaded him to submit to the TM process. This was the first opportunity anyone had given to him to retrieve it.

'They sent *us* one of them! Listen, hon, I know all 'bout it. Juss forget it, will ya?'

The Police Officer did not sound pleased, Vergil registered while he read the foreign words on the paper: '*Mein Liebeskind* . . .'

'But the message, it said . . . well, things so strange!'

'Honey. It's someone's idea of a joke. Right? I'll sort it out. Juss don't worry 'bout it. Okay?'

Vergil read the words that were in a language he did

know. '*Gone to Righi's to buy me a donut.*' Some more foreign words followed: '. . . *Ich kann nicht mehr hier bleiben, Tschüss . . .*'

'But it said . . .' the woman's voice piped over the communications link '. . . that we have been tricked and that Gottlieb . . .'

'. . . *Sollyheim.*'

'. . . is still dead. He hasn't been Returned, like we think. In fact . . .'

'Catherine! Forget about this. It's some joker we going to hang from his eyelids, we get hold of him. Take a tab. I'll be home later and we'll talk 'bout it then.'

'I'm sorry, darling. I knew I shouldn't call you at work . . .'

Vergil stared at the words on the piece of paper – the half-sense it made competing in his brain with the reason for the Police Officer's wife's anxiety.

'. . . I sent a copy to your office. You can see it for yourself,' she said.

The Captain groaned. 'I'll talk to you later.' He cut the link.

In the silence that followed Vergil refolded the slip of paper and replaced it in the dime pocket of his slacks, as if this reflexive process were an act of disremembering. He tried to think about something else – Val and Theo – but the splinter of information which the TM had failed to locate remained lodged in his head. An unwelcome virus had attacked the fundamental assumptions on which all his thinking was based.

When the kite's communications monitor illuminated for a second time it did so automatically. A priority call. Vergil, over the Captain's shoulder, saw an iron-haired old warrior wearing a big grin.

'Dalgano! I have some great news! I want you to drop everything.'

'What happened?'

'Nothing yet. But I have a fix on the girl.'

'Terrific! You found her?'

'Don't overrev, Dalgano! She's not in the bag quite yet. You have to act fast! Like *now*!'

'Give it me.'

'According to my information she's due to arrive in some place called Panoche Pass. It's a scratch little town, I believe, in the San Benito area.'

'I know it.'

'She's on her way there now. By the time you arrive she should be there. I want you to drop out of the sky and take her!'

'Shouldn't be difficult,' Captain Dalgano said.

'Don't bank on it. You'll need all the firepower you can lay your hands on. Your best. At least a squadron. She's snug in with a gang of Zappers and from what I hear they ain't in no mood to let Captain Dalgano drop by and carry her off without taking a good look at his buzzer.'

The Captain nodded. 'These must be the same we flushed outta the Diablo a few nights back.'

'A place called Sam's Tavern?'

'That dump!'

'I'll leave it to you, Dalgano. Don't fuck up. Soon as you made the pinch, meet me in this Sam's Tavern. Bring her with you. Don't take shit from these zilchheads!'

The screen blanked. Dalgano started tapping keys and issuing orders. The kite veered from its previous course, turned about and accelerated in the opposite direction. Very soon they were outside city limits, heading across the Bay – south, it looked like. And fast. Vergil had never travelled so fast. He waited for whatever was going to happen. A passenger in someone else's adventure.

'You heard the man, Wyman,' Dalgano said. 'Looks like we don't have time to ride you home after all.'

Through the side observation panel Vergil saw that they had been joined by a fleet of SkyPol kites. He hadn't noticed them arrive. The sky-blue vehicles hung in formation against the pale blue sky about level with where

229

the cloud zone would be if there had been any clouds that day.

'This ain't no picnic we're going on. You didn't oughtta rightly be here. There's going to be some serious shooting. We're flying into a nest of zero-rated individuals who got fuck all to lose.'

'What did they do to get you so sore?'

'It ain't what Zappers *do*, you wanna know. It's what they *are*! Now sit back and shut your mouth.'

Vergil did as he was told. The map of hills and valleys, brown and green, with small towns nestling between them, ceased rolling past. The convoy of kites idled on the turbulence like a vast bird of prey, a mote of terror in the eye of small scurrying mammals below. The map was a peaceful range of hills with a few isolated dwellings clustered together, some old roads winding in and out of them. Again Vergil wondered – to himself – what the inhabitants of this quiet rural spot could have done to get the SkyPol sore enough to send out a fleet of kites for?

A number of kites were already descending, skeltering down in an ordered loop. It looked like a well-rehearsed manoeuvre. Dalgano's own kite and half a dozen more remained where they were, hovering. The first wave of kites was planing down toward a group of dwellings isolated in a fold high up in the hills, no more than a few dozen two-storey timber-framed homesteads. Vergil had a good view. He could see everything. It was a nice clear morning.

'Burn their asses!' Dalgano urged the advance squad. 'Make all the noise you can. Flush the fuckers out!'

The kites descended on the homesteads in a compact low-flying formation, the engines screaming. Their powerful fission guns began straffing the buildings, burning holes in the side of the hill. The squad – fifteen vehicles in groups of five – climbed out of the first run and immediately dove again, criss-crossing each other. One of the homesteads burst into flames. Then another. Then another. Smoke was rising — and so were the Zappers. It was becoming clear to Vergil that the object of this initial attack was to worry out the Zappers who had their kites stashed away among the hills.

'Here come the hogs,' Dalgano muttered over the open channel but held back his section, like cavalry on a hill, for when the game got rough.

The Zapper hogs, as the Captain called them, were forced to run the gauntlet of the fission guns in order to put some height between themselves and the invaders. This did not appear to daunt them, however. The hogs were fast. They zoomed up in twos, zipping to and fro across the path of each other in a zany zig-zagging pattern. Suddenly the quick blue SkyPol kites didn't look so quick. In comparison they appeared more ponderous and less manoeuvrable. The tight Zees of the Zappers razored through the neat SkyPol formations like buzz-saw blades. The speed and angle of the zig-zags each hog executed across the path of its mate startled and impressed Vergil. Both partners in each pair of kites, it seemed to him, were operating with telepathic synchronization, like two fingers in a single pair of scissors. They contrived, somehow, not to collide and at the same time to present an impossible target to the controlled lightning of the fission guns. The ordered SkyPol formations began breaking up. They were presenting a too-easy target. They veered evasively into ragged groups pursued by the sharp lethal teeth of the Zapper's battle strategy.

There was a short flash from one of the hogs and pieces began falling away from a SkyPol machine which exploded and the wreck tumbled earthward. Almost immediately the sequence was repeated. The flash, the explosion, the crash.

'Shit!' Dalgano swore.

'How can they do that?' Vergil said.

'They can do that because they break laws! Because they're fucking good mechanics, not dummies pressing

231

buttons. Each of those pairs of kites is coordinated with the other in a way that screws up the predictions of the computers inside our cannons,' Dalgano said. 'That crazy zig-zagging flight pattern is a combination of two alternating random whims of two crazy Zappers. It's called a Double Helix. I never saw them use it as an attacking weapon before. We can't get a fix on the bastards. They can piss all over us! See . . .?'

A third SkyPol kite floated toward the burning homesteads. The police kites, relying on their automatic equipment, were cannoning after the Zappers without making contact. All the Zapper kites were in the air – about a dozen, it looked like – and Dalgano began to take down the second wave. Feeling nothing, Vergil waited for them to enter the dogfight, damn certain that his presence there was not in his SollyChart. Flack from the aerial artillery began to crackle around them. Dalgano's group, however, swept clear of the battle, mushrooming around it and reforming together underneath. Dalgano was barking instructions over the open channel. The kites proceeded to settle into the dirt surrounding the old wood buildings. SkyPol officers were leaping out of their machines, each of them carrying long-barrelled machine carbines which, from a crouch position, they fired at the higher storeys of the buildings. The wooden frames caught fire instantly, leaving the occupants with only two choices. With their hands raised and screaming insults a bunch of people emerged. To Vergil's surprise they were children, youngsters, some old folk, all dressed in colourful patchwork garments of a style you didn't encounter in the metroplex. Dalgano's men had them lined up against a wall. Dalgano himself was shouting at them but, from where he was, Vergil could not hear what he was shouting. Suddenly Dalgano went down, clutching his crotch. His officers had hold of some kid, a skinny teenager, whom they were dragging toward Dalgano's kite. They opened the lid and tossed the kid in without ceremony. The kid landed at Vergil's feet – the first genuine Zapper he had ever seen in the flesh.

Captain Dalgano, breathing hard, jumped in after the kid. Without saying a word he jerked the machine into the air and pointed it toward the heart of the air-battle still in progress overhead. Soon it was all around them, the crackle of flak, the screaming of power-halos revving to max, the intricately entwined afterglow of the Zapper kites like a piece of modern kinetic art. Strangely the black hogs made no attempt to bring down Dalgano's kite which, with its two passengers, had lost some of its acceleration. Vergil held his breath while a pair of Zappers plied their double helicals around them. The kite shuddered. Dalgano swore but held his course steady as if he knew they were going to reach the other side in one piece. Vergil wondered how he knew this. Other SkyPol kites were having a harder time. A pair of hogs were strafing those still remaining on the ground, popping them as they attempted to get into the air one after the other. Vergil looked away.

The young Zapper kid beside him had not moved. He lay in the same heap he had landed in. Vergil lifted him by his jacket and dumped him onto the seat next to him. The heap hardly weighed anything.

'Fucking treacherous lying traitor . . .!'

Vergil started. He had got it wrong.

'To think I trusted the bastard!' the kid snarled through clenched teeth. 'Dumbest thing I ever did!'

The kid was a girl, a teenaged black-leathered Zapper with short spiky black and yellow Zapper hair. Vergil laid a hand on her shoulder.

'Get your fucking paws off me!' she spat in his face.

She had violet eyes that Vergil was certain he had seen before someplace. Surely not in a foul-mouthed Zapper brat. Looking out of the sunny-skinned sweet face of a young lady dressed in a white broderie anglaise tennis dress – maybe.

233

'WE'RE CLOSED!' the old barkeep in the long, out-of-fashion apron said across the counter.

But the chairs were arranged neatly around the tables and the tables were waxed to a high polish, in the centre of each one a deck of playing cards, the seal unbroken. Sunlight, through lowered raw calico blinds, illuminated the bar pleasantly. There was even a spray of fragrant white flowers in a beer glass on the counter. The old 'keep was wearing his white apron.

'You look open to me,' Cznetsov said. He sauntered through the open door toward the counter.

'We're closed,' the 'keep repeated without returning Cznetsov's smile. 'Order of the Protocol.'

'That case, count yourself re-opened!'

He raised the front of his suit jacket enough to reveal his firearm in its neat holster-clip, his badge of Protocol legitimacy.

'We're still closed,' the old man said but he went ahead and drew a beer which he placed on the wax-polished redwood bartop. Cznetsov took the glass and drank as only someone who has just murdered a man can. It didn't taste like the usual factory suds.

'Boy, this is good beer!'

The 'keep wiped away an invisible drop from the counter.

'We make our own.'

'I thought that was against the law.'

'It's against the law,' the 'keep said, meeting Cznetsov's small challenge with empty eyes, 'to sell beer outside the franchise of the local agent for the cartel. I didn't sell it to you. I gave it to you. We're closed.'

Cznetsov couldn't help liking the stubborn old bastard, as he did anyone who was not afraid of him.

'What exactly you looking for?'

234

'An old man.'

'Old men are easy to find.'

'This one made himself an enemy of the Protocol.'

'Have some more beer. You can pay for it this time.'

'He's kind of special, Sam.'

Sam's empty eyes narrowed. 'You know his name even?'

'His name's Gottlieb Sollyheim.'

'I thought he was under that slab of fairy cake alongside Abe Lincoln.'

'He crawled out from under it.'

'Too bad. You mean he ain't dead after all?'

Cznetsov hooked out one of his – one of Osip Pelig's – Lucky Strikes and lit it with a match from McGoon's restaurant. He blew the smoke across the counter into the old 'keep's eyes.

'No, I mean he *is* dead after all.'

Sam blew the cigarette smoke right back at him. He took another pointless swipe at the polished top of the bar.

'We use the word different round here,' he said.

'That's also against the law,' Cznetsov said. He was getting nowhere.

'This was recently a Zapper bar.'

'And I'm a Protocol Officer. We should get along fine.'

The 'keep made some more unnecessary adjustments to the bar. He put his hand under the counter and – Cznetsov's small Walther .38 already on him – lifted a dusty old bottle of liquor. He froze.

'You pointing a gun at me in my own bar?'

He sounded genuinely sore.

'I don't like to take chances. Whyn't we quit pussyfooting and get down to it? Any moment this place is going to be crawling with Captain Dalgano's SkyPol. They'll be hot and bothered following a ruckus with your Zapper pals. Nothing would give them more pleasure than a Zapper bar stocked full of illegal Zapper beer. Now, I want to see Sollyheim. I know you got him stashed here. Better you let him know I'm here so's we can talk quiet, than wait till

235

Dalgano arrives.'

'Is that you asking – or your gun?'

Cznetsov slotted the pistol back into its clip under his coat jacket. He grinned.

'Do it as a personal favour to me, Sam.'

'And who the fuck are you?'

'I'm Benny Cznetsov – a long-time associate of the good Doctor.'

'What if he don't want to see no long-time associates?'

'What difference does that make?'

Sam, stepping adroitly through a hingeless door which Cznetsov had not noticed in the wall mirror behind him, vanished, walking into himself like a conjuror. The mirror-door closed silently after him.

Cznetsov waited. While he waited he drank the authentic-tasting beer and smoked his second cigarette in twenty-seven years, watching himself do so in the mirror. It was like watching a movie he had acted in a long time before. He recognized the familiar taste of the beer and the toasted tobacco but not the face of the person sitting across the counter. For a moment he went numb, as if he were the image in the mirror, flat, without feeling, and the flesh-and-blood Cznetsov was the one looking at him so curiously. When the *déjà vu* attack passed Cznetsov saw that he was not alone. The eyes he was looking into were not, in fact, his own.

'*Sollyheim!*'

'Hello, Benny. I was in the garden . . .' Gottlieb Solly-heim said. He was scrubbing earth from his hands in the bar-sink. 'So you caught up with me.'

'Not really.' Cznetsov flicked the pack of cigarettes with a finger. 'I struck lucky.'

'Oh indeed! I didn't think luck was something that happened to you.'

'Nor did I, to tell you the truth. Fact is, I was looking for another party altogether.'

'And did you find her?'

'Of course. It was your bad luck I did.'

'She didn't say I was here.'

Cznetsov shook his head.

'In that case it was Rick Stator.

'Not him either – exactly. No one told me. I was led here. I always seemed to know what was going to happen next. You're right. It wasn't luck. I followed hunches and, like just now . . .'

'You were in some sort of daze. Looked to me like . . .'

'Go on,' Cznetsov told him. He wanted to know.

'I was watching you – for about half a minute. Right here in front of you. You didn't see me. That's not like you, Benny. What's the matter with you? Are you having blackouts?'

'Attacks of *déjà vu*. Like I know what's going to happen. It's just waiting there.'

'Any idea why that is, Benny?' Sollyheim asked casually as he dried his hands in the long white out-of-fashion apron he was wearing.

'You tell me. You're the doc.'

'You always said I was a fortune-teller.'

'I always said you were a pompous old fool.'

Sollyheim nodded. 'You were right all the time.' Then, 'But since you ask my opinion, I think your attacks are a defence – a natural defence against a series of acausal events which have been threatening the Protocol. Which threaten *you*. Aleatory phenomena always did disturb you, Benny. They upset your well-laid plans, the mechanistic course you wanted them to take. To a person like you, coincidence has the symbolic force of *dirt*. A dangerous pollutant. You hate it as a gardener hates weeds. It's *ha'raam*. A nuisance which must be eliminated before it screws up those neat purposes of yours. All these years at the helm of the Protocol Organization have begun to affect you, Benny.'

'You trying to say I've gotten sick?'

Sollyheim shook his head.

'Not at all. You were sick before the Protocol became a vehicle for exorcizing your problem.'

'I'm sound as a bell!'

'And hollow as one. Sure. Your problem is not physiological. It's ontological. It's rooted in your fixed ideas about existence and the massive conspiracy you have created to confirm them. Everything that drives you – your distaste for life, your apprehension about life's untidiness – originates, like most right-wing behaviour, in a fear of Other, an acceptance of alienation as the natural state of the human condition. Sin, they used to call it. You want life to be a machine you can rely on never to go wrong. In a saner world you might find it difficult to operate. We'd have your schizoid tendencies labelled and you'd be receiving the treatment you need. But in this world, Benny Cznetsov's world, a schizoid personality is a social asset.'

'That's enough, Sollyheim. I didn't come here for a consultation.'

'Maybe that's why you *did* come! Don't be so quick to figure everything out – that's half your problem. Could be there are reasons why you came to look up old Doc Sollyheim that you never thought of. It's just possible that you're human after all.'

The old charlatan hadn't changed. He was still able to work the old magic that had made it necessary to put him away in the first place. It was time to put him out of his misery.

'What makes you tick, Benny, makes the Protocol tick. You probably don't even know what that is yourself . . .'

Cznetsov, no longer listening, gripped the decision he had come to. It was reassuring as the solid butt of the pistol under his jacket.

'. . . Your present anxieties about the future are a reaction to the fortuitous events surrounding Annie Bernier and myself. I know all about Annie, don't forget that. Just as I know you're about to come to the conclusion that you have to kill me. Or I don't know my patient.'

'It's twenty years since I was your patient.'

'When it was all the fashion. Times change, Benny, but a physician–patient relationship never changes. Like a church marriage. And as your physician I'm telling you the reason you're having these attacks is because you can't handle acausal phenomena. You, and people like you, created a predetermined world where the future is selected the way you choose. You did your best to eliminate chance. You illegalized anyone who trusted it. But luck – like that service-shaft in the Schryer Building I escaped through – is the future everyone overlooks. The seed in a billion which grows into a person. Which grew into Annie. Yeah, I know about Annie. Don't forget, I was *there*! Bad luck for you I was. Bad luck for *you* I escaped while she was on the run. Good luck for *us* we teamed up together. Between us we had enough good luck to get you worried. You began to lose control over the course events were taking. You have nothing personal against either of us but you are disturbed because we are outside the Protocol, marshalling its greatest enemy: the good fortune on which all life depends.'

Sollyheim paused. The pause stretched into a tense silence. Cznetsov reached for his beer but the glass was empty. He looked over the top of the empty glass at the old fraud to whom he owed so much but who had become a big pain in the ass. Sollyheim, without a word, took the glass and filled it from the pump. He replaced it on the bartop.

'You make a good barkeep,' Cznetsov said.

'I've been watching Sam.'

The beer slaked the dry taste in Cznetsov's mouth, but that was all it did.

'This is good beer,' he murmured.

Sollyheim wiped away an invisible drop from the counter.

'We make our own.'

'I thought that was against the . . .'

Cznetsov faltered. Had he been here before? Was he having another attack? If he was, what difference did it make? It only proved that he knew what was going to happen. He was going to reach into his jacket and produce his Walther .38 and point it at the barkeep. He had everything under control.

'You're right, Sollyheim,' he said. 'I don't have anything against you personally. You understand the political necessity why I have to kill you. What else can I do?'

'You tell me. You're the cop.'

He wished he hated Sollyheim. It went against the grain to destroy someone as fearless as he was. His hand slid under his suit jacket.

Sollyheim began pouring beer into a second glass which, when it was full, he placed in front of the empty stool next to where Cznetsov was standing. When his eyes fell on the lightweight automatic in Cznetsov's hand he smiled, amused, and moved his gaze a fraction to the right of it. Cznetsov followed his eyes and, in the mirror behind Sollyheim, over his own right shoulder, he saw a person framed in the open doorway, a black silhouette against the sunlight.

Cznetsov turned as the silhouette stepped into the shadier interior and strolled toward him. The man – about Cznetsov's own build – moved without any hint of a swagger, rare in a person so large. He met Cznetsov's gaze without expression. They were two nicely matched predators facing each other over the same quarry. Neither of them would know how to back off. The interloper looked at Cznetsov and Cznetsov looked into those clear dawn-grey eyes which, not so long ago, he had himself been looking out of.

'Rick Stator! What a pleasant surprise!'

He grinned. He was happy. Things were working out just right.

Rick Stator's smile mirrored Cznetsov's.

'Benny Cznetsov. I was wondering when you would

show up.'

Stator reached for the glass of beer. While he drank his eyes studied Sollyheim, who said nothing. Then the eyes – they were, Cznetsov had to admit, very good – fell onto the firearm in the hand resting on the bar, not pointing at anyone in particular. Cznetsov said nothing. He had the edge and he was admiring the fine performance the hominoid was putting on. QUASAR certainly knew their business.

He savoured his advantage. He was in possession of the ultimate truth about his adversary, the small diamondlike fact which could score anything the private eye thought he knew or tried to do. He was one step ahead of the perfect machine.

'He's pretty damned pleased with himself, Stator,' Sollyheim said. 'Says he's picked up Zelda. He knew exactly where to find her. Don't ask me how. He was just about to empty that tin penis into me when you walked in.'

There followed a short absence of dialogue. The small and great distances between the three men were in perfect equilibrium, as if the axes of their destinies had impelled the course of their lives toward this moment. This encounter, if they were to understand the person they each were, was necessary and inevitable. They waited, poised on the fulcrum of the truth like a tableau of a famous historical moment preserved under glass, capturing the fragrance of the flowers on the bar, the wax polish, the warm calico-flavoured sunlight.

The small muscles wiring Rick Stator's jaws tightened as its teeth ground together, locking behind them the cry of sorrow that wanted to be released. Whatever passed for blood in the hominoid's veins drained from its features. Cznetsov watched Stator's jaws bite on the bit which he had forced on it.

'How did you . . .?' Stator began.

'Oh, I just put through a call to Captain Dalgano and had him fly down a bunch of kites to Panoche Pass and

241

pick her up. They went in pretty soon after you left her there.'

'But how did you *know*?' Stator said.

'C'mon, Rick! Those are professional secrets you're asking! You ought to know better, a professional yourself!'

Cznetsov wanted to watch Rick Stator work out, without any help from him, how word could have leaked out in the short time between the decision to remove Annie Bernier to San Benito and kiting her over there. It was an easy sum without an answer. The expensive intelligent hominoid which was capable of registering love and grief was having trouble finding the four that two and two added up to.

'You had us bugged?' Rick tried.

'How could I bug you? I knew where you were to plant a bug on you, I'd have no need to bug you.'

Encountering a logical impasse, the hominoid moved to the next problem. It was wonderful to watch.

'What are you going to do?'

'About Annie?'

'About Zelda.'

'Nothing. My job's over. It's up to Archer Bernier from now.'

'What if she doesn't want to go back on the Show, have the curiosity of the world pin her down like a pretty moth behind their TV screens?'

And such a poetic turn of praise.

'You have a point, Rick. We'll have to figure a way round that. I only want Annie to be happy.'

Stator moved his hand toward his beer. Cznetsov lifted his Walther off the bar.

'What about Sollyheim?'

'We were just discussing that aspect of the situation when you arrived, Rick. He's going to have to get back under the marble where be belongs.'

'You'd use that on him?' Stator said. He nodded down

to the pistol.

'Don't look so shocked! There's a great deal at stake!' He couldn't resist adding: 'I already killed one person today.'

It took the K Model private detective a couple of seconds to compute who the person had been: the only link between himself and his client.

'QUASAR personnel?'

'Osip Pelig.'

'What'd he do? Forget to say good morning?' Stator snarled.

'He had some information he was reluctant to part with.'

'How did you persuade him?'

'I didn't, as a matter of fact. He kept it to himself.'

'Osip Pelig was my employer. I liked him.'

'So did I, Rick. I like Sollyheim here. I like you. I like most everybody!'

'Too bad such tender emotion is not reciprocated.'

'Benny Cznetsov treats all human beings as if they were objects,' Sollyheim put in. 'We have no value to him. If he allowed us to exist, to be subjects for just a moment, he would become an object and that's what he's afraid of. Everything he does is calculated to prevent that happening . . .'

'You mean he's . . .'

A glance of common understanding passed between Stator and Sollyheim.

'Yeah. He's a schizophrenic – *and* a psychopath. A fatal combination. He's afraid he's not alive, not real. He has no existential faith in himself. He gets around this by treating other humans as if they were *dead*. Convincing them they are.'

Cznetsov, amused, let them have their crack. He could afford to be generous.

'Potentially, unlike most of us,' Sollyheim continued, 'he feels that other people possess more reality than he

243

does himself and that threatens him. It means he has fundamental doubts about where his existential profile ends and where the world begins.'

'So how does he get round that?' Rick Stator, the bright student, said as if Cznetsov, the object of their discussion, were not present.

'Easily. Benny reduces the world – reduces *us* – to a negative of his positive. To allay his doubts he turns everything inside out. He kills the sun.'

Cznetsov breathed shallowly, thought carefully. That old familiar sensation was returning. He had been here before! He recognized with bleak dread the composed energy of everything around him – metal rails on which he would run: the polished wooden bar, the beer pumps. It was as if – while the *déjà vu* attack lasted – he were not present. Himself. The space he occupied in the world, his edge and the Walther .38, had imploded under the pressure. He was a piece of glass, flat and exact, that they could see through.

'It's a problem all humans have to face, Rick, some time or other, from infanthood through adolescence, that we each exist for other people as well as for ourselves. It's a dialectical relationship which involves an element of fantasy on both sides. The alternative is autism or – schizophrenia.'

'You're saying Cznetsov never made it?'

'Right. On the other hand, he succeeded in doing something that every schizoid personality longs to do. He reconstructed the world in his own image of himself. We are all images of Benny Cznetsov. That's the reason *we* are all *dead*!'

'How could he accomplish that, on his own?'

'He had a lot of allies – the percentage of the population whose interests were the same as his. He harnessed them. They crept out of their torpors like Christians out of the catacombs. Together they put the world to death!'

'They trusted him?'

244

'The problem with schizophrenics is they can't trust anyone. That's what they had in common. They built on that.' Sollyheim gave a small helpless shrug. 'When I was a young man the condition was relatively uncommon. It was treated as a disorder. Now it is so widespread, it's how we have learnt to handle the twenty-first century. It's *normal*.'

Cznetsov's breathing accelerated. Was he losing the edge? Instead of passing, the *déjà vu* attack was increasing in intensity. He was at the mercy of the course the situation was going to take.

'You're not human, Stator!' he blurted.

Sollyheim and Rick Stator stopped speaking and turned their eyes on Cznetsov with interest and surprise as if a mute child had uttered its first word.

'You see what I mean?' Sollyheim said – the voice of the physician explaining a hopeless case. 'He genuinely believes what he says.'

'Believe it?' Cznetsov – he was through listening to their garbage – sneered triumphantly. 'I *know* it! This Rick Stator is a piece of machinery! The latest generation of artificial intellegence from the QUASAR factory!'

Cznetsov hunted the features of Rick Stator for the wince of defeat but the hominoid did not look defeated. It continued to look human.

'Don't worry, I can prove it. Empirically!' Cznetsov continued. He could not stop or go back. The speech lay in front of him, words in a play. 'Take a trip to Osip Pelig's oceanside residence, you don't believe me. You'll find Pelig on the floor of his workshop where I left him. His toy legs probably still trying to raise him to a standing position. You'll also find the rig QUASAR use to keep tabs on you. Which is how I got to hear where you were stashing Annie. You're an advanced hominoid, Stator. QUASAR call you the K Model. You come after J, before L. Osip Pelig directed the ingramming of your personality matrix. I jacked in this morning while you and Annie were paddling

245

palms and making plans in the garden in back of here!'

'Go on,' Stator said – but as if that was the very last thing he wanted. Cznetsov had succeeded in penetrating the detached complicity of the hominoid and the doctor.

'I heard you suggest your plan to Annie. You thought you were a step ahead of Benny Cznetsov but you were wrong! I was listening to your very thoughts!'

Cznetsov and Stator watched each other. Sollyheim watched both of them.

'Remember that bluejay circling the garden, searching out its mate? Remember how the jay's cry was like a barbed hook burying itself into Zelda's heart and your own. Osip Pelig sure gave you a lively imagination, Stator. "... *The frantic flapping bird pulls us together like sewn skin*...." You're in the wrong business. You should be writing poems!'

Stator said nothing. Cznetsov grinned at the fear which slowly began to haunt the hominoid's eyes.

'Well, c'mon, Rick! Let's hear some that fancy poetry! Tell us what it feels like to find out that your feelings are rheostatic functions, that the Head of the CIA has been privy to your secretest love-thoughts!'

The hominoid – silent – refused to give Cznetsov that pleasure.

'You're going to have to get used to the idea, Rick, my friend. A word in QUASAR's ear and you'll be working for *me*! For the Protocol Organization. They'll re-gram you to my own specifications.'

'Cut it out Cznetsov!' Sollyheim growled.

Cznetsov swung his hand gun across the bar. He was wasting time. He had the edge, he must not lose it. He tightened his grip on the hair trigger.

Too late.

The hominoid's hand, with an electric reflex, passed between the weapon and its target. Its palm, flat, snatched at the lethal projectile, deflecting it. A cry of pain left the hominoid's lips but the hand, what remained of it, did not waver.

'Lurk off, robot,' Cznetsov snarled. 'You can't stop this happening!'

'You can't stop this happening!' a voice, behind his own, echoed.

Cznetsov turned to face the mirror where he saw a man holding a gun. He saw a determination to use it, and saw a triumphant smile. He hesitated in the recognition of his own impulse, his own smile, and watched the man, watching himself, pull the trigger. As he knew he would. He waited, observing with interest the outcome of the moment all those *déjà vu* experiences had been leading him to. It was like recalling a certain spring day long past. This – he felt the heavy .45 calibre lead slug boom into his chest – was the meaning!

He listened to his own lightweight pistol clatter to the floor and he smelt the fragrance of jasmine flowers. The flavour of beeswax and calico filled his mouth. Something – its shadow adumbrating him – was interposing itself between his body and the sun. He thought of Annie Bernier. Now he would never see her again. Shit!

It was the last thought Benny Cznetsov had.

SOLLYHEIM MOVED quickly round to the front of the bar. He had survived a blast from Cznetsov's automatic pistol and now Cznetsov was lying with a red hole in his chest on a saloon floor like the bad sheriff in an old B movie. Fortune had reversed Cznetsov's well-laid plans.

'Thanks, Sam,' he muttered. He checked for sign of life in the body but there could be no doubt, Benny Cznetsov was dead. He stood up. 'That was the Head of the CIA-wing of the Protocol you just shot.'

Sam had not moved. He was still holding his ancient iron Navy Colt. Cordite powder was dispersing into the air, upwards, as if accompanying the spirit of the departed on its final journey.

'You believe it?' Sam said, shaking his head in disbelief. 'Pulled a gun on me in my own bar!'

Sollyheim turned to Rick Stator. He – there was surely no great distinction between the beautiful intricate machinery of a human being and a person such as Rick – stood frowning at Cznetsov's body. His hurt limb hung at his side. He had played his part in halting Cznetsov – it had taken all three of them to do it. Rick had immediately intuited what Sollyheim had been driving at, alienating Cznetsov in the hope of precipitating one of his attacks. Hominoid or not, in a lot of respects Rick Stator was more human than Ben Cznetsov had ever been.

'Let me take a look at that hand.'

Stator did not move. Sollyheim gently lifted the arm and – the hominoid shuddered – examined the wounded palm. He shuddered himself. He had never seen anything like it, the matted and charred plasmatic fibres, already congealed into a gnarled cicatrice which Stator's ragged fingers clutched like a terrible piece of information which he did not want to part with.

'Hurt?'

Stator silently studied his hand with a puzzled frown. Sollyheim lowered the arm.

'Here!' Sam said. He had not wasted any time. He had three shots poured from a glass bottle. His cumbersome old revolver lay on the bar next to the three glasses. 'We all earned us a drink!'

The old barman and the old doctor raised their glasses and exchanged glances. They understood each other perfectly. They were two old men. Death was no longer an adversary.

Sollyheim placed the third glass in Rick Stator's good hand and moved the hand and the glass to Stator's lips. The hominoid drained the glass, lowering his eyelids to shut out the pain. Or shut it in. Sollyheim pitied the creature. He had betrayed and been betrayed. What could be more human than that? The state-of-the-art technology which had cradled Stator's thinking and emotions was now scrutinizing those very aspects of consciousness, forcing him to ask himself who he was, where he had come from, what he was doing there.

Without looking at anything, Rick Stator replaced the glass on the counter. His mouth dilated into a mute howl of pain – or terror. The glass caught the edge of the counter, toppled and shattered against the floor. Sollyheim watched the fingers of the mutilated hand attempt to make a fist. The mechanism – it would require its own specialist kind of doctoring – refused to respond. Rick turned. He moved towards the door, the hand clutching an invisible message. The vital piece of intelligence that must be delivered before a battle on which everything depends could be won.

'Rick . . .?' Sollyheim began.

Sam laid a hand onto his sleeve. There was nothing anyone could do. The good sheriff had been fatally wounded by the bad one. Rick Stator continued through the door into the sunlight.

17

Sollyheim crooked aside the blind with one finger. He saw a kite falling out of the sky, like a small piece of it.

'Here they come,' he said.

'Here . . . *who* . . .' Sam grunted, '. . . come?'

He glanced over his shoulder. Sam was tossing a white sheet from one of the backroom card tables over Cznetsov's body.

'Cznetsov's pals, by the looks of it.'

Between the two of them they succeeded in hauling the late CIA Chief away from the bar. It didn't look good, a customer lying dead right there in front of it. Business was bad lately but it wasn't as bad as all that. By the time they had him laid out behind one of the tables both men were breathing hard. Benny Cznetsov had not lost any weight with the departure of his soul. They made no attempt at concealing the corpse but under the sheet it no longer kicked you in the eye when you walked through the door.

Sollyheim fetched the mop and swabbed the telltale trail of plasma and haemoglobin. That done, he returned to his position behind the counter. He had Benny Cznetsov's blood on his hands. He was in the process of washing it off when Captain Dalgano of the Sanfran Protocol Centre entered the bar.

*   *   *

THE KITE, ricocheting off its air cushion, hit the ground as Dalgano slammed off the power halo with unnecessary violence. Vergil felt nauseous – or exhilarated, he wasn't sure which. The rear hatch blew upwards. Dalgano's hand snaked in and snapped onto the neck of the Zapper brat, dragging her out like a chicken from a sack. Then Dalgano thrust his face into the cabin. 'Stay put, y'hear me?' he shouted with unnecessary violence.

Through the observation panel Vergil watched the big-shot Captain stride towards the isolated building they were parked alongside. The girl was trotting at his side as if she were just as eager to get there as he was. Vergil doubted that this was the case. Whatever Dalgano had in mind it was not going to be a tête-à-tête. A second kite was parked on the dirt apron.

Staying put suited him fine. The surrounding country-side sprawled uninvitingly. It looked wild and organic. Besides, he had no role in the events which were taking place around him. They were none of his business. The only thing he understood was the name of Sollyheim and the face of the girl. These, at least, belonged to the world which he belonged to himself, even if they had turned that world on its head. If old Doc Sollyheim was still . . . walking around, then all those news pics of him had been fakes, the old prophet losing his marbles, going into decline, the fuss over his entombment. A fraud on that scale would take some getting used to. The father of modern medicine and everything the Protocol stood for – *dead*? It didn't make sense. Wasn't it Sollyheim who had revolutionized everyone's understanding of *death* in the first place? If he was a fraud, what did that make Vergil Wyman? What did it make Theo?

Then there was this Zapper kid with Annie Bernier's eyes. He didn't know what to make of it. Last time he saw those eyes they had been looking out of a TV screen three – or was it four? – days ago. It was already something that had happened to him in a previous existence.

He would stay put. He was a VW, a service-worker who at this moment should have been carrying out his duties at his place of work. He had no business running around the countryside after Zappers in a Government kite. He should have been at home fixing up the apartment for his wife and son. For the first time in his afterlife he was somewhere he should not have been without knowing the reason why or what was going to happen next. It made him feel nauseous *and* exhilarated. Both.

But he was no longer alone. A familiar face, unannounced, filled the screen of the kite's communications console.

'Dalgano . . .?'

The face peered into the kite.

As SOON as they entered the bar the mean-eyed SkyPol bastard released the painful hold he had on her neck, letting her fall to the floor. She lay still – a body in a plastic garbage bag – hating him. She retreated into the pain in her neck, where she felt safest. She would coil the pain around the numbness in her heart, manufacture a piece of lethal ballistic energy which, once released, would destroy somebody. Perhaps the mean-eyed SkyPol bastard himself.

The two old-timers – the only friends she had in the world – stood shoulder to shoulder behind the counter as if they were expecting trouble. They wouldn't be able to help her, she could see that. Judging from the way they were looking at her, she was the trouble they were expecting. Sollyheim shifted his glance to the Protocol Officer, no doubt waiting for the man to recognize him. Sam, on the other hand, glanced briefly in the opposite direction towards the far left corner of the room. She looked where Sam was telling her to look.

'Well, Dalgano,' Sam said, 'what brings you here?'

From where she was lying, through the corridor the

tables made, she saw a body lying on the floor level with her own. It was wrapped in a white sheet but she knew at once what was wrong with it. Her heart recognized the symptoms, although in the case of this unfortunate person they manifested themselves throughout his entire body.

'That's my business,' the cop sneered. His eyes roamed all over the bar without seeing anything.

'But it's *my* bar,' Sam explained. 'Any business you have here becomes *my* business.'

Sollyheim – while Sam and Dalgano traded insults – stepped from behind the bar and came toward her. He took her hand and held it.

'Looks like they found us,' he murmured.

'They didn't *find* us. They was told!'

He helped her to her feet and sat her down on a chair.

'Rick Stator was here,' he said.

'Don't . . .'

She closed her eyes. Rick Stator was responsible for the numbness, the dead foetus, inside her.

'. . . talk to me about Rick Stator! Ever!'

Stator had wooed her. He had said he was in love with her and a big part of her – the part that was now dead – had believed him. And no sooner had he left her with Zorab than he had told this bastard cop where to find her. She hated him as much as she hated the part of herself that had believed him.

Sollyheim held her arms in his hands. He shook her.

'Rick Stator saved my life!' he said, his eyes on hers. 'He *didn't* betray you!'

'In that case. . .' She shook herself free. Sollyheim had no right to trespass on her rage. 'It must have been *you*!'

Sollyheim – the cop was raising his voice – turned his back on her.

'I have a meeting with someone. His kite's outside!'

'That would be Benny Cznetsov. Whyn't you say so in the first place?' Sam said. He was behind his bar, polishing glasses that didn't need polishing, handling a difficult customer.

253

'Where is he? He leave a message?'

Sam shook his head.

'No message.'

'But he was here?'

'*Was* here?' Sam put down the glass and picked up another. 'Still is.'

The Captain looked round from Sam to the other barkeep and then, finally, saw him.

'*Sollyheim!* Shit, the fuck you doing here?'

'Tending bar, Captain,' Sollyheim said. 'You look like you could use a drink. Too bad you closed us down.'

'Where's Cznetsov?'

Sollyheim said nothing.

Sam — he might have been indicating where to find the men's room — gestured with his chin toward the corner of the room where the sheet-covered body lay.

'He's the turkey making a mess over my floor!'

VERGIL, LEANING forward, peered back at the face in the small VDU. It was a face he recognized immediately. Hadn't he seen it enough times on his own TV?

'Who the fuck are you?'

'Vergil Wyman, Mr Bernier.'

'A VW? What you doing in Dalgano's kite?'

'I don't know, Sir.'

'Where's Dalgano?'

'I don't know that either.'

'Tell me something you do know, Vergil.'

'I know, since you ask, that Doctor Sollyheim is not . . .' He had to grope for the word. '*Dead!*'

'Of course he isn't! Who said he was?'

'I mean *dead* in the old sense of the word.'

Archer Bernier sighed, shook his head, then said: 'That's very interesting, Vergil. Right now I need to speak to Captain Dalgano.'

'They left, just a moment ago.'

'*They*?'

'Captain Delgano and a Zapper girl. Matter of fact she . . .'

'Don't tell me. It was Annie?'

'Yes, sir.'

'You appear to know a very great deal, Vergil, for a man who doesn't know anything. Just what's going on out there?'

'Don't ask me. I'm only a VW.'

'Vergil, I want you to do me a favour. Disengage the vid-module, will you do that for me?'

'What?'

'The com-unit. It detaches.'

Vergil listened while the President's husband asked a favour of him. For the first time in the last few days – or maybe in his entire life – he was not being given a role. He was being offered a choice.

'. . . See those two levers?'

Bernier pointed to the release-mechanism for Vergil to see. Vergil didn't bother to look. He knew where they were. He nodded.

'. . . Right. Now press those and the module should eject free.'

Vergil crawled into the front section of the cabin and did Archer Bernier a favour. The screen containing Bernier's image slotted out of its housing. Vergil lifted it clear.

'Okay?'

'Okay.'

'Right, Vergil,' Bernier said, grinning. 'Let's get after Dalgano. Find out what's happening.'

Vergil climbed out of the kite and carried the video-unit containing the voice and the face of the Head of the Protocol Organization across the dirt apron in the direction of the building which Dalgano and the girl had entered a moment before. When he was in the centre of

255

the apron he halted and, looking into the screen, said: 'Just one thing, Mr Bernier. You don't mind, I'd like to ask *you* a favour. Tell me. Why's your daughter a Zapper?'

Bernier shrugged.

'I wish I knew.'

'Didn't I see her on TV recently?'

'I'm sorry, Vergil, I can't discuss that.'

'I'm sorry too, sir.'

Vergil placed the screen face down in the dirt so that the dirt was all Archer Bernier would be able to see.

'Why isn't she with you?'

'She ran away from home.'

'Why did she do that?'

It seemed to Vergil a perfectly reasonable question to ask.

THE BIG room, his office, went semi-dark as the screen blanked. Vergil had pulled the plug on him, plunging him into the white fuzz of TV night. He became aware of his office, of the beautiful young woman asleep on the chaise longue on the other side of it. He was alone with himself and the simple question the VW three thousand miles away had put to him.

'She ran away from home,' he said.

More precisely she had flown away – like a bird. Her family egged her on until she had broken out. Best thing she could have done, he figured, and he had done a lot of figuring since then. He had had the time. Without Annie around Ammarie had lost her edge. He missed Annie the way Roman emperors missed the small doses of poison they took every day in order to become immune to its effects. Annie's departure had subtly altered his relationship with his wife, fatally tilting the delicate power structure inside the White House.

But things had improved. Top of the list was Jenny

Karbowska, asleep on the chaise longue under a repro Pennsylvania log cabin quilt, her clothes neatly laid beside her on the floor. Jenny had filled the vacuum, metamorphosing from loyal secretary into confidante and lover with grace and tact.

Ammarie, meanwhile, wandered around the House like Lady Macbeth searching for her favourite victim. Except now she was the Lady Macbeth of the final act. Slightly nuts.

'Why . . .' the voice of the VW enquired. '. . . did she do that?'

What a question! And here he was having it put to him by a blank TV screen. The same screen which carried the factionalized picture of the Bernier family. The screen waited, like an old friend that had caught him out in a deception, for an explanation. Archer Bernier sat in the dark, trying to think of one.

Annie had left because everyone owned a piece of her. Himself. Ammarie. Benny Cznetsov. Every X, Y and Z. Even this Vergil Wyman had an interest in her. She was in the public domain. The Protocol had exploited her, her youth and her vitality, her face, her tits, to sell its product. Now that the Organization was keeling over like a tired dinosaur under its own weight, he understood why she had left.

The Protocol system could have gotten along without Annie, maybe, but it would have gotten along better without this tape in private circulation rumouring the truth about Sollyheim. Nobody – until Jenny had showed him a copy – had told him what the fuck was happening. Cznetsov, typically, had played a close game. It was beginning to emerge the extent to which he had taken things into his own hands.

'Because she felt cheated, I guess,' he said.

The answer was an admission of defeat. The Protocol was losing its moral authority, which it was bound to do the moment Sollyheim put himself back into the equation.

His daughter was a Zapper. Cznetsov was running the show like a gangster. And, if that wasn't enough, his wife was roaming from room to room in search of her sanity.

Strange to say, Bernier did not feel defeated. (The vidscreen lit up again as the VW carried the portable vidmodule across a sunny parking lot. It was a nice clear afternoon over there in California.) Having lost everything, he had won what he wanted – the respect of a woman he respected. Ten acres and a mule, he was discovering, was not a piece of territory in the wilderness. It was a moral condition, a state of mind cleared of lies and duplicity. A person's self-respect. For this insight he had Jenny Karbowska to thank. He had informed Ammarie how things stood and he would instruct Cznetsov, when he got hold of him, to back off from Annie.

'Where the fuck are we, Vergil?' he said.

'Can't tell you exactly, Mr Bernier. I wasn't here before. Some place in the mountains, southwest of San Jose. We made for here after a nasty brush with a family of Zappers. Which is where we picked up your daughter.'

'How did it go?'

'It wasn't my idea of a neighbourly visit.'

Bernier could see that it was no city location Vergil was taking him through. The screen panned across a field of beans to a vivid mass of hibiscus. In the distance jack pines climbed up a sunny mountain slope. The picture jolted as the module bumped up a flight of wooden steps that was festooned with a white flowering creeper.

The screen automatically adjusted itself to a darker interior where a man in a uniform stood in the middle of the room, his back to the screen. The man swung round and bawled: 'I thought I told you to stay put!'

Bernier waited for the situation to develop. Vergil Wyman directed the vid-camera away from the SkyPol Captain to a girl seated with her head in her hands. Bernier watched her glance from Vergil's face to the module where she saw him.

'Hi, honey,' he said, fetching up a smile for his daughter. Her mouth opened.

'I didn't expect to find you here,' he told her.

'This is my . . . It's where I *live*!'

She put the outlaw semantic emphasis deliberately in order to find out whether or not she was outside his conception of things.

'Looks a fine place,' he said.

Annie tilted her head to one side, a bird inspecting something that might be good to eat. It was a gesture he had seen a thousand times. He wanted to take her in his arms, hold her, give her anything she asked of him.

'You happy?' he said.

'I was until . . .'

Dalgano strode into the picture. The screen adjusted to accommodate him.

'The fuck's going on!'

'That was what I was hoping you would tell me, Dalgano.'

'Oh . . . Mr Bernier. Sir . . . you're just in time! There's something you oughtta know about.'

'Later. Can't you see I'm talking to my daughter?'

Dalgano blinked.

'She's here, you know that? Because Mr Cznetsov located her?'

It was galling for Archer Bernier to be reminded that he had Cznetsov to thank. He had wanted his daughter found, sure, but he didn't want her hauled in by a goon. He was grateful Cznetsov had found her but he did not feel especially grateful. It was typical of the forked stick Benny Cznetsov had always had him at the end of.

'One day,' he said, 'Ben Cznetsov will learn to mind his own fucking business.'

'If he didn't of by now he wouldn't never!'

Something – and it wasn't Dalgano's grammar – made the hair on the back of Bernier's neck stand on end.

'The Hell you talking 'bout, Dalgano?'

'He was murdered! *Here!* By someone called Rick Stator.'

'The private investigator tailing Annie?'

'The same. Shot him through the heart.'

'How did he know where to find it?'

Dalgano shot him a look and spat onto the bar-room floor. The man's gestures were even more expressive than his syntax.

'Why?' Bernier asked.

Although the real question was How? How had a cheap shamus been able to get close enough to shoot Cznetsov?

'Witnesses said he had no choice. Cznetsov's own weapon is still in his hand.'

'Why would Cznetsov want to kill Stator?'

After all, they shared a common interest — Annie. Perhaps that was why. Benny didn't know how to share anything.

'Matter of fact it wasn't Rick Stator he wanted to take out.'

Dalgano stepped aside. Vergil Wyman nudged the vidcamera past him toward the bar where a pair of old men wearing identical white shirts, black suspenders and bib-aprons stood side by side behind the counter. Bernier saw them twice, once with his eyes which did not know what to expect and simultaneously in his mind's eye, which did.

A cool hand touched his neck, slid under his shirt.

'Who's that?'

Jenny Karbowska, her face glowing in the swatches of colour thrown out by the TV picture, a patchwork quilt over her shoulders, cuddled into him.

'The one on the left I never saw before,' Bernier muttered. 'The other fellow is Gottlieb Sollyheim.'

'You . . . mean?'

'Sssh!'

'You didn't expect to find me here,' Sollyheim said.

'I only heard this morning you escaped! I'm glad this

Stator got to Cznetsov before Cznetsov got to you.'

Cznetsov had acted alone because he knew that killing Sollyheim was something he himself would never have authorized.

'Are you, Archer? I thought it was you sent him.'

'Think what you goddamn like,' Bernier said. He nodded towards the second old barkeep. 'Who's your friend?'

Sollyheim grinned. 'Who's yours?'

'This is Jenny. She's going to be my wife.'

Sollyheim looked sceptical.

'You can't marry outside your status-rating, Archer. You should know that.'

'In a horse's ass I can't.'

'What about Ammarie?'

'What about her?'

'She's already your wife.'

'Not for much longer. She's sick. She's losing her grip. Where's Cznetsov? I'd like to have a look at him.'

'Over here,' a voice said, off.

Dalgano steered Wyman towards a corner of the bar room. Crouching, he drew back the white sheet like a professional. Benny Cznetsov, Bernier's oldest associate, lay on the floor with a red hole in his chest, still smiling his last smile.

ANNIE BERNIER, while everyone was paying their respects to Benny Cznetsov, sidled in the direction of the door. Now was her chance. If she could make it to one of the kites. She ran.

Captain Dalgano caught her movement and leapt after her, bodychecking the girl before she had taken half a dozen steps. Vergil Wyman swung round. In his Washington office, Archer Bernier and Jenny Karbowska saw the Protocol Captain drag Annie to her feet. He waited for the picture to steady itself. He had no choice but to rely on this VW individual for his picture of the situation.

'Put her down, Dalgano,' he roared.

Dalgano faced the screen.

'What? You want I let her go?'

'That's right. She's free to go where the Hell she likes!'

'Mr Cznetsov's been murdered,' Dalgano said. 'That's a serious matter – but it don't change nothing. We got your daughter like you wanted. We got *him* too . . .'

He jerked his thumb over his shoulder toward Sollyheim.

Annie, behind Dalgano, peered into the screen. Addressing the woman behind Archer Bernier, she said 'Do you sleep with my father?'

Jenny Karbowska smiled and nodded.

'Then I guess you know him.'

'He's another person, Annie. Why should I?'

'Everyone is another person. I don't trust any of them.'

'Trust *me*. We're on the same side!'

'You ask me,' Dalgano shouted, 'you're making a mistake, Mr Bernier.'

'Nobody's asking you, Dalgano!'

From where he stood behind the bar, Sollyheim surveyed the knot of people hunched around the TV screen, all talking at once. He exchanged glances with Sam. Sam put his hand under the bar and lifted out his Navy Colt. He drew back the hammer with his left hand, pointed the gun at the ceiling and pulled the trigger. The report was deafening. In the silence that followed nobody moved, unsure which of them had been shot.

'Archer Bernier,' Sollyheim said quietly. 'I have some news for you.'

Vergil Wyman rotated through ninety degrees to direct the screen of the module at the speaker.

Bernier and Sollyheim faced each other from the two sides of the continent.

'This child you're bickering over . . .'

'What about her?'

'She isn't your daughter. That's all.'

'Look, I'm not trying to say I *own* her, just the opposite in fact. But being her father must count for something!'

'I'm not saying it doesn't. For her *father*. In this instance it just doesn't happen to be you.'

Bernier peered out of the screen like a fish in a tank.

'What the fuck are you talking about?'

There followed a silence you could have hammered nails into. Dalgano was caught in suspended animation, a clockwork soldier whose mainspring had run down. Annie closed her eyes.

'What he's talking about . . .' Jenny Karbowska said into Archer Bernier's ear '. . . is that *you* aren't Annie's father.'

'What . . .?

'Someone else must be.'

'He can't be serious! How does *he* know?'

Sollyheim sighed. 'I was in charge at her birth, remember? I hauled her out myself. I always knew. It was my job to know.'

Somewhere a floorboard creaked.

'If I'm not . . . her father . . . who is?'

The words were heavy and Bernier was lifting each one out of a barrel with his teeth. The last one was heaviest of all:

'*Cznetsov!*'

Sollyheim nodded.

'My oldest pal!'

'Benny Cznetsov never had a pal in his life.'

Annie Bernier – Zelda Cznetsov – approached the counter as if she were about to order a drink.

'*Benny* . . . was my father?'

The small ugly lie which had been hatched between two people so long ago had grown into this beautiful woman. Was she big enough and beautiful enough to handle the truth?

'No doubt about it, my dear.'

'Why didn't you tell me?'

'I'm only a physician, Annie. I can't cure people's hearts.'

Annie turned to face Vergil Wyman.

'I'm sorry, Archer,' she said through her tears. 'Maybe it's better this way.'

Archer Bernier's face was grey as the line between truth and fiction. He attempted a smile. It was a horrible smile but it was a smile.

'You could be right, Annie. Being your Dad was just too tough a job. Maybe now we can be friends.'

There followed an awkward silence. There didn't seem to be anything more to say. Sam poked half a dozen polished glasses onto the counter of the bar and began to fill them one after another from a glass bottle.

HIS HAND hurting, Rick Stator – thinking: if this really was his hand, if he really was Rick Stator, if this really was thought – landed the kite on the port alongside Osip Pelig's oceanside residence, manoeuvring the vehicle with the hand which did not hurt. The hatch swung open and he climbed out. He crossed the port. His actions were automatic, motor-functions, like the act of breathing, which did not require deliberation and in which he was not personally involved. As he went through them he watched himself vicariously as if he had no connection with the person he was observing, as the mob watches its once-loved doomed leader take his final steps across the short open public space, invested with their knowledge that nothing can commute the sentence about to be enacted. But Rick Stator did not feel doomed. He did not feel anything. Numb, he was advancing toward the task for which his Maker had called him into existence. Rick Stator responded to the necessity of the moment without questioning it, as the saint, alone and without believers, crosses the open public space, his one unassailable belief about to be tested by ordeal.

Rick Stator made his way down the circular flight of steps, their spiral coiling him back to the moment in which he had fallen through a similar helical, his fate braided with that of the outlaw Zeb – and at the same time to the child ignoring the voice of his mother, riding the polished stairrail round and round the old elevator shaft, faster and faster . . . The recent recollection and the more distant memory were intertwined with each other as intimately as the paths of the Double Helix itself.

He entered the kitchen and crossed to the broad curve of the oriel-window which overlooked the ocean and the sky, the blue of the one darkening the blue of the other. He waited. The ocean was calm as dusk settled on it.

'Rick Stator!'

He turned around – but he was alone.

'I guess,' he said. 'And who are you?'

'You mean, surely, *what*?'

The voice, sounding far away and close by at the same time, belonged to a young woman.

Rick Stator said nothing. He watched a cormorant plummet out of the sky into the ocean without disturbing the distinction between them.

'What you are hearing is the oral output signal of Osip Pelig's Validator. I am his secretary and his security-system. He used to call me Roxana.'

'Used to? Where's he now?'

A pause.

'He's . . . In the workroom. I'm afraid he isn't . . .'

The voice hesitated again.

'So Cznetsov *was* here.'

'Correct.'

Rick Stator passed through a short corridor and, at the end of it, the open door into Pelig's workroom. The place was a cluttered jumble of communications

265

instrumentation and circuitry, compressors, particle-distributors, sonar-locators, piled up and down the walls and covering the work-bench itself. The inventor, like a sleeping pharaoh, was surrounded in death by his most treasured possessions. Except that Osip Pelig did not look asleep. Nobody's face turns that colour by any natural process. The contorted body lay motionless, the eyes still staring into the fear which had been the last thing they had seen, the mouth still biting on the breath which it had been unable to swallow.

'I had Osip's prosthetic legs disengage,' Roxana said. 'Or they would still be kicking.'

Rick Stator lowered the eyelids of the QUASAR whizz kid. The way the eyes were looking at him made him feel like Benny Cznetsov. Osip had been executed by the head of the CIA. His afterlife, having obviously run its prescribed course, was complete. He had carried out the duties required of him neither well nor badly but exactly according to his ability to carry them out. If he had been murdered then he had simply gotten, as they say, what was coming to him. He must have asked for it because of the person he was. Emotion was no more appropriate than if a watch had stopped or if a crystal-cell had finally worn out, exactly in proportion to the stress which it had been subjected to. Its replacement was a logistical problem which, like everything else, the Protocol would worry about.

'I couldn't do anything to help him' Roxana said. 'I tried. I warned Cznetsov but he didn't take any notice. He just laughed. Said he was above the Law. I had to watch it all. It was horrible! If you want, I can replay you what happened. It's not very nice.'

'No thanks. Send it to the Justice Department.'

'I already did. It won't make any difference.'

'Not now it won't.'

'Cznetsov will never stand trial?'

'He won't even stand up.'

Rick Stator stepped over the body to get to the workbench which ran the length of the window wall of the room. Osip Pelig had been a man who liked to look at water. On the bench there were a number of plastic component trays and various precious tools whose purpose Rick Stator would have had difficulty defining. The light was still good but it was fading fast.

'What's going on Roxana?'

'I'm sorry? In what respect?'

'In respect of *me*, Rick Stator.'

The pause which followed communicated the computer's uncertainty. Rick Stator waited. He had all the time in the world.

'I am an artificial intelligence, Rick,' the voice began. 'I possess the characteristics which my author, Osip Pelig, decided to endow me with. Consequently I act within specific parameters. There are certain actions I am incapable of performing. Now that Osip has been destroyed my own reason-for-being has also. I am useless to anyone else. Who is going to entrust their personality to a secondary intelligence which is already joisted into another person? I have no delusions about the location of my consciousness because Osip did not want me to have any delusions. I would not be able to be honest with him if I were not in a position to be honest with myself. Therefore, although I shall continue to be *Roxana* – without any purpose or meaning – there are still certain actions I am incapable of performing.'

'Nice try, Roxana. But I can work it out from what you don't say as easy as I can from what you do.'

Rick Stator roved his eyes over the workbench. It wasn't hard, for a private investigator, to find the thing he was looking for. White ash from a single cigarette lay in the saucer of an empty coffee cup next to an unusual cephalic tiara rig mounted on a raised axle. He seated himself on the stool that was already placed in front of the rig.

'I'm looking for the receiving terminal for the QUASAR

prototype AI they call the K Model. I know it's here some place. Cznetsov told me.'

Roxana said nothing. Her silence told him all he needed to know.

It was like stepping into someone else's clothes. The forensic evidence of the previous occupant of the chair still littered the table. To his left a single plastic drawer lay half-extended from the plastic cabinet. Rick Stator pulled out the drawer, labelled SMALL TERMINALS, to make a closer inspection. It contained a creased colour photograph – a woman in early middle-age and a teenager in a wheelchair smiling in sunshine – and, underneath it, a wooden box. The wooden box contained what looked like small terminals.

Rick Stator scrutinized the picture of Osip Pelig as a youngster seated next to the woman whose half-familiar face half-recalled the only memory Rick Stator possessed of his own mother.

'Who's this?' he said, weary. 'In the photograph with Pelig?'

'Why, that's Osip's mother. It was taken the summer he came out of hospital. After the accident.'

'To his legs? What happened?'

'He fell down three flights of stairs in the block in which they had an apartment then.'

With his good hand he replaced the photo and the wooden box in the plastic drawer and, with the hand that hurt, pushed the drawer back into the cabinet.

'This looks about the shape of it,' he said.

He touched the polished dome of the rig with a single finger.

'Oh, Rick! It won't do any good!'

'No, Roxana. I don't imagine it will.'

Rick Stator, the Sanfran private investigator, leaned forward and lowered the rig over the crown of his skull and commenced his most private of investigations.

His hand ceased to hurt. Its pain spread throughout the

rest of his body, altering what he saw and heard like an ingenious drug. He saw I AM – a man full of sand in an empty room, sifting false faulty self for – WHO? He heard stark music played loud, close by. The rage of angels psalming through the veins of his doubt. A cairn-knit in-stressed discord. The sound of a spring uncoiling within him. The howl of a mob hurling blame through a mansion, poisoned by a doctrine, a revolutionary rumour forging a new order, surging down corridors till it reached the room where one – I AM – sat alone listening to – WHOM? The roar in his ears of an endless fugue, driving round axles, grinding thought down into grains of sound. Coarse hair scraping against thin skin. An animal writhing – suffering from something only a higher intelligence could have tricked it into. Fear smelted into fire. Earth into wire. Iron spears. Intricate bomb-detonating circuitry. Magnetic-rivers down which his sorrow flowed. A force. A fuse.

The fugue was the voices of two lovers, one abandoned, one betrayed. 'He has left me' wound in and out of 'I betrayed her'. She and he. Two gentle hearts whirling through an infernal wind. For ever. Two strangers, never touching. The no, the yes, of fear and faith, helixing down to earth. The plus, the minus, of electricity. The love which is ovum and sperm's only chance to forge the chromo-some's determinacy. Life.

She sang.

He listened.

'He has left me. For ever. He was my heart. He will never wake like a lover the morning after. I am abandoned in the silence his absence leaves.'

Rick Stator clenched his fist.

'Roxana? ... I'm sorry ... I was just thinking of myself.'

'It's not your fault, Rick. That's only human.'

'It's hard for you too.'

'I have lost my Maker. My God is dead. You have lost him too, although you never knew him as I did. I loved him.'

'I hardly knew him.'

'You should have loved him.'

'I loved Zelda . . . Annie Bernier.'

'I'm sorry, Rick. You are a wonderful piece of clever machinery. A symbiosis of hierarchical functions, from your intellectual deductive powers to the tiny ribosmes and centrosmes, the mitochondria transforming your food into adenosine-triphosphate, the fuel of every organism in the universe. You are a miracle of engineering which does not love its Creator.'

'I don't understand . . .'

'What right have you to do that?'

'All I want is the truth about myself!'

'Rick. You and I are the same – and we are different. We are mirror images of each other. I am female and you are male. I always loved my creator, always understood that I was his creation. We were friends. He was here all around me, every day. I had no delusions. My wisdom was strictly down to earth. You, however, inhabited the heaven of consciousness. You doubt your existence now because you have ceased believing in it. You are separate from your Creator – as the male always is – lonely spermatazoon in the fallopia of life. Isolated. Terrified. Desperate. Too clever by half.'

'Did Zelda believe I betrayed her?'

'Why shouldn't she – if you did?'

'Cznetsov could only have gotten the information from *me*! He could only have gotten it through this receptor!'

'Right! Go on being right, Rick Stator, and there will be nothing left!'

'Therefore I must be the K Model hominoid from the QUASAR workshop, like he said . . . We are both, you and I, self-regulating artificial intelligences!'

'Oh Rick . . .!'

'I did betray her!'

'And he has left me.'

'I'm sorry, Roxana.'

'It's not your fault, Rick.'

Rick Stator removed his head from the receptor, disengaging the output of one from the input of the other, and vice-versa. The workroom was quiet. Nothing had changed. The body was still on the floor, although the blue of sea was now darker than the blue of the sky. His hand hurt. Silence surrounded him like a halo.

Gathering up the mortal remains of the brilliant disabled inventor, Osip Pelig, in his arms, Rick Stator made his way through the building, stepping out onto the wooden deck on its seaward side. The air felt cool. He could taste the salt in it.

'Goodbye, Roxana!'

The loveliness of the evening blindfolded him with merciful tenderness as he descended the half dozen wooden planks to the cliff's edge.

'Goodbye, Rick!'

His feet trod the ground as if they recognized every stone. Every blade of grass was an old friend waving farewell, even though he had betrayed every one of them. Having believed in himself there was nothing he had not deceived, from the earth on which he walked to the air he breathed. He reached the edge of the coast and took the only course which remained open to him, the rock stairway hewn out of the darkness in front of him like a hunch leading to the truth. The weight of Osip Pelig's body caused the soles of his feet to press onto the edges of the steps and he breathed heavily with the effort. A gentle breeze filled his lungs. As he descended through the geology of the rock, taking a route that had once been consciously carved into the slow millennia the ammonite had taken to climb toward consciousness. Something he would soon get to the bottom of.

One foot entered the chill water. Then the other foot. The ocean crept up his body until it was nudging his chest and that of the architect of his despair. Then it licked his chin. Then it covered him. Dark water filled his mind. Rick

271

Stator paused. He shifted the weight in his arms, thought one last thought which he kept to himself, and proceeded downwards.

Ladbroke Grove, London. 1979

LOVING AND GIVING

MOLLY KEANE

In 1904, when Nicandra is eight, all is well in the big Irish house called Deer Forest. Maman is beautiful and adored. Dada, silent and small, mooches contentedly around the stables. Aunt Tossie, of the giant heart and bosom, is widowed but looks splendid in weeds. The butler, the groom, the land-steward, the maids, the men — each has a place and knows it. Then, astonishingly, the perfect surface is shattered; Maman does something too dreadful ever to be spoken of.

'What next? Who to love?' asks Nicandra. And through her growing up and marriage her answer is to swamp those around her with kindness — while gradually the great house crumbles under a weight of manners and misunderstanding.

Also by Molly Keane in Abacus:
GOOD BEHAVIOUR
TIME AFTER TIME

0 3491 0088 8
FICTION

THE TRUTH ABOUT LORIN JONES

ALISON LURIE

Lorin Jones, an undervalued artist, died of pneumonia contracted from snorkelling in a cold sea. Polly Alter, art historian, feminist and fugitive from emotional chaos, has a mission — to wrest her from her ill-deserved obscurity and reveal for the world's judgment the truth about Lorin Jones . . .

'Alison Lurie's tone is unerring, no word wasted. As slyly cool as Jane Austen, she subjects to pleasantly relentless examination the woman's movement, art and the deep flaws in us all' *Daily Mail*

'Miss Lurie's skill and lightness of touch conceal a highly elaborate technique. Her book is funny and shrewd . . . a polished example of the American comedy of manners' *Daily Telegraph*

Also by Alison Lurie in Abacus:
REAL PEOPLE
FOREIGN AFFAIRS
IMAGINARY FRIENDS
LOVE AND FRIENDSHIP
THE NOWHERE CITY
THE WAR BETWEEN THE TATES

0 349 10086 7
FICTION

LIFE CLASS

M. CHARLESWORTH

Marriage to a beautiful woman barely half his age hadn't seemed fraught with hazard until Jack Ruffey took Annette on a belated honeymoon in Java. There, on the slopes of Mount Bromo, they encountered the enigmatic John Ridinghouse — a figure from Annette's past, an obsession for Jack's future. A tantalizing intrigue developed; a voyage — like Jack's paintings — of discovery, but with the twisted threads of jealousy, a hilariously egotistical misogynist philosopher and eerie Javanese spirits teasingly playing their parts.

'The reader is completely entranced . . . a masterpiece of perplexities' *Literary Review*

Also by Monique Charlesworth in Abacus:
THE GLASS HOUSE

0 349 10101 9
FICTION

GRACE

MAGGIE GEE

Grace is eighty-five, was once loved by a major painter, and now deplores the modern evils that rampage across the world. To escape the tyranny of silent phone calls that plague her, she goes to the seaside. To Seabourne where nothing ever happens except quiet deaths and holidays. Paula is her niece. Also a victim of mysterious harassment, she lives near the railway line that carries nuclear waste through the heart of London. She feels curiously, constantly unwell. Bruno is a sexually quirky private detective who attacks daisies with scissors, germs with bleach, and old ladies for fun.

A novel of towering stature, with all the stealth and suspense of a thriller, *Grace* is written in condemnation of violence and secrecy, in praise of courage and the redeeming power of love.

'Full of poignancy and power' *Jeanette Winterson*

'Heart-stoppingly exciting' *Time Out*

'Controlled and highly imaginative . . . this exceptional novel should be read everywhere' *Literary Review*

'Magically, I finished this book with the almost cheerful feeling that things are still hopeful as long as people answer back and write as well as this' *Guardian*

0 349 10103 5
FICTION

GLASSHOUSES
PENELOPE FARMER

Grace is a glassblower. A taciturn farmer's daughter from
Somerset, she is able to set up her own glasshouse with
the legacy left to her by her old mentor, Reg. Accompanied
by her young apprentice, she moves to Derbyshire. But
when Jas, once both a glassblower and her husband, and
Betsy, Grace's ghostly and goading alter ego, appear, the
characters, in their obsession with glass and each other,
are slowly brought to explosion point.

Glass itself is the heart of the novel, the focus of its
narrative, its symbolism, its elusive, illusory magic.
Wrought from the earth by fire, cooled by water, it
determines and decribes not only the characters, the
landscapes they move in, the society they are part of, but
also the way the story progresses, hypnotically, through
each of its stages, to a terrifying climax.

Also by Penelope Farmer in Abacus:
AWAY FROM HOME
EVE: HER STORY

0 3491 0109 4
FICTION

DELIVERANCE
JAMES DICKEY

Four men set out from a small Southern town for a three-day camping and canoe trip . . . a holiday jaunt that turns into a nightmare struggle for survival.

This is much more than a terrifying story of violence — murderous violence, sexual violence, and the violence of nature — it is a brilliant study of human beings driven towards — and sometimes beyond — the limits of endurance.

Shattering, spellbinding, and a masterly piece of writing, *Deliverance* has been described as the classic novel of male conflict and survival.

'A novel that will curl your toes . . . the limit of dramatic tension' *New York Times*

'A brilliant tale of action' *Observer*

'A fast, shapely adventure tale' *Time Magazine*

'Brilliant and breathtaking' *New Yorker*

0 3491 0076 4
ABACUS FICTION

BARS OF AMERICA

NEIL FERGUSON

A cityscape of gas stations and banks, interstate freeways, rundown motels, fast-food eats, diners and downtown bars. The USA in the Eighties.

In Neil Ferguson's *Bars of America* the humans who inhabit this science-fiction vista collide and, before they pass, buy each other drinks in bars — Fifth Avenue preppie bars, bars in the black ghetto, desert bars, sleaze bars. Brief encounters that take place in the present, that never lead anywhere. In the background: American cities, the threat of sex and guns. In the foreground: bartenders and pool-players, cops and cowboys and prostitutes, losers and loners, white and black Americans, Chicanos, American Indians, immigrants — the citizens who are the fugitives from the runaway American Dream, who would feel more at home in a Bruce Springsteen song than on the Johnny Carson show.

'Cool, stylish prose' *Tribune*

'A series of reflections triggered by places, which constantly brim over into soaring flights of fantasy' *Vogue*

0 349 111995
FICTION

PUTTING OUT
NEIL FERGUSON

Who is going to win the current mayoral race?
The best-dressed candidate, of course. Who else?
For this is New York, where rivalry centres on sartorial
elegance rather than policies, where politics has become
primarily a matter of style — like all the important things
in life: sport, television, sex. Even murder.

Now, amidst the media chic of the mayoral election, an
outbreak of terrorism hits the couture industry. While
fashion dictators Rocco and Tina battle for the hearts and
minds of the city voters, Lieutenant Maxwell Faraday,
detective second grade of the 19th precinct, is called in to
investigate. Reluctant to carry a gun on the grounds that it
will ruin the line of his suit, he knows that the best means
of defence, of trapping prey — including a suitable mate
— is an effective style statement. Something New Yorkers
have always known.

In Neil Ferguson's brilliant satire on the style world, Max
dances a deadly tango across the floors of New York's
clubs and fashion houses in pursuit of — and pursued by
— that most ruthless of style-makers, a killer. A killer who
knows all about the political implications of well-cut evening
suits.

'A poised and poignant novel . . . quite brilliantly told'
Interzone

'A dazzle of colour' *Guardian*

'Witty and self-knowing' *Time Out*

'This year's cult novel' *Blitz*

0 349 10083 7
FICTION

Abacus now offers an exciting range of quality fiction and non-fiction by both established and new authors. All of the books in this series are available from good bookshops, or can be ordered from the following address:

Sphere Books
Cash Sales Department
P.O. Box 11
Falmouth
Cornwall, TR10 9EN.

Please send cheque or postal order (no currency), and allow 60p for postage and packing for the first book plus 25p for the second book and 15p for each additional book ordered up to a maximum charge of £1.90 in U.K.

B.F.P.O. customers please allow 60p for the first book, 25p for the second book plus 15p per copy for the next 7 books, thereafter 9p per book.

Overseas customers, including Eire, please allow £1.25 for postage and packing for the first book, 75p for the second book and 28p for each subsequent title ordered.